T0333008

UNIVERSITY CHALLENGES

1989/90

Jack Sheffield

bantam

TRANSWORLD PUBLISHERS
Penguin Random House, One Embassy Gardens,
8 Viaduct Gardens, London SW11 7BW
www.penguin.co.uk

Transworld is part of the Penguin Random House group of companies
whose addresses can be found at global.penguinrandomhouse.com

First published in Great Britain in 2024 by Bantam
an imprint of Transworld Publishers

A CIP catalogue record for this book
is available from the British Library.

ISBN 9780857505231

Typeset in 11/15 pt Palatino by Falcon Oast Graphic Art Ltd
Printed and bound by Clays Ltd, Elcograf S.p.A.

The authorized representative in the EEA is Penguin Random House Ireland,
Morrison Chambers, 32 Nassau Street, Dublin D02 YH68.

Penguin Random House is committed to a sustainable
future for our business, our readers and our planet. This book is
made from Forest Stewardship Council® certified paper.

For Larry Finlay and his Transworld family

Contents

Acknowledgements

In the late eighties I moved from my headship into higher education. It gave me the opportunity to teach again and encourage the next generation of teachers. I remember this time in my life well and have recounted it in this, the second in the University series, through the eyes of my hero character, Tom Frith.

It was a wrench to leave behind my Teacher series of fifteen novels but refreshing to have this new impetus to my writing. The University series became the new project and for that I have to thank my hardworking editor at Penguin Random House, the ever-patient Imogen Nelson.

I have been fortunate over the years to have had the support of the excellent team at Transworld led by the remarkable Larry Finlay, now retired following decades of loyal service. His first words to me back in 2007 were 'Welcome to the Transworld family.' How true those words turned out to be.

Special thanks must go to Viv Thompson who puts up

with the fact I am a frustrated copy editor at heart. Her cheerful and understanding correspondence keeps me grounded and she continues to improve my novels.

There is a terrific literary agent out there who usually phones me when he is walking his dog. I refer to Phil Patterson of Marjacq Scripts. It was a partnership that began with a chicken and lettuce sandwich at the Winchester Writers' Conference in 2006. Bribery was never this cheap! In return he promised to read my first novel, *Teacher, Teacher*, and we've never looked back since. If you're ever interested in Airfix modelling kits circa 1980, he's the man for you.

My main supporter is, of course, my wife Elisabeth. Her patience is remarkable. The discussions we have about developing plots while enjoying her latest culinary creation are always eventful. Writing novels is a way of life for me now. With the support I have around me, may it long continue.

There are a host of wonderful booksellers and events managers out there. Particular thanks must go to Steph at Waterstones Milton Keynes, Laura at Waterstones York, Kirsty at Waterstones Alton and Sam at Waterstones Basingstoke.

Finally, if you've borrowed this book from your local library, keep in mind they are the cornerstone of a cultural society. The eight-year-old Jack who visited Compton Road Library in Leeds began a journey that is now well travelled.

Prologue

Consequences . . . we all suffer them from time to time.

Some matter little whereas others have a more serious outcome. Occasionally they begin with an innocent gesture, a smile or the hand of friendship. Such a day began for Tom Frith, a thirty-three-year-old lecturer at Eboracum University in the city of York on a bright sunny morning in the early autumn of 1989.

When he arrived in the porter's lodge for his second year as a lecturer he was unaware it was the day he was destined to meet a strange and unconventional woman. Her name was Rosie Tremaine.

So began a year in his life he was destined never to forget.

Peter Perkins, the university's head porter, was immaculate as ever in his navy-blue jacket and regimental tie. He smiled up at the tall man before him. 'Good morning, Dr Frith, and welcome back. I have a message for you.'

'Morning, Perkins, good to see you again. What is it?'

'Professor Grammaticus wants you to call into his study before the faculty meeting.'

Tom put down his leather satchel on the counter. 'Thanks . . . Did he say why?'

Perkins nodded. 'It'll be to meet your new colleague.' He glanced up at the clock with its faded Roman numerals. 'She arrived on the dot at half eight. Tall lady. Kept looking at her watch.'

'Ah, yes,' said Tom. 'Dr Tremaine . . . I heard she might be arriving today.'

Perkins gave a knowing look. He had a few doubts regarding the newcomer. 'Well, she's here now.'

Tom nodded. 'OK, thanks. Catch you later.' He picked up his satchel and strode off towards the quad.

Perkins called after him, 'And Dr Larson arrived half an hour ago. She said she would be in the common room.'

Tom gave a wry smile. He already knew where Inger Larson would be this morning. An hour ago the dynamic Norwegian music lecturer had mentioned she had an early meeting.

It was about the time she had climbed out of his bed.

Chapter One

A Woman of Precision

Tom walked through a Victorian archway to the ancient quadrangle and paused at the top of a flight of stone steps. Before him was a view that still filled him with awe and wonder. A huge, manicured lawn of verdant green was bordered by a wide pathway of worn cobblestones. It was surrounded by towering red-brick walls topped by turrets of sash windows. Another archway led to the modern buildings of the university, including lecture theatres, a vast refectory and pebble-dashed blocks of student accommodation. All seemed quiet on this sunlit morning. It was Monday, 11 September 1989 and for Tom Frith the start of classes was still a week away.

He walked around the quad and opened the door marked 'Alcuin'. Then he climbed the stairs to the top floor and stopped outside a study on which a brass plate read:

Professor Victor Grammaticus
Head of Faculty of Education

He tapped on the door and walked in.

'Morning, Tom,' said Victor with a welcoming smile. 'Thanks for calling in. I wanted you to be the first to meet your new colleague.' The dapper professor, in his crisp white shirt, waistcoat, bow tie and with his grey hair tied back in an incongruous ponytail, gestured towards the woman beside him. 'This is Dr Rosie Tremaine from Cornwall.'

Tom studied the figure before him with interest. A tall, graceful woman in her early thirties, she had auburn hair in a short-cropped boyish style. Her green linen trouser suit matched the colour of her eyes.

'Rosie, this is Dr Tom Frith. You will be working alongside him with the students who are training to be primary teachers and whose main subject is English Literature.'

'Pleased to meet you, Tom,' she said confidently. Her handshake was cool and firm.

'Welcome to Eboracum,' responded Tom with a smile. 'I'll look forward to working with you.'

Rosie regarded Tom, taking in his six-feet-two-inch, broad-shouldered frame, long wavy brown hair, denim shirt and creased oatmeal cord suit. 'Professor Grammaticus tells me you're to be my buddy tutor,' she said.

Tom looked puzzled. *'Buddy tutor?'*

'It's a new initiative, Tom,' explained Victor. 'The Vice Chancellor proposed it to give new members of staff some in-house support.'

'Good idea,' said Tom. 'I suppose I had Owen doing that job for me last year.'

'Exactly,' said Victor.

'Owen?' queried Rosie.

'Owen Llewellyn,' said Tom. 'I share a study with him on

Cloisters corridor. Teaches physical education. A Welshman and a great friend. I've been fortunate.' He smiled at Rosie. 'So I'll do what I can to help.'

She shook her head with a moue of dissent. 'Thanks but to be perfectly honest I've done this job before so I should be fine.'

Victor raised his eyebrows but said nothing.

'Well . . . I'm sure you will,' said Tom hesitantly. There was a moment's pause before he pressed on. 'We have some terrific students here training to be teachers.'

'As I had at Exeter University,' was the crisp reply.

Tom continued, eager to help. 'Well . . . thinking ahead . . . I'm happy to go through the English syllabus with you if you wish . . . perhaps after the faculty meeting?'

Rosie gave a brief nod. 'Thank you. My specialism in Victorian literature will no doubt be included.'

'I'm sure it will,' said Victor evenly.

Tom glanced at the clock on the mantelpiece. 'Well, if you'll excuse me, Victor, I've some papers to collect from my room before the meeting.' He looked at Rosie. 'No doubt I'll see you there.'

'Of course,' she said with confidence.

After Tom left, Rosie glanced at her watch. 'Your clock is two minutes slow.'

Victor nodded sagely. 'Close enough for me. A present from Brighton. My partner liked the art deco style.'

Rosie looked concerned. 'The faculty meeting is at nine, I believe.'

'Yes,' said Victor. 'I'll collect my notes and take you down there. It's in the common room. Early birds usually arrange the seating.'

Rosie had an aversion to lateness and frowned. 'It's seven minutes to nine.'

'Don't worry,' said Victor and picked up a bulky Manila folder from his desk. 'Shall we go?'

The door to Room 7 on Cloisters corridor was open when Tom walked in. A pair of ancient oak desks were butted up against each other in front of the latticed window. Owen Llewellyn was crouching down next to the coffee table and rummaging through his sports bag. In his mid-thirties and wearing a T-shirt and tracksuit bottoms, he looked superbly fit. He had been a loyal companion during Tom's first year. Owen looked up at his friend. 'Welcome back, boyo.'

Tom grabbed a folder from the bookcase. 'Come on, the meeting starts in a few minutes.'

Owen stood up and grinned. 'So . . . how was Miss Norway this morning?'

A few colleagues were now aware that Tom and Inger Larson, the Music tutor, had been an 'item' during the summer vacation.

Tom shook his head. 'She's fine.'

'Lucky bugger,' muttered Owen. 'Come on, Romeo,' and he followed Tom down the steep metal staircase and back into the quad.

Elizabeth Peacock, the sparky Dance and Drama tutor, was sitting on a bench outside the common room, staring at an agenda and smoking a cigarette. She was known to her colleagues as Zeb, and with her flaming red hair and outspoken manner, she was a lively member of staff. In her late thirties, and with an acerbic wit and a lithe ballet dancer's figure, she had a regular supply of young, athletic boyfriends.

'Morning, Zeb,' said Tom.

'Bloody hell!' exclaimed Zeb. 'Couldn't you get your little friend to tidy himself up a bit?'

'It's my rugged look,' said Owen with a grin. 'Women love it.'

Zeb stood up. 'Give me strength,' she muttered and stubbed out her cigarette. 'Come on, Tom, and bring your Welsh degenerate with you. The meeting is about to start and there's a lot to get through.'

They followed Zeb into the common room and found seats on the back row. Zeb, as the recently appointed Deputy Head of Faculty, sat down next to Victor behind a table at the front. The two of them made a formidable team. Tom noticed Rosie Tremaine had taken a seat on the front row with a notebook in hand.

On the far side of the room Inger Larson was in conversation with Professor Richard Head, the tutor in charge of the science department. Richard, a short, intense academic with spectacles and a goatee beard, was ticking off items on his clipboard while Inger spoke quietly to him. She caught sight of Tom and Owen and waved.

'OK, lover boy,' muttered Owen. 'Do you want to sit next to your girlfriend or stay here with me?'

'No . . . she's busy,' said Tom. 'She had a meeting first thing with Richard about sound and lighting for the Freshers' Concert next week.' He looked appreciatively at the blue-eyed Norwegian in her floral summer dress. Inger's long blonde hair hung loosely over her tanned shoulders.

'She looks good after the holiday,' said Owen. 'How did it go with her mam and dad?'

'OK,' said Tom. 'Nice people. Bit apprehensive at first but they made me welcome.'

Tom and Inger had flown to Oslo in August and Inger's parents had met them at the airport before driving back to their home in the tiny village of Langøy. There they had enjoyed some lively nights out with Inger's younger brother, Andreas, a concert violinist, and his girlfriend, Annika. For Tom it had been the happiest time of his life.

'Anyway,' said Owen. 'Looks like we're starting.'

Victor stood up, shuffled a few sheets of paper and scanned the faces of the forty members of staff in front of him. 'Thanks, everybody, welcome back and I hope you have all had a good break. We have a busy year ahead and I should like to welcome two new colleagues who have joined the faculty. Dr Rosie Tremaine from Cornwall will be working with Tom in the English department.' He gestured towards Rosie, who nodded in acknowledgement. 'We also have a new tutor in the science department, Dr Sam Greenwood from Manchester, and he will be working alongside Richard.' A lanky, fair-haired, cheerful-looking man in blue jeans and a T-shirt emblazoned with '$E=mc^2$' grinned broadly from the second row and tapped the name badge on the lanyard that hung around his neck. 'So please make them welcome, and, with that in mind, Zeb has arranged for a social gathering for all faculty members here in the common room on Friday afternoon. Refreshments will be served, so do come along.'

Victor pointed to the huge noticeboard at the back of the room and gave a smile of satisfaction. This was his pride and joy, namely the faculty timetable. On large sheets of graph paper was displayed a veritable cornucopia of coloured squares, times, groups and rooms. 'So here we have it,' said Victor, 'our first draft timetable for the autumn, spring and summer terms.' There were appreciative nods of approval. 'As always there will be minor amendments so please check it out and get back to myself or Zeb by Thursday evening at the latest.'

Victor picked up a typed sheet and studied it for a moment. 'I have here lists of admissions for each department so please collect them before leaving. You will see we have a few overseas students swelling the numbers and I know you will make every effort to integrate them into our community.' He paused and glanced at Zeb. 'Also Freshers' Week is fast approaching and Zeb has a few arrangements in place.'

Zeb stood up and gave a broad smile. 'Now, pin your ears back, everybody, because I want us all to play our part. There's a list of events from next Monday onwards and throughout the week, including an introduction to sports and societies, health and safety issues, a tour of the campus, a quiz night in the Students' Union and a dance on Friday evening. About twenty students have volunteered to return early and help and I trust all of you will be around to assist whenever needed. That apart, Victor and I are here to support so don't hesitate to contact us.'

It was a brief, confident address and she sat down again.

Tom looked across the room at Inger, who was scribbling notes on a pad. She leaned forward and her long hair hid her face. Although they had been on holiday together and he had met her parents, working alongside her would be different now. Back in Eboracum life had subtly changed. His reverie ended when Owen dug him in the ribs. 'Wake up, dreamboat,' he whispered. 'Victor's got more to say.'

Victor was on his feet again and he pushed his notes to one side. 'Just a personal message before we close.' He surveyed the room and all the expectant faces. 'It's been a great privilege to take on the post of Head of Faculty. You are aware that the conclusion to last term was difficult for us all following the tragic accident that befell Dr Wallop.' There was an uncomfortable silence and a few murmurings.

'Good riddance,' muttered Owen, who was never the most forgiving of souls.

The previous Head of Faculty, the infamous Dr Edna Wallop, had died after falling down the metal staircase outside her study. She had been deeply unpopular and Tom knew he would not be here now but for this twist of fate. His lectureship had been about to be terminated by the malicious woman. Instead he had been welcomed back by Victor, who recognized his value to the university.

Victor held up a letter. 'The Vice Chancellor has written to me suggesting I put it to you that there should be some form of memento, possibly a plaque or a tree in the grounds. So, if you have any suggestions please let me know and I'll circulate responses.' He turned to Zeb, who was clearly keeping her thoughts to herself. If Dr Wallop had stayed in post she would also have moved on. 'Finally, Zeb has an update on arrangements for the annual field week which will be earlier than usual this academic year.'

Zeb rose to her feet once again. 'The new bursar had a word with me and he's keen the costings for our various field week activities are on his desk in good time. The date that's now in the diary is Monday, twenty-sixth of March, a short while before we go down for the Easter holiday. So we shall need estimates from all department heads by November at the latest.' She smiled and gestured towards two members of the ancillary staff who had appeared behind a long table set out with coffee pots and an array of croissants and cake. 'Unless there are any questions, there's coffee and cake for everyone . . . so enjoy!'

Predictably there was an immediate scraping of chairs on the wood-block floor and an exodus towards the refreshments. Inger was pouring coffee when Rosie appeared beside her. She looked up and smiled. 'Hello, I'm Inger, would you like a coffee?'

'Yes, please,' said Rosie.

Inger poured a second cup. 'So, how are you settling in?'

Rosie nodded. 'Fine, thanks. I've been given a study on Cloisters corridor, number two.'

'Oh, that's next door to me. Call in for a chat if you wish.'

'I shall,' Rosie said and sipped her coffee.

Inger spotted a spare table next to the wooden pigeon-holes where a few tutors were collecting their mail. 'Shall we sit down?' and Rosie nodded.

Inger was intrigued by a tiny wooden cross tied with fine red ribbon hanging from a silver chain around Rosie's neck. 'I love the pendant.'

Rosie fingered it protectively. 'My mother gave it to me. She's a faith healer. It's from a rowan tree . . . Meant to keep me safe.'

'That's wonderful,' said Inger. 'So I guess she believes in prayer.'

'Yes, unlike me,' replied Rosie. 'She has firm religious beliefs.'

'I see,' said Inger cautiously.

'So what do you teach?' asked Rosie.

'I'm in the music department . . . mainly piano and voice.'

They sat down and Rosie studied the woman before her. 'So, Inger . . . what brought you here?'

Inger sipped her coffee and thought for a moment. 'I worked as a peripatetic music teacher in schools in Norway where I was brought up. My parents still live there. I simply wanted a fresh challenge and I spotted an advertisement for Eboracum. I'm pleased I did; it's a great place to work. What about you? I love Cornwall. Why did you leave such a beautiful part of the country?'

Rosie placed her cup in her saucer and looked down. She touched her left ear almost unwittingly as if pondering a reply. 'It seemed an attractive opportunity . . . and York is such a wonderful city.'

'I presume you've discussed your work with Victor,' said Inger. 'He's very supportive.'

'Yes. He had just taken over as Head of Faculty when I was interviewed.' Rosie turned and glanced across the room at Tom, who was enjoying a lively conversation with Owen and Zeb. 'I'm working with Tom. Apparently he's my so-called buddy tutor.'

'That's right. I heard the Vice Chancellor thought it would be helpful for new members of staff. You're fortunate. Tom will provide excellent support.'

Rosie looked at Tom once again. 'So . . . what's he really like?'

Inger was beginning to wonder where this conversation was heading. 'He's a kind, hardworking man.'

Rosie gave Inger a level stare. 'Yes, I imagine he is.' She stood up. 'Thank you for the coffee,' and she glanced at her wristwatch. 'I had better start unpacking in my study.'

Inger rose from her seat. 'Pleased to have met you, Rosie, and let me know if you need anything.'

Rosie gave a nod and strode away confidently while Inger looked after her with curiosity.

Later that morning, Tom walked up Cloisters corridor and tapped on the door of Room 2. Inserted in the metal name slot was a white card with 'Dr R. Tremaine' printed carefully.

'Come in,' called a voice.

He walked in to find Rosie at her desk, unpacking a box of books.

'Hi,' said Tom. 'I thought I would drop off the reading lists for each year.' He put a stapled sheaf of paper on her desk. 'There's plenty of flexibility, particularly with supervision of final-year theses. We could divide these up according to your interest.'

'Thanks, and speaking of interests, I'm busy at present with a book on Oscar Wilde. He's my favourite author.'

'That's great,' said Tom with enthusiasm. 'Coincidentally, Inger and Zeb were discussing producing *The Importance of Being Earnest* next summer. You must speak to them about it.' He walked back to the open door. 'So let me know when it's convenient to discuss the syllabus. This week I'm in the refectory most lunchtimes if that suits.'

'Thanks,' said Rosie. 'I'll do that.'

'Anyway, I can see you're busy.'

'Yes, I need everything in its place. I'm simply replicating the arrangement I had before in my study at Exeter University. It's important to be organized.'

'I agree,' said Tom. 'Good job you've got a study to yourself and you're not sharing with Owen. He's not exactly the tidiest.'

Rosie pursed her lips. 'Oh no! That would be unbearable.'

Tom realized she meant it. 'I'll leave you to it.'

When he returned to his study he tripped over a pair of rugby boots before clearing some space on his desk where Owen had been sorting the contents of his filing cabinet. He thought back to the order and precision that Rosie Tremaine was creating in her study and muttered a few of the choice Welsh swear words that his colleague had taught him last term.

At midday, Tom walked into the vast refectory, a huge building of glass and steel, and joined the queue. He chose quiche and salad and joined Zeb and Owen on a table in an alcove favoured by tutors.

'Hi, Tom,' said Zeb. 'I haven't caught up with Rosie Tremaine yet. How about you?'

'She's fine. Just sorting out her room. Looks to be a seriously tidy person.'

Owen grinned. 'Like me, you mean.'

Zeb shook her head, glancing at Tom. 'I really don't know how you cope with Mr Messy.'

Tom raised his eyebrows. 'Yes, we have our moments. But he has his good points.'

Zeb stood up. 'Like being a bloody good tutor who has the misfortune to wander around looking like a tramp.' She ruffled Owen's curly hair. 'I'll leave you two lovebirds; I've a meeting with Victor,' and she hurried away.

Owen had finished his scampi and chips and began flicking through the pages of his newspaper. He had spent 22p that morning on a *Daily Mirror*.

'So, what's new?' asked Tom as he tucked into his quiche.

Owen shook his head. 'Nineteen thousand ambulance crew members are going on strike tomorrow. Good luck, I say. Without them we'd struggle.' Then he turned to a photo of Lady Diana on the front page. 'Meanwhile, check out this special lady.' Owen wasn't a royalist but made an exception for Lady Diana.

'What's the story?' asked Tom.

'She was giving out prizes at the Burghley Horse Trials and bumped into Mark Phillips who had designed the course. It says here she's the first member of the royals to meet him since he separated from Princess Anne ten days ago.'

'So what happened?'

'Typical! She gave him a great big kiss.' He sighed. 'Lucky sod!' He looked across the table at Tom. 'By the way, speaking of tall, slim, attractive women, your new friend, the Cornish cream tea lady, knocked on our door looking for you. Something to do with a list. She didn't stay long and I don't think she approved of me. I was sorting out my filing cabinet and there was paper everywhere.'

'OK, I'll find her. Her name's Rosie by the way and I'm her buddy tutor.'

'Good luck with that. Looked a bit of a cold fish to me.'

Tom shook his head in despair, finished his meal and set off to find her. Going up the steps to Cloisters corridor he met Inger. 'Hi,' he said. 'You look busy.'

'Meetings,' she said simply. 'Lots of them. One more to go with the Vice Chancellor about funding.'

'That shouldn't be a problem. He thinks you're wonderful.'

Inger smiled. 'Maybe, but this is for a new baby grand piano. The old one has had it.'

'Oh well, good luck.'

There was a pause as Tom looked into her blue eyes. 'What are you doing tonight?'

Inger pushed a lock of blonde hair from her face and looked calmly at this eager and caring man. 'We agreed weekends . . . in term time. This is term time . . . well, almost.'

'Yes, *almost.*'

Inger smiled. 'Come round to mine. I'll cook something.'

Tom gave her a peck on the cheek. 'I'll bring a bottle.'

Rosie Tremaine's study had been completely transformed when Tom knocked on the door and walked in. A shelf on the bookcase was filled with a selection of Victorian novels and there were labels on each drawer of the filing cabinet. A photograph of a younger version of Rosie receiving her doctorate was displayed on the mantelpiece next to a small brass clock, and a row of notepads neatly arranged on her tidy desk. Her green linen jacket was hanging on a wooden coat hanger on the back of the door and a collection of fine china crockery was displayed on a shelf above the small sink. The coffee table sported coasters of Cornish beauty spots.

Tom took in the sight. 'I'm impressed. You've worked wonders in here.'

Rosie smiled. 'Thank you. We all have our foibles. I simply like to have everything in its place.'

'Owen mentioned the list I left with you. Would you like to go through it now?'

'Yes, please.' Rosie gestured towards one of the armchairs next to the coffee table. 'I have it here with a number of changes that I believe would be advantageous.'

Tom sat down and stared at a sheet of paper covered in red lines and neat notes in the margin. During the next hour he realized he was dealing with a very determined woman.

By late afternoon members of staff were beginning to drift away. Owen cycled to his home on the Hull Road to meet up with his wife, Sue, and take his son, Gareth, to the children's playground. Inger drove her bright red Mini out of the university car park to her flat on the Knavesmire opposite the racecourse and then searched in her fridge for sufficient ingredients to produce an evening meal for two.

Meanwhile, Tom had climbed into his 1980 hatchback Ford Escort and was driving north to his rented cottage in Haxby in order to change and collect a bottle of wine from the supermarket across the road. As he drove up the A19 he turned on the radio. Kylie Minogue was singing 'Wouldn't Change A Thing' and he smiled.

Zeb was busy with Victor in his study checking on student numbers when she leaned back in her chair with a thoughtful expression. 'Just a thought, Victor . . . but what do you make of the new bursar?'

Victor put down his pen and stared out of the window. 'Ah yes, Gideon Chalk, an interesting name and an equally interesting man. Can't quite make him out. The Vice Chancellor introduced me to him. Apparently he's a very highly qualified accountant from Herefordshire. Spends his spare time fishing in the River Lugg which pleases Edward. They both love their country pursuits.'

'Yes, but what's he really like? When I met him he treated me like a servant. He clearly has a high opinion of himself. The contrast between him and our previous bursar is huge. I was sad when Frank Bottomley retired.'

Victor paused, seeking the right words. 'I would only say be watchful and stay on your guard.'

At that moment Gideon Chalk was sitting quietly at his desk. It reflected his personality: he liked order and precision. It was this very attribute that had secured his latest post, along with the excellent references from his previous employer. His accountancy skills had never been in question but he had ruffled a few feathers. So the agreement had been that he leave at once with high-quality references or face an internal enquiry. The job at Eboracum was a perfect opportunity to start again. He had the Vice Chancellor in his pocket. The old man was easily impressed, a skill Gideon used when needed. Manipulating others was his mantra. He smiled as he considered the financial opportunities that lay ahead.

Back in his study Victor glanced up at the clock. 'Is that the time? Sorry, Zeb, I need to leave,' he said suddenly. 'Things to do.'

Zeb was surprised. It was unusual for Victor to depart so early. 'That's fine, Victor. We can finish up in the morning.'

Minutes later Victor was walking out of the university and driving home. He had begun to be concerned about his partner, Pat, a man of huge talent and charisma. Victor had sensed there was a problem when he had left that morning and he was thoughtful as he drove up the A19 towards Easingwold.

What Victor did not know was that during the early afternoon Pat had closed up his artist's studio at the foot of their spacious back garden and booked an appointment with a private doctor; he'd been feeling unwell for some time and experiencing regular back pain. He had not shared the problem with anyone else. He was working towards an exhibition of his work in December and put his symptoms down to the long hours of recent weeks.

Zeb decided to call by Rosie's study to check all was well after her first day and she tapped gently on her door.

'Come in,' was the muffled call.

When Zeb walked in Rosie was standing at her desk and had clearly just replaced the phone. Her cheeks were flushed.

Zeb stopped abruptly. Something seemed amiss. 'Oh . . . sorry to interrupt.'

Rosie glanced back at the phone. 'Not a problem,' she said hurriedly. 'It will keep. Not important.'

Zeb took in the situation. 'Well, I can catch up with you tomorrow if that's more convenient. Just checking you were OK.'

'Yes, thanks,' said Rosie. 'Tomorrow sounds good.'

'Right,' said Zeb. 'Until then.'

Rosie took her jacket from the back of the door, slipped it on and began to pack some papers into her leather shoulder bag. Then she closed her study and walked quickly downstairs to the quad. As she passed through the porter's reception area Perkins called after her, 'Good afternoon, Dr Tremaine.'

She looked up rather nervously. 'Oh, yes, thank you,' and hurried towards the winding driveway that led to Lord Mayor's Walk and the city walls. Out on the pavement she walked briskly up Gillygate, past the Theatre Royal, and turned right. After passing the library she reached the tall metal gates of the Museum Gardens. Rosie checked her wristwatch. It was precisely four thirty.

She walked purposefully towards the ruins of St Mary's Abbey where a tall man in an expensive business suit was waiting. He beckoned her towards the shadow of the ancient walls. It was only when he had checked they were out of sight that he took her in his arms.

Chapter Two

The Freshers' Ball

It was lunchtime on Friday, 22 September and Freshers' Week was drawing to a close. Zeb had worked hard to ensure its success and the rest of the tutors had played their part. When Tom and Owen walked into the refectory they surveyed the scene before them. It was good to see so many young students enjoying what was for some their first taste of freedom. Eighteen- and nineteen-year-olds were gathered around tables discussing aspects of their new life, everything from the consequences of an excess of alcohol to what to wear for the Freshers' Ball or how to work a washing machine. Tom smiled at the buzz of excited conversation.

'Lucky sods,' said Owen. 'I remember it well. Rugby twice a week and beer at 25p a pint.'

'They all look so young,' said Tom as he collected a tray.

'Fresh out of sixth form,' said Owen. 'What do you expect?'

'Maybe it's just us getting old,' added Tom with a grin.

Today's special was a ploughman's lunch and they

collected generous portions and looked for an empty table. Richard Head, the science nerd and astronomy buff, was sitting alone.

'Come on,' said Tom. 'He looks lonely.'

'OK,' said Owen somewhat reluctantly.

'He could probably do with some company,' said Tom.

Owen nodded. 'Wonder who christened him Richard. It must have been tough going through his early life being called *dickhead*.'

'Maybe keep that to yourself,' muttered Tom as they sat down.

Richard's eyes lit up and for a moment he forgot to separate the peas from the carrots and arrange them in neat sectors on his plate. His obsessive-compulsive disorder was well known among his fellow tutors. 'Oh, hello, good of you to join me.' His baggy Aran sweater looked out of place on this warm autumnal day.

'So, how's the world of astronomy?' asked Tom, eager to find something to kickstart a conversation.

'Good question, Tom.' He was suddenly enthused. 'Actually these are really exciting times. Yesterday Neptune ended its retrograde motion and today we have the conjunction of the Moon and Jupiter. It's almost too much to ask for.'

'Definitely,' muttered Owen through a mouthful of cheese and without conviction.

'That's fascinating,' said Tom. There was a pause while he thought of another subject. 'And what about tonight's Freshers' Ball? Inger said you've been busy.'

Richard's cheeks reddened slightly. The thought of the beautiful Norwegian always had that effect on this dedicated academic. 'Yes, it should be a good event. Inger has invited a final-year student to come back early to be DJ and I've set him up with a really sophisticated sound system.'

'Well done,' said Tom.

Owen decided to join in with a pertinent question. 'So . . . how's Felicity?' he asked.

Again, Richard's cheeks flushed. Felicity Capstick, a lecturer from Ely in Cambridgeshire and a fellow stargazer, had made his acquaintance last term when she had applied for the vacant Head of Faculty post. Since then she had secured a new post at Sheffield University. They had begun to spend occasional dark evenings beneath the skylight window in his study while peering through his telescope.

'She's calling in next week. It's Sextantid time again.'

Owen's eyes widened and he almost dropped his knife and fork. 'Pardon?'

Richard nodded enthusiastically. 'We decided to enjoy Sextantid together.'

There was a pause. 'I see,' said Tom quietly . . . but he didn't.

'Yes,' said Richard. 'It peaks on the twenty-seventh.'

Owen could stand it no longer. 'What does?' he asked bluntly.

'The Sextantid meteor shower,' said Richard. 'Comes round every year. Should be spectacular so we decided to share the experience.'

'Ah,' said Owen. 'I guess you would.'

Eventually Richard took his leave and Tom and Owen gave each other a knowing look. Conversations with the slightly eccentric professor were always eventful. They finished their meal and returned their trays to the collection rack.

'Are you going to the Freshers' Ball?' asked Owen.

'I told Zeb I would help out for the first part of the evening.'

'I'll be there later after we've fed Gareth and put him in his cot.' The two men spotted Rosie Tremaine hurrying into the refectory and joining the queue. 'So . . . how's it going with your buddy Cornishwoman?' asked Owen with a grin.

Tom was thoughtful. 'Not seen much of her this week and when we last spoke she seemed preoccupied.'

'Fair enough,' said Owen. 'I guess she'll speak up when she needs some help.'

'Maybe,' said Tom.

'Anyway,' said Owen, glancing at his watch, 'must go. I'm meeting a guy about a new trampoline for the gym.'

Tom resisted the opportunity to quip about the ups and downs in their lives and set off for his study. As he reached the quad he heard a familiar voice.

'Hi, Tom.'

'Ellie,' said Tom in surprise. 'You're back early.'

Ellie MacBride was a so-called 'mature' student, one who had entered university later in life. The attractive twenty-nine-year-old with black hair and a South Yorkshire accent had proved to be an outstanding student in her first year. She was training to be a primary school teacher and her main discipline was English Literature, so she had seen a lot of Tom. He had soon realized she was a bright woman and eager to learn. However, it had been clear from the outset that Ellie had hoped for more than a simple tutor–student relationship. Eventually it had reached a point where Tom had stepped back before it went too far. Following a few awkward moments both of them appeared to have moved on, much to Tom's relief.

Ellie smiled. 'I'm back to write an article about the Freshers' Ball for the *Echo*.' The *Eboracum Echo* was the students' monthly newspaper and Ellie was on the editorial team.

'I see,' said Tom. 'It promises to be a lively affair.'

'I remember last year's,' she said wistfully. 'I felt as though I had crashed a teenage rave party. It wasn't really my scene.'

'I can understand that,' said Tom. 'Have you got a photographer?'

'Yes, John Wright from Year Three maths, one of Victor's protégés.'

'In that case I'll see you later. I've offered to help with the bar.'

Ellie stared up at Tom. 'And how are you? Did you have a good holiday?'

Tom didn't want to discuss his visit to Oslo. 'Yes, thanks. What about you?'

She pursed her lips. 'Bit mixed, to be honest. I spent a few weeks helping out my mum and dad on their stall.' Ellie's parents sold fruit and veg in Barnsley Market. 'That apart I had a few days away. Nothing special.' She paused and looked reflective, her green eyes soft and warm. 'By the way, are we still fine for my special study on Jane Austen this year? You agreed to supervise.'

'Of course. We can get organized after one of the lectures next week.'

For a moment she looked a little sad. 'Thanks, Tom. I always appreciate your help.'

'Catch you later,' he said and Ellie watched him a little wistfully as he walked away.

*

It was mid-afternoon when Tom closed his Primary One folder, left his study and wandered downstairs. It was usual to meet up in the common room around this time and Victor and Zeb were drinking tea in a quiet corner near the television set. *Weekend Outlook* on BBC 2 had just begun with the sound turned down. They waved when Tom walked in. He collected a mug of tea and a couple of custard creams and sat down at their table.

'Hi, handsome,' said Zeb. 'Thanks for offering to help out tonight.'

'Looking forward to it,' said Tom, munching on a biscuit.

'In that case let's get the bar under way at seven and then we can pass it on to some of my students later in the evening.'

Tom smiled. 'That's fine by me.'

'How's Rosie?' asked Victor. 'I presume all is well.'

'I'm meeting her at three,' said Tom. 'A final run-through of our timetable and syllabus.'

Victor looked pleased. 'That's good. It's important she has a good start.'

'I've not really caught up with her,' said Zeb. 'She doesn't seem to have been around much this week.'

'Probably busy in her study,' said Tom.

'I heard she's writing a book about Oscar Wilde,' said Zeb. 'That should be interesting,' she added with a grin. 'Quite a character.'

'That's right,' said Victor. 'We discussed it at interview.'

'Is she coming along tonight?' asked Zeb. 'Many hands and all that . . .'

'I'll ask her,' said Tom.

Zeb glanced at the television screen. There was an image

of Paddy Ashdown, the leader of the Liberal Democrats. 'He's got it right,' she said with determination. The fiery dance tutor was a supporter of the middle ground of politics.

'What do you mean?' asked Tom.

'Well, in his address at last week's party conference he vowed to gain power and end Thatcherism.'

Tom nodded. 'Owen would be with you on that.'

Zeb raised her eyebrows. 'Except he's just a bolshie socialist and would have us all working down the pit.'

Victor grinned. 'I wouldn't tell him that if I were you.'

'So . . . is your little Welsh comrade coming tonight?' asked Zeb.

'Yes, after a few domestic chores by all accounts,' said Tom.

Zeb gave Tom a mischievous wink. 'Well, tell him not to turn up looking like a tramp. I might even teach him to dance.'

Victor leaned forward conspiratorially. 'Coming back to Rosie,' he said quietly. 'Were you aware she was a south of England chess champion?'

'Impressive,' said Zeb. 'Brains as well as beauty.'

'I used to play chess in school,' said Tom. 'I enjoyed it.'

'Maybe you should challenge her to a game,' quipped Zeb.

'Wouldn't do any harm,' said Tom. 'I might learn something.'

The conversation drifted back and forth until Tom realized it was three o'clock and time to move on.

Rosie Tremaine was sitting at her desk when Tom tapped on the door and walked in. It was five past three and Rosie checked her wristwatch and gave an imperceptible shake of her head. In Rosie's world timekeeping was important.

Tom took in the view of the surroundings. 'Your room looks terrific.'

There were fresh chrysanthemums in a vase on the coffee table, books were arranged in Dewey Decimal order on the bookcase and on top of the filing cabinet was a framed photograph of Rosie holding a silver trophy.

'Thanks,' she said. She passed over a carefully typed and colour-coded sheet of A4. 'Here's the final draft of my time-table for the first semester.' It appeared there was no time for small talk.

Tom took it and studied it carefully. 'Looks perfect. Well done.'

'You'll see I've responded to the option for Victorian literature in Year Three and I've added the names of four final-year students whose theses I could definitely assist with. So, if it's fine with you, I'll arrange tutorials next week so we can make an early start.'

Tom sensed it was a rhetorical statement and merely nodded. This was a determined, well-organized and dynamic woman. She clearly didn't suffer fools gladly. It also occurred to him she hadn't asked him to sit down.

She gave him a direct stare. 'Will you be giving me a copy of *your* timetable?'

'Yes, I'll drop one in.' There was a pause. 'I was wondering if you were thinking of calling in at the Freshers' Ball this evening?'

Rosie sat back in her chair. 'Is it compulsory? Back in Exeter we weren't expected to give up our evenings for events such as this.'

Tom hesitated before replying. 'No, it's not compulsory. It's mainly so that the first years can put names to faces in an informal setting. I'm just helping on the bar for an hour or so. After that I'll probably head for home.'

Rosie leaned forward in her chair. 'Will Victor be there?'

'Probably, but not for long.'

'In that case I'll call in for a short time.'

'Can I give you a lift?'

Rosie hesitated. 'Thanks but no. I'll drive myself.'

'I've never asked where you live.'

'Wigginton. I'm renting there.'

'I live in Haxby. I pass Wigginton on my way in.'

'Yes, you will.'

It was left hanging in the air.

'In that case I'll see you later,' said Tom. 'I can buy you a drink,' he added with a smile.

'I don't,' said Rosie brusquely.

'Don't?'

'Drink . . . I don't drink.'

'Ah . . . I see. Fine.' He headed for the door. 'Thanks for your time. I'll call back with my timetable.'

As Tom returned to his study he wondered if he had somehow got off on the wrong foot with this woman. If so, he couldn't understand why.

At seven o'clock Tom entered the students' common room, a huge space of alcoves and seating. Tables and chairs had been pushed to the sides to create a dance floor. It was already crowded with young people making new friends and sharing experiences of the past week. He had made an effort to look smart in his new blue cord trousers and a white collarless shirt he had bought in Oslo while shopping with Inger. He spotted her talking to Richard in front of the window at the far side of the room. She was backlit by the setting autumnal sun, her blonde hair a halo of light. Tom thought she looked stunning in a cream halterneck summer frock. It seemed an intense conversation and Inger kept pointing to the sound system set up on stage blocks under the canopy of the mezzanine floor above.

The student disc jockey, Barry Crookshank, also known as Bazza, was already in full swing, setting the mood with Alice Cooper's hit record 'Poison' followed by Madonna's 'Cherish'. The noise was deafening and Tom made his way towards Inger. He leaned towards her. 'I'm working on the bar. Shall I see you there?'

She seemed preoccupied with Richard. 'Too loud,' she was saying and then turned to Tom, gave a wan smile and nodded. 'Sorry, Tom, the balance isn't right. I'll catch up with you later.'

Tom walked over to the makeshift bar to join Zeb, who looked amazing in a close-fitting bright red dress that matched her lipstick and emphasized her slim figure. She was smoking a cigarette and had two punch bowls in front of her. One had a cardboard label that read 'Non-alcoholic cocktail'. The other clearly wasn't as Zeb added half a bottle of vodka to the evil brew.

'Hi, Tom,' said Zeb. 'Try this. It'll blow your socks off.' She scooped a spoonful into a plastic cup. 'I'm only serving it to special friends.' She gestured towards the cans of beer and lager. 'The students can have this stuff.'

Tom coughed and spluttered after taking a sip. 'My God! It's liquid dynamite!'

'One of my best,' said Zeb with a contented smile. 'So . . . how long can you stay? I'll be here until around nine.'

'I could do a couple of hours as well, I guess.'

'Perfect.' She stubbed out her cigarette and smoothed her dress over her hips. 'I've got a date later with a guy who works at the Theatre Royal. He's new there. Has a body like Nureyev. I'm meeting him in the Hole in the Wall pub.'

Tom grinned. 'Well, good luck.'

'Cheers, Tom.' She raised her plastic cup and smiled. 'I'm always lucky.'

Suddenly a crowd of students appeared, seeking solace and companionship in a can of Theakston's Bitter. The music seemed to get louder, the dance floor was filling fast and 'Too Much' by Bros was blasting out on Bazza's turntable.

It was then that Rosie Tremaine arrived, wearing a blue silk blouse and tapered blue jeans. She immediately sought out Victor, who was sipping a beaker of red wine in a secluded corner behind a pillar. He was watching the new intake of students and seeing if he could spot any problems.

'Glad you could make it,' said Victor. 'Thanks for calling in.'

Rosie scanned the room. 'It's not really my scene, to be honest. Hope you don't mind.'

'Quite frankly, it's not mine either,' he said with a smile. 'I won't be staying for very long. I love music but not this loud.'

'Likewise,' said Rosie.

'So, all set for next week? Tom mentioned you seemed to be very well organized.'

'Yes, I should like to think so.'

'Can I get you a drink?'

'No, thanks, but I'll pick up a soft drink before I go and check in with Zeb and Tom.'

'Enjoy your evening. Have you any other plans for the weekend?'

Rosie hesitated, touched her left earring and stared out of the window. 'Nothing special, simply checking all is well for next week.'

'In that case I'll bid you goodnight.' Victor headed out to the quad and on to the car park. Minutes later he was driving north to Easingwold to relax with his partner, Pat, who had convinced him he was fine when he went home earlier in the afternoon.

As darkness fell, Owen arrived to help behind the bar. A muscular young man in a Rolling Stones T-shirt had just collected two cans of John Smith's bitter.

'Enjoy yourself, Chris,' said Owen with a smile, 'but I need you fit for training next week.'

'OK, sir,' Chris said and wandered away, beer in hand, to join the rest of the rugby team at the far end of the room.

Owen grinned. 'Fresh from school. Still calls me sir.'

'So what's special about him?' asked Tom.

'Rugby,' said Owen. 'Chris Scully is one of the best prospects I've ever had. He's a natural. Played blindside wing forward for Yorkshire schoolboys, then a trial for the England under-nineteen team. Best tackler I've seen. He has a great future. The problem is keeping him. Headingley and other big clubs will be checking him out. I don't want to stand in his way but I could make him even better.'

'Good luck,' said Tom. 'I hope it works out.'

Tom was aware of Owen's dedication to his Physical

Education courses and in particular his love of rugby. Every year his 1st XV proved formidable in the north of England. As a coach Owen was respected by all the students who saw him as their mentor. Tom watched the young man join in a raucous rugby song with his friends and recalled what it was to be eighteen years old.

Rosie suddenly appeared at the bar. 'Hi, Rosie,' said Tom. 'There's a non-alcoholic punch here if you would care for some.' He scooped up some of the fruit-laced concoction.

'Thank you.' She sipped from a plastic cup and looked thoughtful. 'Tom, I've just been speaking with Victor and he said you had reported to him that I appeared well organized.'

'That's right, you are.'

'I was wondering if part of the remit of being a so-called buddy tutor was to pass on reports of my progress.'

'Really?' Tom looked puzzled. 'No, I don't see it that way. It was simply a supportive comment to say that you seemed to have settled in well.'

Rosie remained phlegmatic. 'I think it's important we get off on the right foot, don't you?'

'Yes, of course. I presumed we had.'

She replaced her drink on the table, stood back and folded her arms. 'You see, I have always preferred independence. It's not necessary for me to rely on other colleagues who will have had different experiences to mine.'

'I see,' said Tom doubtfully. 'I have no wish to interfere, merely to help whenever it's needed.'

'That's good, Tom. So, no hard feelings. I'll bid you good-night,' and she walked out into the twilight of the quad.

'What was all that about?' said Owen. 'Sounded like she had got her knickers in a twist.'

'Nothing really,' mused Tom. 'It's just that I find women are hard to understand.'

Owen raised his can of Theakston's and supped deeply. 'Join the club, boyo . . . join the bloody club.'

At nine o'clock Tom was finishing his stint on the bar when there was a tug on his sleeve. It was Ellie MacBride in a floral summer dress. 'How about a dance, sir?' she asked coyly and then stared up at him. 'What's wrong? You look miles away.'

'Oh, sorry, Ellie. How's the report for the *Echo* going?'

'Fine – finished it now. The usual one-liners from the first years, a sanitized comment from Victor plus a great photo of Zeb on the dance floor. So enough for a decent article.'

'Would you like a drink?' Tom felt this was preferable to dancing.

'Thanks.' She smiled. 'A white wine, please.'

Two of Zeb's final-year students were now running the bar. 'What about you, Tom?' asked one of them. She was dressed incongruously as a 1920s flapper girl.

'No, thanks.'

They moved away from the crush at the bar. Ellie was standing close to Tom while sipping her wine. 'Is everything OK?'

'Fine. Just a bit preoccupied.'

Ellie moved a little closer to make herself heard. 'What do you think of the music?' Bazza had begun to play 'French Kiss' by Lil Louis.

Tom considered this for a moment. 'Mixed,' he said cautiously.

'I agree,' said Ellie.

On the other side of the room Inger had spent much of

the evening with her prospective choir members. She saw it as a good opportunity to get to know them a little better. They looked relaxed as they drank and discussed ideas for the annual autumn concert. It was only when she spotted Tom and Ellie in close conversation that she frowned for a moment.

Half an hour later Tom and Inger walked out to the car park.

'What a relief,' said Tom. 'That music was simply too loud for me.'

Inger had her head down, deep in thought. 'I saw you talking to Ellie MacBride. I did warn you about her. You need to take care. She's clearly fond of you. It's important you don't offer any encouragement.'

Tom looked surprised. 'I only did what I would do with any other student in those circumstances.'

Inger sighed. 'But she's not simply any other student.'

They stopped next to Inger's Mini under an ethereal sky and a blizzard of stars. There was a moment of quiet on this balmy autumn evening. 'So . . .' said Tom, 'would you like to come back to mine?'

Inger sighed. 'I'm a bit tired. It's been a long day and a busy week.'

Tom didn't take the hint. 'It's the weekend. Let's spend it together.'

Inger looked down at the ground. 'To be quite honest, Tom, I feel as though my weekend will begin tomorrow morning after a good night's sleep.'

Tom frowned. 'I guess we've both been busy but time together is important.'

Inger turned towards her car. 'I'm going now.'

'I'll ring, shall I?' asked Tom.

Inger looked up at him and replied quietly, 'Maybe not at the moment.'

'Why?'

'It's just that sometimes I simply need some space.' There was caution in her words. A *permanent* relationship wasn't what she wanted at this time. 'Sorry. I'll say goodnight.'

Tom looked anxious. 'We're still OK, aren't we?'

'We're fine . . . I just don't want to be rushed.'

She climbed in her car and drove away. Tom stood there as her red tail lights disappeared into the distance. As she drove home she turned on her car radio. Tears for Fears were singing their hit 'Sowing The Seeds Of Love', and, for the first time, she began to reconsider her relationship with Tom.

Chapter Three

Unwillingly to School

Tom was driving on the Malton Road towards Broad Hutton Primary School where two of his first-year students were experiencing their first taste of teaching. It needed to be a brief visit as he was teaching English Two at eleven o'clock. The countryside was always spectacular at this time of year but Tom's mind was elsewhere. It was Monday, 2 October and the season was changing. Leaves were tinged with gold and in the hedgerows, beneath a hammock of spiders' webs, goldfinches were seeking out the seeds of tall teasels.

His radio was tuned in to BBC Radio 2 and Derek Jameson was playing 'You're History' by Shakespears Sister and that was how he felt. The relationship with Inger had cooled slightly and he didn't understand why. She was consumed with her work and there had been little communication between them since the new term began.

Finally a pretty village came into sight and he slowed until he spotted the school sign. Yorkshire stone cottages with pantile roofs huddled next to a whitewashed pub and the clock in the tower of the local church was announcing the beginning of a school day. A red sports car sped by as he parked on the main street behind a van with a sign on the back that read 'No Pies Are Left in this Van Overnight'. He followed a parent and child hurrying towards the school where a tall, craggy sixty-year-old in a collar and tie and brown overalls was standing by the gate like a guardsman, holding a large broom. 'C'mon, Mrs Pickersgill, yer late again,' he bellowed.

A rotund lady with her hair in curlers under a head-scarf looked up at him fiercely. 'It's my Ernie,' she yelled. ''E's neither use nor ornament. Couldn't find t'keys for 'is van,' and she dragged a small bristle-haired boy down the cobblestone path towards the school entrance.

He was shouting, 'Don't wanna go t'school. Wanna mek pies wi' m'dad.'

'C'mon, y'soft ha'porth. Gerrin t'school an' do as yer told.'

'Y'need t'get 'im sorted out,' the guardsman called after her.

Tom paused at the gate. 'Good morning,' he said, unsure whether to proceed as this huge figure was blocking his way.

'And can I be of assistance, young sir?' the man asked with affected politeness.

'I'm Tom Frith from the university, here to see the students.'

'Are you expected?'

'Yes, I spoke on the phone last week to the headteacher.'

'In that case welcome t'Broad 'Utton an' enjoy yer visit. Allus pays t'be careful when *outsiders* turn up.' He stood to one side. 'Great lady is Mrs Wigglesworth. Tough as old boots. They don't make 'em like 'er any more.'

An imposing grey-haired lady in a tweed two-piece and pince-nez spectacles was standing in the entrance hall when Tom walked in. She had rosy cheeks and there was a twinkle in her eyes. 'Mr Frith, I presume,' she said and smiled. 'I see you've met Mr Baldwin, known locally as Long John. He's very protective.'

'Very wise,' said Tom. 'You can't be too careful these days.'

'Quite right.' She gestured towards a door labelled 'Mrs Enid Wigglesworth, Headteacher'. 'Shall we have a word before you go into class?'

Tom sat down in the visitor's chair and admired the tidy desk before him with its vase of sweet williams, a glass paperweight and a jar of sharp HB pencils.

'Thank you, Mrs Wigglesworth, for taking on two of our students. You'll recall they are just here for a week to give them a taste of the profession.'

Mrs Wigglesworth nodded sagely. She had seen it all before. 'Yes, they look very young, don't they? Yet it's possible to spot potential even at this early stage.'

Tom glanced down at his carbon-copy notebook. 'Where have you placed Mr Scully?'

'He's with Mrs Etherington in the top class. Definitely a good prospect, polite and prompt. He arrived early, looked smart and was well prepared.'

'That's good,' said Tom. 'And what about Miss Picard?'

There was a pause while Mrs Wigglesworth chose her words carefully. 'A few concerns here, I'm afraid. I saw her arrive from my window only a few minutes ago in a sports car that peeped its horn after dropping her off. In my view her appearance is inappropriate – a very short skirt – and she seems half asleep. I've put her in the class of six- and seven-year-olds with my most experienced teacher, Miss Pritchard.'

Tom considered this for a moment. It was mixed news. 'I appreciate your thoughts, Mrs Wigglesworth, and I'll have a word with both of them if I may.'

'Assembly is at ten and morning break at twenty past. You're welcome to have a hot drink with us if you have time.'

'That's kind but sadly, no. I'm teaching again at eleven and it's more than a half-hour drive back to York.'

'Very well,' she said. 'I'll show you to the classrooms.'

Chris Scully was engrossed with a group of children who were discovering the properties of isosceles triangles when Tom entered the classroom. The young sandy-haired rugby star looked very much at home in this environment. Tom introduced himself to Mrs Etherington and they stood by the chalkboard and watched the children at work. They were all busy completing workcards from the *School Mathematics Project*. Tom nodded in appreciation. There was a positive hum of activity with children weighing, measuring and writing results in Manila-covered exercise books.

'He's made a good start, Mr Frith,' said Mrs Etherington, a vibrant lady in a mustard blouse and suede skirt. 'One for the future.'

'That's good to hear. Thank you for giving him this opportunity.'

After watching Chris Scully at work for twenty minutes Tom sat down and wrote a summary in his notebook. He tore out a carbon copy and placed it on the teacher's desk before inserting his own copy in the student's folder.

The contrast in the next classroom was noticeable. Miss Pritchard, a fifty-year-old woman with over twenty-five years' experience, frowned when Tom walked into the classroom. There were brief introductions.

'Good morning, Mr Frith. Not one of your best, I'm afraid,' she said quietly. 'I've sent her into the Book Corner to listen to children read.'

Sienna Picard was sitting with two small children while yawning and looking out of the window. She was wearing a tight polo-neck jumper, miniskirt and high-heeled boots and looked out of place in this well-ordered environment.

Tom beckoned her towards the door and they walked out into the corridor.

'Hi, Sienna. How are you getting on?'

She shrugged her shoulders. 'It's fine.'

'The headteacher mentioned it was close to nine when you arrived. Was there a problem? We had organized a bus from the university that should have dropped you off at eight thirty.'

Sienna smiled, bright red lipstick, white teeth and false eyelashes. 'My boyfriend dropped me off. We were at a party last night and I slept at his so I wasn't in halls.'

'So what's the plan for tomorrow?'

She gave Tom a mischievous look. 'I guess it depends where I spend the night.'

'Clearly that's your business, Sienna. My concern is that you arrive in good time to be well prepared to support the children in your care.'

'I get the message, Tom. So don't worry.'

'OK, go back into class and do your best. You're working alongside a really experienced teacher so make the most of this opportunity.'

Tom followed her into the classroom and, after having a quiet conversation with Miss Pritchard and watching Sienna at work, he scribbled a few helpful comments on his carbon notepad and made his way back to the head-teacher's office.

'Pleased to have met you, Mr Frith, and do stay longer next time if your schedule permits.'

'Many thanks, Mrs Wigglesworth. I certainly shall.'

'And don't worry, your students are always welcome here . . . After all, they're the future.' She walked with Tom to the entrance door and waved goodbye.

The roads were busy when he drove back to York and there was no time for a mid-morning coffee as he gathered his notes for English Two and an analysis of *Tess of the d'Urbervilles*. As he hurried through the quad it occurred to him there was a sharp contrast between Thomas Hardy's heroine and the unceremonious Sienna Picard.

His lecture on the works of Thomas Hardy, the renowned Victorian poet and novelist, was well received by the eighteen students in English Two. The discussion ranged from the striking characters and evocative landscapes in *Far from the Madding Crowd* and *The Mayor of Casterbridge* to the heart-rending story of *Tess of the d'Urbervilles*.

Amy Fieldhouse and Liz Colby had become firm friends during their first year and were often found in the library together. Both had done extensive research into Hardy's works and were particularly impressed with the character Bathsheba Everdene and her desire to break free of the expectations of Victorian society in *Far from the Madding Crowd*.

'I don't think feminism in Victorian times is what it appears to be today,' said Amy.

'I read it was called *protofeminism*,' said Liz. 'I had to look it up.'

'Good point,' said Tom. 'That's the term we use when the modern feminism we know today is described in an era such as this when it was comparatively unknown.'

Two Liverpudlian students, Tommy Birkenshaw and Billy Whitelock, were looking completely blank during this conversation. The male-dominated households in which they had been raised included few liberated women. A lively debate ensued and, as the bell for the lunch break rang, it was Ellie MacBride who had the last word.

'Tom, I noticed that Hardy described happiness as simply an episode against a background of pain. I wondered if you agreed.' She gave him a long knowing look and, as always, Tom guessed there was a subliminal message here. Like Rosie Tremaine, Ellie had green eyes but there was a difference. Ellie's look was soft and tinged with sadness.

When Tom walked into the refectory he spotted Rosie Tremaine sitting alone at a table at the far end of the room. She had just finished her meal and looked deep in thought. He collected a ham salad and approached her. 'May I join you?'

She looked surprised for a moment, shaken from her contemplation. 'Of course.'

Last week all the students had returned and Tom's teaching had gone well. He had also received positive reports from students who were being taught by Rosie. Her preparation was excellent and her calm, precise manner seemed to have gone down well. At the end of the week, late on Friday, they had met briefly and identified the very few students with whom they had a concern. They also listed the fifteen first-year Main English students who would require a brief visit during the following week's school placement.

'How are you?' asked Tom. 'Busy times.'

Rosie sipped her herbal tea and replaced her mug on the table. 'I was intending to have a word with you about that,' and she gave Tom a hard stare. 'You listed seven students for me to visit and I checked the mileage over the weekend. They're in four different schools. Fitting them in is almost impossible along with the final-year tutorials I've planned on top of the weekly schedule of lectures.'

'I do my tutorials at the end of the working day . . . after lectures and visits. Otherwise you can't fit them all in.'

Rosie frowned and shook her head. 'But that would mean not finishing until after six and I have commitments in the evening.'

Tom recognized the impasse. 'In that case give me a couple of your first years and I'll fit them in during one lunchtime this week. These visits are just to check they feel comfortable in a school environment. It's also an opportunity for a brief chat about any concerns they might have.'

Rosie sighed. 'I may have a word with Victor. In Exeter we didn't organize our timetable in this way.'

Tom was concerned. It was essential every first year received a visit, not least to reassure the schools they were taking an interest in their students. 'Shall we meet tomorrow after final lectures for a catch-up? I'm sure we can resolve this.'

Rosie picked up her tray and stood up. 'In the meantime,

I'll have a word with Victor,' she said with finality and walked away.

After his one o'clock lecture with Primary Three, Tom joined Zeb and Owen in the common room during afternoon break. They sat there drinking tea until Zeb made a surprise announcement. 'I'm thinking of buying a house.'

'That came out of the blue,' said Owen.

'Why now?' asked Tom.

Zeb put down her cup, lit up a cigarette and leaned forward. 'I don't know if you guys have noticed but property is suddenly a lot cheaper. Prices have fallen by almost four per cent since May and sixteen per cent since last year's boom. So maybe now is the time. I've waited long enough.'

'Sounds good,' said Owen. 'Where are you thinking of buying?'

Zeb leaned back and blew a plume of smoke towards the closed window. 'To be honest I really like those houses near the racecourse where Inger has an apartment but they're too expensive. So I'm looking at the outskirts of York. Maybe up the A19 in Easingwold where Victor lives or one of the villages, Stillington, Huby, Sutton-on-the-Forest. It's lovely around there.' She paused, looking pensive. 'It's just such a big decision and a lot of money. I've got savings but it will be tight.'

Owen grinned. He loved to tease Zeb. 'Maybe you ought to write a children's book like Fergie and earn a fortune.' Sarah Ferguson was in the news again for cashing in on her children's books about Budgie the Little Helicopter.

Tom nodded. 'I read she's due to receive £126,000.'

'Bloody hell!' said Zeb. 'That's crazy. I despair sometimes.

What on earth does she think she is doing? It was bad enough when she appeared in *It's a Royal Knockout*.'

Owen grinned. 'Even I thought the press reports were a bit harsh. They said she resembled a cow that had just charged through a washing line.'

Zeb sighed. 'I wouldn't have gone that far.'

'We should get rid of the lot of them,' declared Owen.

'There speaks a disciple of Lenin,' muttered Zeb.

'I read that Labour are ahead in the opinion polls,' said Tom.

'That's some consolation, I suppose,' said Zeb, who wasn't a fan of Margaret Thatcher. 'We need tomorrow's prime minister – not yesterday's woman.'

Tom looked at the clock. 'And on that note I have some tutorials.' He left them engaged in a stormy conversation about politics while knowing deep down their respect for each other knew no bounds.

When he reached the quad he saw the new bursar, Gideon Chalk, in a heated conversation with a group of students. It was strange to see discord of this kind in full view. Chris Scully and three other members of the rugby team had surrounded the diminutive, balding accountant. Gideon, a skeletally thin man in a dark three-piece suit, was shaking his head. His gaunt and cadaverous face was grey and he was raising his voice with a furious response. Tom was in a hurry and decided to leave them to it but thought he would mention the incident to Owen, since he coached the rugby team.

It was four thirty when Ellie MacBride knocked on Tom's door and walked in. He was sitting at his desk listing some background reading for her in preparation for her Year Two special study on the works of Jane Austen. She had changed from the jeans and sweatshirt she had worn in the morning lecture and was now wearing a new V-neck dress.

'Hi, Tom, thanks for your time,' she said with a smile and sat down in one of the armchairs. She placed her notebook and pen on the table.

'Would you like a coffee?' asked Tom.

Ellie jumped up. 'I'll make it, shall I?'

'If you wish,' he said.

She knew where everything was and two mugs of hot coffee appeared with a plate of biscuits. 'They're for you,' she said. 'I'm watching my figure.' She opened her notebook, sat back and crossed her legs. Then she looked expectantly at Tom and smiled. 'So where to begin?'

Tom sat down opposite her. He had always been impressed by her willingness to learn. 'This is a perfect study for you,' he said. 'Austen's novels have universal appeal.'

Ellie opened her notebook and began to write.

'You need to concentrate on her six major novels, *Sense and Sensibility, Pride and Prejudice, Mansfield Park, Emma, Northanger Abbey* and *Persuasion*. Make sure you focus on her comedy of manners and the fact that her world followed stricter rules than ours. Identify them as you read through the text and emphasize why her work was so groundbreaking.' He sipped his coffee and munched on a digestive biscuit while she scribbled.

A half-hour seemed to fly by in a lively exchange of views. It was five o'clock when Tom called a halt.

'Thanks, Tom. I'm looking forward to this. I appreciate your guidance.'

Tom opened the door and Ellie paused in the corridor. 'Just a thought, Tom. A few of us are calling into the Keystones at Monk Bar if you would like to join us.'

'Sorry but I've got some work to finish off. Thanks anyway.'

'If you change your mind it would be good to see you.' He stood in the doorway and watched her walk away. Suddenly she stopped and turned. 'Everyone needs a chance to relax. Thomas Hardy can be great but it makes you think about life sometimes. We can't all be Bathshebas, even if we want to.'

Tom smiled. 'Maybe not.'

Then Ellie looked beyond Tom and waved. 'Hi, Inger.'

Inger had left her study and was walking down the corridor.

Tom turned in surprise. 'This is unexpected! Come on in.'

Inger stepped into the study and closed the door behind her. 'I've just had a conversation with Rosie and I thought I had better share it with you.'

'Fine. Take a seat. Coffee?'

'No thanks.' Inger sat down in the chair Ellie had just vacated. 'So why are you seeing Ellie MacBride?'

'I'm supervising her special study. She's one of the four students I'm monitoring in English Two.'

Inger sighed and looked pensive.

'Her work is really good,' enthused Tom. 'Anyway, what did Rosie have to say?'

'We can get to that,' said Inger firmly. 'Sometimes, Tom, you are so naive.'

'Naive?'

'You don't see it, do you? People notice things. There have been conversations among my students that, quite frankly, have made me feel embarrassed. She's obviously still infatuated with you.'

Tom looked nonplussed. He was frustrated that Inger and the rest of his colleagues did not see that his relationship with Ellie was entirely innocent. Ellie was simply a student whose work ethic he admired. The woman he loved was standing before him.

'I don't see it that way. It's good to have students of her quality and dedication. Makes the job worthwhile.'

Inger looked sad. 'I thought you had dealt with this last year.'

'So did I.'

There was silence until Inger stood up. 'Anyway, Rosie is not happy. I popped next door to see how she was. It's these extra school visits that she can't cope with. Apparently she saw Victor, who was sympathetic, but said there are busy weeks like this one and we all have to manage the best we can.'

'I agree,' said Tom. 'I even offered to take on some of her visits.'

Inger stared forlornly out of the window. 'It's tough to make contact with her and feel at ease.'

'Well, we're both trying our best.'

Inger gave Tom a wry smile. 'With others . . .'

Suddenly Tom stood up. 'Let's get out of here for a while. It's a lovely evening. Simply a walk . . . fresh air and a bit of freedom away from this place.'

Inger stood there filled with indecision. 'There's so much to do. The concert is close now and requires a huge commitment from me.'

'I know that, but we both need a break. Let's have a coffee

in the Museum Gardens. It's lovely at this time of year and it's ages since we've been there.'

Inger gave a deep sigh and smiled. 'You're right, I'll get my coat.'

Twenty minutes later they were sitting on a bench beneath a tree in the Museum Gardens and sipping coffee from cardboard cups. It was a sunlit, balmy, autumnal late afternoon. Leaves, red, gold and amber, fluttered down and swirled around their feet.

'Thanks,' said Tom. 'I'm glad we've done this.'

Inger sat back and pushed her long blonde hair from her face. 'I'm sorry, Tom, if this is not what you want. It's difficult sometimes. We've had good times together and Oslo was great. My parents really liked you. But since we've been back I've found sometimes you're simply too intense. I need to keep my independence. It's difficult to explain but that's how I feel.'

Tom stared into the distance at the ruins of the abbey. His thoughts raced. Was he losing the woman he loved? 'If I'm misjudging situations, I'm sorry. This is new to me as well. I felt we were good together. But I understand your dedication to the concert and your students. It's plain for all to see.'

'They depend on me, Tom, and this is their chance to shine. I owe them my undivided attention.'

Tom leaned forward and touched her hand gently. 'Thanks for coming here. It's good to talk.'

Inger smiled. 'You're right. I guess we both did need a break.' Suddenly she looked up. 'Hey, look who's there.'

Higher up the hill, through the trees and beyond the

grassy bank, Rosie Tremaine was walking along the path in front of the museum.

'Wonder where she's going,' said Tom. 'She looks to be in a hurry.'

'Probably towards the other end of the gardens into Marygate.'

It was then they saw her step off the path and skip along the grass towards the shadows of the abbey walls, where a tall man in a pinstriped business suit stood smoking a cigarette. For a brief moment they held hands and she kissed him on the cheek. After exchanging a few words they both went their separate ways. The man set off for Marygate while Rosie turned round and hurried back the way she had come.

'Well,' said Tom. 'What do you make of that?'

'A mystery,' said Inger.

'How strange,' said Tom.

Inger looked intrigued. 'Particularly as I recognized the man.'

'Really? Who was it?'

'Julian Meadows, local solicitor and a neighbour of mine.'

'So you know him?'

There was a long pause. 'I do,' said Inger quietly. 'He's married with two children.'

Chapter Four

The Dying of the Light

Victor Grammaticus looked out on a ghostly dawn. Each day the temperature had dropped and an autumn mist covered the distant countryside with a mantle of silence. Outside his bedroom window teardrop cobwebs hung like pearls and beyond the fragile gauze the trees were spectres against a gun-metal sky. On the radio Fantasie in F Minor was playing. Schubert's piano duets always touched his soul and suited the mood of the morning. It was Tuesday, 17 October and an early meeting with Zeb and Tom awaited him; a few students had begun to cause concern and needed to be discussed. That evening was Inger's autumn concert so a long day lay ahead.

Downstairs, Pat was preparing eggs Benedict on toasted muffins with hollandaise sauce and a garnish of chopped chives. Victor's partner was not only an outstanding artist but also a talented cook.

'Hurry up, lazybones,' he called out. 'It's ready.'

When Victor walked into their spacious art deco kitchen,

not for the first time he realized just how lucky he was. Pat was a very special man. Even so, there was something that wasn't quite right. The flamboyant artist was quieter than his usual effervescent self.

Three miles away in his Haxby cottage Tom was munching on a slice of burned toast and drinking a mug of instant coffee. On BBC Radio 2 the Beautiful South were singing 'You Keep It All In' and he knew how they felt. His relationship with Inger was on hold at present and he was hoping this evening's concert would be a success. Perhaps then they could rekindle those halcyon days of summer. Now it was time to hurry. Victor had asked him to call in before lectures for a brief meeting so he grabbed his duffel coat and walked out to his car. He drove towards York through a countryside shrouded in a blanket of mist and past hedgerows rich in wild fruits. The season was moving on, nights were closing in and it was the time of the dying of the light.

In her apartment opposite the Knavesmire, Inger was sitting at her Challen baby grand piano and checking the scores for Vivaldi's *Gloria* and Handel's *Messiah* while sipping on a herbal tea. The annual concert had dominated her waking thoughts for weeks. She was pleased with her choir, particularly a gifted first-year soprano, Arabella Esposito, who would be singing 'Pie Jesu', made popular by Andrew Lloyd Webber in his 1985 *Requiem*.

She glanced across at her ageing record player. On top was the Lloyd Webber LP, *The Premier Collection*, a gift from Tom, and she sighed. He was a good man but the thought of a permanent relationship still made her feel uneasy.

There were scars from a previous life that had never fully healed and it was important to keep active to stay ahead of the memory.

Zeb, in her city-centre apartment, was standing at the breakfast counter and swaying her hips while eating a bowl of chopped banana and muesli. She was in a good mood following a night of passion with Tony, the Theatre Royal box office manager, who had left early for work.

After tying back her spiky red hair with a yellow ribbon, she donned skintight leggings, a brightly coloured sweatshirt and her favourite *Fame* leg warmers. She then slipped on a pair of Doc Marten boots before setting off to walk to the university. After calling into the newsagent on Parliament Street and buying a packet of twenty John Player Superkings, she lit up a cigarette and skipped along. Life felt good for the flame-haired Deputy Head of Faculty.

She had two meetings before her first lecture, one with Victor and Tom and then another with Royce Channing, the enigmatic head of the art department, to discuss scenery for next summer's drama production of *The Importance of Being Earnest*. It seemed a long way off but it was best to be well prepared.

Tom walked into Victor's study to find Zeb had just boiled a kettle. 'Hi, handsome,' she said. 'Coffee?'

Tom smiled. 'Yes please.'

Victor gestured to one of the comfortable armchairs. 'Thanks for calling in, Tom. I was keen for you to be involved. Zeb has prepared a list. It's only a short one this month.' He sat down as Zeb served coffee in matching mugs featuring

Van Gogh's *Starry Night*. 'Zeb, do you want to kick off with one of your drama students?' He looked down at the typed list and smiled. 'It's Robson Luís Moreira de Souza. I'm told he's discarded the patronymics of his birth name and shortened it to Robbo.'

'That's right,' said Zeb with a smile. 'Quite simply he's a lazy sod. He's just discovered girls and booze and failed the first three assignments, two of them through non-submission. So far I've admonished him with the usual censures but I'd like to escalate it and send him to you for an official first warning.'

Victor nodded. 'Yes, let's do that.'

He returned to the list. 'So, two of yours, Tom. I'm surprised to see young Whitelock here. He's in your English Two, isn't he?'

Tom looked thoughtful. 'Keen young man. Did well last year until he witnessed the Hillsborough disaster. Since then his grades have plummeted. There're family problems back in Liverpool. He really needs some counselling.'

'We can help with that, Tom. I'll organize some professional in-house support. Let me have his timetable.' He returned to the list. 'Meanwhile, what's the problem with Sienna Picard?'

'Non-submission of assignments and a really poor attitude during her first school placement. Plus regular lateness to my sessions.'

Victor scribbled a note. 'Have a meeting with her. Issue a first warning and keep me informed.' He studied the next name and looked concerned. 'That apart, there's a final-year student who needs our support. She's pregnant. Siobhan Malone. One of Richard's scientists, talented by all accounts.

Zeb, check in with Richard, get some background and then have a word. We'll need to give her every chance to achieve her degree.'

'Fine,' said Zeb. 'I'll do that.' She paused and spoke quietly. 'There's a rumour the father is a member of staff.'

Victor sat back and sighed. 'Oh dear. Well, see what you can discover, discreetly of course. So, anyone else?'

'Yes,' said Zeb. 'I've heard there're a couple of women in the Art Faculty who are taking those guar gum slimming tablets that have been banned by the government. They're dangerous. We need to take some action.'

'I've heard about this,' said Victor. 'There's a guy called Peter Foster who has made a fortune claiming they soak up calories. Apparently a nutrition expert said they could kill you.' He made a note on his pad. 'Again, I'll pull in some professional help.'

'I could have a word with Ellie MacBride and ask her to write an article in the next issue of the *Echo*,' said Tom.

'Thanks,' said Victor. 'Yes, do that.'

'One more thing,' said Zeb. 'A couple of girls have told me that they think some of the lads have been messing about and looking in their bedroom windows at night.'

'Do they know who?' asked Tom.

'No, they aren't sure. It's only happened a couple of times but it's worth mentioning to the students.'

Victor nodded. 'Good idea.'

'Maybe it's time to review existing pastoral care for female students,' said Zeb. 'There're some vulnerable kids out there.'

'I agree,' said Victor. 'Get it started and we'll meet again.' He stood up. 'I'll see you both this evening at the concert.'

*

Tom had finished his lecture on the novels of John Steinbeck with English Three and was on his way to the refectory when Richard caught up with him. He was holding a clipboard covered in copious notes. 'I think we're all set, Tom,' he said. 'It's really the same as last year: you working the spotlights again while I do the sound.'

'OK, Richard. So, what time?'

The myopic scientist peered through his smeared spectacles. 'Six thirty should be fine.'

'See you then,' Tom said and headed for the queue in the refectory. He collected a portion of cottage pie and spotted Billy Whitelock, the Liverpudlian in English Two, sitting alone at a table. He was staring out of the window, deep in thought.

'Hi, Billy,' said Tom, sitting down. 'What did you think of last week's England game in Poland?'

The young man suddenly returned to the here and now. 'Oh, hi, Tom. Yes . . . good enough. A goalless draw but it qualified us for the World Cup in Italy.'

'That should be special,' said Tom with an encouraging smile. 'Looking forward to it. It will be wall-to-wall telly in the common room, I guess, next summer.'

Billy seemed to relax. 'Definitely.'

'So . . . how're things?' asked Tom. He would be studying Billy's response carefully.

It took a while for the lad to speak. 'My mam's not good. I rang up last night. She lost one of her nephews at Hillsborough. My cousin Harry.'

'I'm sorry,' said Tom. 'Must be tough. Keep in mind, whenever you want a word just call into my study.'

'Thanks,' Billy said quietly, but the light in his eyes seemed to dim. He had finished his meal and sat back.

'I fancy a coffee,' said Tom. 'How about you?' He glanced at his watch. 'It's only twelve thirty. What have you got next?'

'History of Education at one.'

'So there's time,' said Tom. He stood up and headed back to the coffee machine next to the serving counter.

After fifteen minutes of conversation about football, friends and family, Billy looked more relaxed as he set off for the main lecture theatre and the 1944 Education Act. It had changed post-war education in Britain but the only changes that mattered to Billy Whitelock included the fact his mother's hair had turned white in the past few months.

Ten miles away in his art studio, Victor's partner, Pat, was in despair. His head ached and the slanting sunlight bludgeoned his senses. He didn't feel well, although he had done his best to hide it from Victor. Following a second medical appointment, the results of his X-rays and a follow-up consultation with Dr Stern in York were imminent and he was worried about the diagnosis. His illness had gradually worsened over the past weeks but he had been determined to sustain his general joie de vivre at all costs during his time with Victor. He was aware that his partner needed all his energy to meet the demands of his new role as Head of Faculty. Victor's workload had increased and, after their evening meal, he would invariably retire to his study to prepare for the next day.

Pat wiped his brushes, dipped them in poppyseed oil and cleared away his latest painting, a huge canvas of magenta hues. It was time to turn his attention to food preparation, even though he knew Victor would be late. He had excused himself from attending the concert, saying time was of the essence to complete the vast portfolio of work for his forthcoming exhibition in mid-December. As always, Victor was understanding. Both of them were making sacrifices at present. Life was busy.

It was late afternoon and Victor was in his office. He glanced out of the window at the setting sun and sighed. It was that time of year again: the clocks were due to go back at the end of the month. There would be more daylight in the morning for children to walk safely to school but darkness was returning once again. His thoughts drifted on a stream of consciousness. There were occasions when life appeared fleeting and he treasured the special moments.

The nefarious activities of his predecessor, the late Dr Edna Wallop, were always at the back of his mind and he was determined not to return to those tyrannical times. He wanted to be a democratic leader rather than a so-called 'enlightened despot'.

At that moment there was a knock on the door. It was Rosie Tremaine.

'I'm so sorry to trouble you, Victor,' she said. Her cheeks were flushed.

'Not all all. Come in and sit down. It's good to see you.'

'I don't want to take up your time.' She stood there rather awkwardly.

Victor stood up and filled the kettle. 'I have some excellent herbal tea and I'm ready for a short break, so do join me.'

Rosie sat down a little nervously. 'Very well. Thank you.'

Soon they were sipping camomile tea and only the ticking of the clock on the mantelpiece touched the silence.

'So . . . how can I help?'

'It's really an apology.' She put down her cup. 'I'm afraid something has come up and I can't make tonight's concert.'

'Oh dear. That's unfortunate. Is there anything I can do to help?'

She put down her china cup and touched her left earring. 'It's rather personal.'

Victor studied her carefully. He intuited there were hidden depths to this intense lady. 'I'll pass on your apology to Inger.' He picked up the teapot. 'Meanwhile, more tea. It really is delicious, isn't it? I find it very calming in our busy lives.'

'No, thank you, but that was lovely,' and she replaced the cup. As she leaned forward the cross around her neck hung free on its silver chain.

Victor decided to engage her in conversation a little longer. It was clear his young colleague was troubled. 'I've often admired your pendant.'

She fingered the two small rowan twigs tied with red ribbon. 'My mother is a folk healer. She gave this to me. It's intended to protect me from evil spirits.'

Victor cast his mind back to his predecessor, Edna Wallop, and gave a wry smile. 'That could be useful in this profession. And are you finding time to pursue your chess? My partner is an enthusiast and we enjoy the occasional game, although I expect that compared to you we are both neophytes.'

Rosie seemed to ignore the compliment. 'I do have some dates for competitions but obviously out of term time.' She stood up and glanced at the clock on the mantelpiece. 'I had better get going, Victor. Thank you for the tea.'

After she had left, Victor collected the crockery and washed it in the sink. He wondered what it was that could be so important for Rosie to miss the concert. *A very intense lady*, he thought as he dried the cups and saucers. He reflected on the games of chess he enjoyed with Pat. They were simply a battle of wits whereas for Rosie Tremaine it appeared that it was almost a religion.

At four o'clock there was a knock on Tom's study door and Sienna Picard walked in. There was a smile on her face. She was wearing a micro miniskirt, high heels and lots of make-up. Under her denim jacket was a skintight T-shirt and it was obvious she wasn't wearing a bra.

'Hi, Tom, can you spare a minute?'

'Of course. Take a seat.'

She sat down and crossed her long legs. There was a shiny bracelet on her right ankle.

'So, how can I help? Is it the latest assignment?'

She stood up. 'It's warm in here,' she said and slipped off her jacket. She draped it on the back of the chair and sat down again. Then she fussed with the hem of her miniskirt before once again crossing her legs and sitting back in the chair. 'It's partly the assignment, Tom.'

'Partly? You had better explain.'

'Well, you gave me an official warning after our last session.'

'That's right. It's inevitable if you don't hand in assignments.'

She leaned forward and looked eagerly at Tom. 'It's just that life's really busy for me at present. I've got an evening job in a cocktail bar.'

'And how is that going?'

'Bit tiring, to be honest. Late nights, but the tips are great.'

Tom was beginning to wonder where this was going. 'So, are you saying it's having an effect on your work? Is that it?'

'That and other things.'

'Go on.'

'I'm a bit behind with your assignment on classroom management. I just can't get my head round it.'

Tom stood up and walked to the filing cabinet. He opened it and took out a folder. 'I've got some background notes here that might help.' He handed over a sheet of closely typed script. 'Photocopy this and let me have it back tomorrow. It will help you get started.'

She stood up and walked over to him. 'Thanks, Tom.' Then she took the sheet and looked up at him. 'The thing is, without your help I don't think I can achieve the grades I need to pass my first year.'

'Obviously I'll help as much as I can but you have to put in the time and the effort.'

Sienna moved closer to Tom. A strong scent of cheap perfume hung about her. 'I need you to give me good grades, Tom.'

'Well, that's possible if you earn them like everyone else.'

'That's just it. I'd like to earn them. So maybe we can come to some arrangement.'

'I don't follow.'

She placed the sheet of notes on the top of the filing cabinet and then leaned closer and put a hand on his shoulder. 'You're a great-looking guy, Tom. I could give you what all men want when they look at me. The owner of the cocktail bar has already propositioned me but I said no. I'm more interested in a man like you.' She stretched up and put her hands around his neck.

Tom took a firm hold of her wrists and stepped away. 'You're making a big mistake, Sienna. I'm not interested. You need to leave and we'll discuss this further at another time.'

She picked up her jacket, slung it over her shoulder and leaned provocatively against the chair. 'I'll look forward to it.' She gave him a wide-eyed smile. 'In the meantime you don't know what you're missing.' As she stood in the doorway she blew Tom a kiss before clipping away down the corridor on her high heels.

Tom folded his arms and shook his head. He would need to deal with this carefully and make a definite point of seeking Victor's advice. He glanced across at the filing cabinet. The sheet of notes was still there.

By seven o'clock the music room was packed with staff, partners and students. Inger was having a final word with her choir, who were all dressed in matching black blouses and shirts. When she finally stood in front of the microphone to introduce the concert, Tom sat back and drank in the image of this beautiful woman. In a classic black dress and a diaphanous blue silk scarf, she looked stunning.

Next to him sat Richard with his detailed list of instructions in front of him. Tom was relaxed. He had experienced all this last year and knew what to do. His scientist friend was concentration personified and everything went to plan. Lights faded, spotlights highlighted the soloists and the sound system was perfect.

As one piece of music began to segue into the next Tom

gradually understood the purity of Inger's seamless transitions. As a conductor and a pianist she was superb. The evening was a triumph and, at the end, the soprano, Arabella Esposito, received a standing ovation for 'Pie Jesu'.

After the concert there were drinks and congratulations. Inger was surrounded by well-wishers while Tom helped Richard clear the stage. Finally, Tom walked with Inger back to the car park. It was past eleven and a chill wind was blowing in from the north-west; Inger shivered and pulled her coat around her a little tighter. They stopped next to her Mini.

'Thanks for your help,' she said quietly.

'You're cold,' said Tom. 'Let me give you a hug.'

She gave a wan smile and unlocked her car. 'I'm really tired, Tom. We can catch up tomorrow.' She kissed him quickly on the cheek, climbed in her car and drove away.

As he drove home, Tom's thoughts were filled with this remarkable and unconventional woman. She was a conundrum and, on occasions, her words rankled and tugged at his thoughts. On the radio Wet Wet Wet were singing 'Sweet Surrender' as he wondered about the enigma that was Inger Larson.

Chapter Five

The Price of Wisdom

On an iron-grey morning in Haxby village Tom was scraping ice from his windscreen. It was Friday, 17 November and the first harsh frost heralded the onset of winter. A frozen cloak of mist covered the land and the smell of woodsmoke hung in the air. As he drove towards York beneath the torn rags of cirrus clouds, Cher was singing 'If I Could Turn Back Time' on the radio and Tom wished he could. During those far-off summer days Inger had been relaxed but since then their relationship had stalled. A month had gone by since Inger had requested some space and Tom had tried to tread carefully. He didn't want to rush her towards a more committed relationship and respected her need to step back for a time and concentrate on her work. Problems seemed to lie around every corner and solutions were elusive.

Meanwhile, a busy day lay ahead. A full timetable of lectures and seminars was in store followed by a sherry soirée for his English Two students in the Vice Chancellor's residence. There would be the compulsory poetry readings and

Rosie Tremaine had volunteered to organize that part of the evening. He hoped all would go well. The Vice Chancellor, Canon Edward Chartridge, was an influential man. He missed nothing and it helped to have him on your side.

The car park seemed more full than usual. It was a vast area the size of several football pitches but there was always room at the far end next to the dense evergreen bushes and the perimeter of sodium lights. The reception area was welcoming on this bitterly cold day and Perkins, the head porter, was his usual cheerful self.

'Morning, Dr Frith.'

'Hello, Perkins, how are you?'

He smiled, stood to attention and pretended to salute. 'All shipshape and Bristol fashion, thank you.'

'That's good to hear.' Tom rested his heavy satchel on the counter. 'Any news?'

Perkins pointed towards the tree-lined path that led to the Vice Chancellor's residence. 'Yes. Wilf the gardener has dug the hole for Dr Wallop.'

'Hole . . .? Oh, you mean the tree planting?'

'Yes, the memorial tree to remember our departed Head of Faculty.' Was there a hint of irony in this generally strait-laced man's voice?

'Do you know when it is?'

Perkins glanced down at his leather-bound day book. 'Yes, Professor Grammaticus said twelve forty-five. So, during lunchtime and just before afternoon lectures. Bit of a ceremony, so I understand. That nice lady governor, Miss Glendenning, will be in attendance and the Vice Chancellor will be saying a few words.'

'Thanks, Perkins, I'll be there.'

It occurred to Tom that Perkins was a useful confidant. He was the wise owl of Eboracum University with all its idiosyncrasies. It was a wisdom that had grown over generations of students.

After his tutorial with English Three and a discussion on the use of iambic pentameters in Shakespeare's sonnets, Tom caught up with Owen in their study.

'Coffee time, Englishman,' said Owen with a grin as he grabbed his *Daily Mirror* from his sports bag.

'Let's go,' said Tom after collecting his notes for his next session. As they scampered down the stairs from Cloisters corridor, Tom asked, 'How's Gareth?'

'*Gwych*, boyo. Brilliant. Six months old this week. Crawling like a clockwork mouse and feeding for Wales. He's a fit boy.'

'That's great. How about Sue?'

'Busy but her mum seems to call in every weekend. I find it a bit much, but I can't complain because they've been really helpful. They paid for our caravan holiday in Skegness in the summer and they worship their grandson.' He opened the door to the quad.

'Sounds a bit hectic,' said Tom as they hurried outside.

'Sorry,' said Owen. 'I shouldn't grumble.'

In the warmth of the common room they collected hot coffee and a handful of biscuits and sat down at a spare table. Tom began flicking through his diary while Owen was shaking his head in disgust at an article in his *Daily Mirror*.

Suddenly Zeb appeared with a mug of coffee. She sat down and lit a cigarette. 'So what's the news in your socialist rag, my little Welsh comrade?'

Owen pointed to the front page. 'Don't knock it, Dancing Queen. It was voted colour newspaper of the year with nearly four million sales.'

'Which just shows the state of the nation,' grumbled Zeb. 'We really have to get rid of this Tory government.'

'I agree,' said Owen. 'Have you seen the pay rises the water bosses are giving themselves?'

'I saw it on the news,' said Tom. 'The salaries are eye-watering.'

Owen pointed to his newspaper. 'It says here the Chairman of Yorkshire Water expects to double his £54,825 salary and, if that wasn't bad enough, the South West Water bosses intend to triple theirs to £232,000.'

'Obscene,' said Zeb. 'The gap between the rich and the poor simply gets bigger every year.'

Owen tossed the paper across the coffee table to Zeb. 'Meanwhile, Richard Branson, the Virgin boss, says he's planning to fly a balloon higher, faster and further than anyone else.'

'More money than sense,' muttered Zeb. She turned the pages of the newspaper and smiled. 'Looks like Fergie has been given the hard word. It says here that after giggling her way through last year's Remembrance Day service at the Cenotaph she managed to remain serious this year. How the other half live.'

'By the way, Zeb, what's got into the new bursar?' said Owen. 'He's giving a group of my students a hard time. Something to do with their rent. They think they're paying too much and he keeps giving them the cold shoulder.'

'I've had similar stories from some of my students as well,' said Tom. 'His responses have been a bit caustic, so I've heard.'

Zeb looked pensive for a moment. 'I'll follow it up,' she said.

'Thanks,' said Owen, 'and have you seen he has his own reserved parking space next to the Lodge?'

'Plus a seriously flash new car,' said Zeb.

'I've seen it,' said Tom. 'A new Audi 100, high tech and no change out of eight grand, so I've been told.'

'As you've just said . . . how the other half live,' muttered Owen.

Tom looked out of the window. 'Are you going to the tree-planting event this afternoon?'

'Sadly, yes,' said Zeb, 'if only to support Victor. I've seen the plaque in his office. The usual hypocritical stuff . . . "In memory of Dr Edna Wallop", et cetera. I know we shouldn't speak ill of the dead but, be honest, we would all have been kicked out if she had still been Head of Faculty.'

'Perkins told me the tree has arrived,' said Tom, 'and Wilf the gardener has dug the hole.'

'What time do we need to be there?' asked Owen.

'Twelve forty-five according to Victor,' said Zeb, 'and, thankfully, it should only take five or ten minutes.'

'We'll be there,' said Owen.

After lunch it was a sombre group that huddled in warm coats on the winding tree-lined path outside the university entrance that led to the Lodge. Owen, Tom and Rosie stood with Victor and Zeb along with a few of their faculty colleagues. Their breath steamed in front of them as they waited for Wilf the gardener to pat down the frozen earth around the young cherry tree and erect the metal plaque. Then an elegant woman representing the governors said a few words, followed by a brief prayer from the Vice Chancellor. It was over quickly and everyone hurried back to the warmth of the reception area.

Canon Edward Chartridge caught up with Tom and Rosie. 'I'll see you this evening, Thomas,' he said. 'And you too, Rosemary.'

'Thank you, Vice Chancellor,' said Tom. 'Looking forward to it.'

'Likewise,' added Rosie and they watched him take a left turn to the Lodge.

Rosie spoke quietly to Tom. 'It's only my mother who calls me Rosemary.'

'And *my* mother only calls me Thomas when she's angry,' replied Tom with a smile.

'I can't imagine that's very often.'

'You'd be surprised,' said Tom, grinning more broadly.

'So what's in store this evening?'

'Thankfully you don't drink so you won't have to suffer the copious glasses of sweet sherry. Otherwise it's simply to be on your best behaviour and let the students do their stuff with the readings. It's all very civilized and strait-laced. However, he's very perceptive and his apparently innocent questioning always has an ulterior motive. So beware.'

'Thanks for the tip.'

It was after Tom's lecture with Primary Two that Ellie MacBride touched his sleeve. 'Did you read my article in the *Echo*?'

Tom smiled. 'It was excellent. You researched it well, not just those illegal slimming tablets but all the other products that are popular today.'

'Thanks. It was a bigger job than I first thought but I've had positive feedback.'

'Also, I heard you're now second-year rep on the Students' Council.'

Ellie swept back her long black hair from her eyes. 'Yes. I'm trying to make the most of my time here.'

'Oh, and I've checked through your Jane Austen notes. They're fine.'

'Thanks, Tom.' She glanced at the clock. 'Anyway, mustn't keep you but I'll see you this evening at the VC's event. I remember when it was our turn last year. We all had to be on our best behaviour.' She smiled. 'Rosie has given me a T. S. Eliot poem to read, one you introduced me to last year, so I'll try to do it justice.'

'I'm sure you will. Catch you later.'

At four thirty, Rosie tapped on Inger's study door. Inger was sitting at her desk marking essays. The curtains were closed, the room was warm and cosy and prints of popular operas lined the walls. A photograph of a pretty Norwegian village stood on top of the filing cabinet and the bookcases were filled with ring binders of music manuscripts. Her denim jacket hung on the back of her chair.

'Hi, Rosie, come on in. How's your book on Oscar Wilde progressing?'

'Really well, thanks.'

'You must catch up with Zeb some time. It's definite now. She's producing *The Importance of Being Earnest* next summer with her drama group. You may be able to contribute. They're always brilliant productions, one of the highlights of the year.'

'In that case I shall.'

'So . . . how can I help?'

'It's the VC's soirée tonight . . . my first.'

'Ah, yes . . . well, nothing to be concerned about. They're usually convivial events: a surfeit of sherry, his favourite tipple, and students standing up and reciting poetry.'

'Yes, I've arranged the readings. It's the English Two group.'

'Well, Tom will be there. I'm sure he can let you know the format.'

'Actually, it's not that. I'm wondering if it's *formal*, in other words what to wear. Is it casual or smart?'

Inger smiled. 'Definitely smart but maybe understated. Edward is a bit old-fashioned, I'm afraid. Still living in the era when women had to wear skirts. Also, I recall he doesn't like women wearing too much make-up.'

'Fortunately that doesn't apply to me,' said Rosie with a forced confidence. 'I believe it's important to have a clear skin.'

'In that case you're *very fortunate*,' said Inger. 'Either way, I'm sure you'll enjoy it. Just follow Tom's lead and you'll be fine.'

'Incidentally, I've warmed to him lately. At first we didn't hit it off. It was as if I was a junior to him, a trainee.'

'I'm sure he wouldn't have wanted you to think in that way. Tom is a kind and generous man, always willing to help his colleagues.'

'You're clearly fond of him. My students say he's your partner.'

Inger looked down at her desk before she replied. 'I tend to ignore student gossip, Rosie, and what we do in our private lives is our own concern.'

Rosie sensed the finality of Inger's words. 'Well, thanks . . . you've been really helpful. I know what to wear now.'

'That's good,' said Inger evenly. 'Have a good evening.'

After Rosie had left, Inger stared at the closed door and wondered why so many of the conversations with her neighbour were far from comfortable.

It was shortly before seven o'clock when Tom arrived at the university and followed a group of students along the path to the Lodge, a distinctive Victorian building with churchlike roof finials and a pair of octagonal towers. Miss Hermione Frensham, the Vice Chancellor's personal assistant, was there to welcome the arrivals. It had been a pleasant change for her by mid-afternoon to put the cover over her IBM Selectric typewriter with its golf-ball head and prepare the main reception room for a sophisticated soirée. In her new pinstriped Jaeger business suit she never looked quite off-duty but this was as near as she would probably get.

Tom walked into a room of old-school refinement, with beautiful furniture and watercolour paintings. The cherubic figure of Canon Edward Chartridge welcomed everyone while Miss Frensham served sweet sherry in crystal glasses and the occasional soft drink to the assembled throng. The bursar, Gabriel Chalk, was strolling around the room, glass in hand and keen to impress. He didn't propose to converse with the tutors, merely those with real power. As he scanned the gathering he noticed various individual idiosyncrasies. The new female English tutor had caught his attention and he decided to have a quiet word with the Vice Chancellor.

Rosie Tremaine was standing alone and sipping a glass

of lime cordial. She had dressed very formally in a high-buttoned blouse, long skirt and a jacket, and Tom moved through the crowd to join her.

'Hi, Rosie. Love the outfit.'

She smiled. 'I thought I had better make an effort. It's my Edwardian schoolmarm look.'

'Appropriate for this evening,' said Tom. He glanced down at his slightly rumpled blue cord suit. 'This is the best I've got. Not very stylish, I'm afraid.'

'It's fine, Tom. Reflects you . . . the casual academic.'

He and Rosie were slowly developing as a team and they had both found a middle ground of respect as time went by. She looked around the room. 'Impressive place. I only caught a glimpse of it when I was interviewed.' She pointed up at a magnificent print above a drinks cabinet filled with bottles of sherry. 'Remarkable picture.'

'Apparently it's Lord Nelson on Plymouth Hoe,' said Tom. 'He's surveying his fleet before setting off for Spain. I've had the full guided tour a few times now.'

Rosie nodded. 'I guess you have.' She held her glass in both hands and gave Tom a level stare. 'This might be a good moment to say thanks.'

'What for?'

'For all your help. We didn't get off on the right foot. I was a bit defensive. Just me clinging to independence, I suppose. I'm enjoying the work now.'

'Good to hear. We're colleagues, Rosie, and I'm here to help whenever I can.'

For a moment there was silence and they looked across at the Vice Chancellor, resplendent in his three-piece suit and clerical collar. He was regaling a group of wide-eyed students with the fact that a seismic change was about to occur in modern politics when the House of Commons was televised live for the first time next week.

'Anyway,' said Rosie. 'I had better get the readers organized.'

'Good luck,' said Tom and he watched her walk away. It occurred to him that she was the only woman in the room completely devoid of eye shadow and lipstick. Her porcelain skin was clear and fresh. What he didn't know was that her lover, Julian Meadows, insisted she must never wear make-up and she always did exactly as he said.

Gradually everyone settled on the comfortable chairs and sofas, with a few sitting on the soft carpet. Rosie introduced each reader as Miss Frenshaw, the Vice Chancellor's personal assistant, dimmed the lights and everyone listened carefully to the poems of Emily Dickinson, Robert Frost, T. S. Eliot and Edgar Allan Poe. It was followed by polite applause and a vote of thanks from Edward. Then he took Rosie by the arm to the far corner of the room next to the canted bay window and the mahogany bookshelves. 'Congratulations, my dear, a triumph and an excellent selection.'

'Thank you, Vice Chancellor. We're fortunate to have some talented readers in English Two.'

'And how is your work progressing?'

'To be honest, it was tricky at first. Everything was new and a little different to my work down south, but I'm really enjoying it now.'

'What about your buddy tutor? Is that working well? I've had good reports from Professor Grammaticus.'

'Yes, Dr Frith has offered constant support. I'm fortunate.'

'Well, these are still early times in your career at Eboracum.' He gave a twinkling smile. 'You're still in your salad days, my dear.'

Rosie gave him a knowing look. 'I suspect we both love our Shakespeare, Vice Chancellor.'

'Yes indeed. *Antony and Cleopatra*,' said Edward.

'Act one, scene five, to be precise,' responded Rosie. '"My salad days when I was green in judgement."'

'Precisely,' said Edward knowingly. Then he pondered for a moment while assessing the competence of the young woman before him. 'I do hope you're not still green in judgement, Rosemary. It would be such a waste after the good start you have made.' He raised his glass and clinked it against Rosie's. 'Anyway, time to circulate. Thank you once again and enjoy your evening.'

Rosie watched him walk across the room to join Gideon Chalk and considered the Vice Chancellor's choice of words. She recalled that Tom had said he never missed a thing. She touched the lobe of her left ear and sipped her drink.

Ellie approached Tom and looked up at him appreciatively. She had always liked his wavy hair and hazel eyes.

'Well done,' said Tom. 'You read beautifully.'

'It was one of your favourites from "Little Gidding" in the *Four Quartets*. There's a great message there from T. S. Eliot about the cyclical nature of life and arriving back where you started and knowing the place for the first time. I felt that when I went back to my mum and dad's house in Barnsley during the summer. It seemed like a different world to the one I'm experiencing now.'

'I can understand that. How are they?'

'Mixed at present. They're having a big argument now about football.'

'Football?'

'Yes, apparently the FA have invited Argentina to play at Wembley next May prior to the World Cup in Italy.'

'There will be a lively reception for "Hand of God" Maradona,' said Tom. 'No one will forgive him for cheating. I'm guessing it's being seen as an ending to the hostilities with Argentina after the Falklands War.'

'Exactly. That's what the argument is about. My mother wants to put it all behind her while Dad will never forgive. It changed my life as well when my fiancé never returned.'

Tom was quiet for a moment. He knew of Ellie's history with a young man who lost his life in the Falklands. He was also aware that she had been to Greece during the summer break with Ricky Broadbent, a librarian from Barnsley. Apparently his wife had left him the previous Christmas and then he and Ellie had met in the library café, but it had proved to be an unsuccessful liaison.

'Difficult times,' said Tom quietly.

'Never ending,' murmured Ellie. Then she looked up at him and smiled. 'Just a thought – why don't I make some curtains for your study? It's pretty sparse at present, a sort of functional man-cave.'

Tom grinned. 'Not sure, particularly as I'm sharing with a Welsh cave-man. Owen's not into soft furnishings.'

'Well, have a think about it, and while we're talking about improvements, how about a haircut? Your hair is nearly as long as mine.'

'I've not really considered it,' said Tom.

Ellie leaned forward and grasped a lock of his hair. 'I could really do something with this.'

Tom stepped back, embarrassed, but not before Rosie had looked curiously in his direction.

'Thanks anyway, Ellie, but not now.'

Edward had persuaded Victor to have another sherry and he ushered him to a quiet corner. 'A splendid evening, Victor. Thank you for your support.'

'Always a pleasure, Edward. Your hospitality is legendary.' He gestured towards the students. 'This is a special experience for them.'

'Victor, I gather a certain Miss Picard is leaving us for pastures new.'

'Ah, yes. You've heard.'

'A wise decision, as always. It was clear that teaching was not for her. The incident in Dr Frith's study was reported to me by Miss Frenshaw. As you well know, she is my eyes and ears.'

Very true, thought Victor but kept his own counsel. 'It's taken a while, Edward, but it's settled now. I've helped her move on to another career path. I spoke with the person in charge of management training at Marks and Spencer's. Sienna starts there next month on their fast-track training scheme. It will be much more suitable for her.'

'I agree. You've done well, Victor. Good judgement . . . A wise move.'

Victor gave a wry smile. 'As you well know, Edward, it comes with age. We both know that.'

'But of course. For us age is a constant companion.' He placed his hand gently on Victor's shoulder. '"The price of wisdom is above rubies." Proverbs chapter eight, verse eleven.'

Victor smiled. 'You have a quotation for every occasion.'

Edward was aware of Victor's agnosticism but that had never clouded his judgement of Eboracum's finest academic. He leaned forward and lowered his voice. 'Not quite all, Victor. Your Dr Tremaine remains a conundrum. I hear things.'

'Really, and what might they be?'

'We can discuss it another day. In the meantime do keep your eye on her. She could be an excellent addition to the faculty so long as there are no pitfalls along the way.' He glanced around the room where some of the students were staring up at a collection of valuable first editions on one of the bookcases. 'Forgive me, I must play the host,' and he walked away to discuss the works of Percy Shelley with a group of over-awed students.

Tom and Rosie were the last to leave and, after shaking hands with the Vice Chancellor, it was after nine o'clock when they walked out into the darkness of the car park. It was almost deserted now. Around them the trees stood like sentinel shadows, stark in the moonlight. A ghostly mist hung in the air and the sodium lights in the distance were reflected in the crystals of frost that covered the ground.

'I'm on the other side of the car park, Rosie, so thanks for everything and safe journey home.'

'Goodnight, Tom.'

Rosie walked to her two-door Opel Manta and climbed in while Tom strode away in the darkness. As he breathed on his key before inserting it into the lock of his hatchback Ford

Escort, in the far distance he saw a long sleek car suddenly turn on its lights and cruise gently towards Rosie's. It circled round in front of her and stopped so that their driver's windows were adjacent and then turned off its lights. It was a strange cameo, two cars in that vast space side by side. It was impossible to see who it was; the other car was a shadow in the darkness, almost a hole in the air. It was only a matter of moments before it drove swiftly away.

Tom sat in his car and switched on his headlights. He saw Rosie drive out of the exit, following the other car. Then the mist descended once again and he guessed it was probably her solicitor friend. It was a brief incident at the end of a long day and for Tom Frith it was one that mattered little at the time. Only later did it begin to make sense.

Chapter Six

Queen's Gambit

It was early on Friday, 1 December and the first snow of winter had covered the countryside in a white shroud. The land was gripped in an iron fist and a severe frost covered the streets and pavements of Easingwold town. All sounds were muted apart from the cawing of the rooks in the tall elms. For Victor Grammaticus it would be a tough journey into York on this bleak morning.

Victor and Pat were sitting at their breakfast table staring at the cafetière of coffee in front of them but neither was drinking.

'Are you sure?' asked Victor.

'Yes, Victor, I'm sure.'

'So the diagnosis is prostate cancer.'

Pat waited a moment, choosing his words carefully. 'Yes, but fortunately at an early stage so the prognosis is positive.'

'He's good, is he . . . this Dr Stern?'

'The best.'

Victor clasped his hands. 'It's breaking my heart thinking about it.'

Pat stretched across the table and placed his hand on top of Victor's. 'It will be fine. We've had setbacks before. This is simply another one and we shall see it through together.'

There were tears in Victor's eyes. 'I pray you will be fine.'

Pat smiled. 'Ah, yes, prayer . . . it's never too late even for an old agnostic like you. Now drink some coffee while it's hot. It's bloody cold out there and you've got a faculty to run and I've got one more painting to finish for the exhibition.' He poured two mugs of coffee and they sat there drinking in silence.

In his Haxby cottage Tom was also sitting at his kitchen table putting the final touches to a huge list of students and their grades. It was important to check everyone's progress before going down for the Christmas holiday. Flakes of snow pattered against the window while the television was burbling away on the kitchen worktop. The newsreader had just told the nation that a man had left £50,000 to the Queen's corgis in his will, much to the disgust of his stepson.

His steaming bowl of Scott's Porage Oats was welcome on this bitter morning. Finally he packed his satchel with his lecture notes and, as he wrapped a scarf around his neck and donned his duffel coat, he thought of Inger. Tickets for the Faculty New Year Dinner Dance in the Assembly Rooms in York had gone on sale and he was hoping she would be his partner.

Owen was in their study when Tom walked in.

'Hi, Tom. I'm seeing Zeb this morning to pick up my New Year tickets. She's organizing sales, so are you going?'

'Nothing certain yet,' said Tom a little gloomily.

'Well, shape yourself. I'm taking Sue. Her mum and dad are coming over to stay.'

'Inger's been busy. I'm waiting for the right moment.'

'Bloody hell, Tom. Stop shilly-shallying. Just ask her. This is no time for dithering. What are you . . . a man or a mouse?'

Tom shrugged. 'It's tricky.'

Owen looked at the clock on the mantelpiece. 'I've got to go. Primary One in the gym. Remember, Englishman . . . hesitation will get you nowhere,' and with that he grabbed his clipboard and left.

Tom shook his head, emptied his satchel, selected his notes on J. D. Salinger and a copy of *The Catcher in the Rye* and ran downstairs to the quad and his tutorial with English Four.

At morning break Tom hurried back upstairs to Cloisters corridor and tapped on Rosie's study door.

'Yes?' was the call.

When he walked in she was sitting in an armchair deep in concentration. In front of her was a beautifully carved ivory chess set displayed on her coffee table.

She glanced up. 'Hi, Tom.'

He waved a stapled list of names and numbers. 'I'm just dropping off the list of English grades for you to check.' He placed it on her desk. 'Impressive . . . What a beautiful chess set.'

She smiled. 'A gift from my parents after I won my first tournament.'

'It looks terrific. So are you practising a few moves?'

'Yes. To be honest, it relaxes me. I've got a tournament back in Cornwall over Christmas.'

'I enjoy a game,' said Tom, 'but you're clearly in a different league.'

'It began as a hobby but in recent years I've taken it more seriously.' She checked her wristwatch. 'Are you teaching at eleven?'

'Yes, Primary Three. Their two-week placement in school starts next week.'

'Would you like a coffee? We've got time.'

'That's kind. Yes, please.'

Rosie stood up and switched on the kettle. 'Take a seat.'

On the table was a paperback describing the 1972 World Chess Championship between the American Bobby Fischer and the defending champion Boris Spassky of the Soviet Union.

'I remember this,' said Tom, tapping the cover. 'A remarkable win for the American.'

'Yes, probably the greatest match of all time. I use some of their moves in my practice games.' She selected two matching St Michael's Mount mugs, spooned in some Nescafé Gold and poured in the boiling water. Then she placed on the table a jug of milk, two spoons and a small plate of Cadbury's chocolate biscuits.

'Thanks, Rosie. This is really welcome. So what exactly are you practising?'

She stirred her coffee and gave a wry smile. 'One of my favourites. It's the Queen's Gambit, probably one of the oldest openings in chess and involves a bit of cunning. It's when white appears to sacrifice a pawn then black struggles to recover.'

'I've heard of it but I'm not sure what it is.'

'I could teach you. It's subtle but fairly simple.'

Tom grinned and selected a biscuit. 'About right for me then.'

At lunchtime Tom joined Owen in the refectory queue. A group of young men stood in front of them, including the rugby player, Chris Scully.

Owen tapped him on the shoulder. 'Hi, Chris, all set for tomorrow?'

'Oh, hi, Owen.'

'Big game coming up,' said Owen. 'Looking forward to it?'

'Definitely. My mum and dad are coming to watch.'

'That's good. Make sure I get a chance to meet them.'

'Will do. My mother was born in Cardiff so she'll love you.'

'What about your dad?'

'He's a Yorkshireman. Hates the Welsh every time they beat us at rugby.'

'In that case I'm looking forward to meeting your mum.'

After reaching the front of the queue, they collected their trays of food and went their separate ways to find a table.

'Confident young man,' said Tom. 'Good to see and he's done well on all his teaching placements so far.'

Owen smiled. 'One for the future in more ways than one.'

They found a table in the alcove where staff tended to gather and sat down.

'So remind me,' said Tom. 'What's the match tomorrow?'

'It's in Hull. Perfect for Chris. Last week when we were playing in Nottingham a couple of scouts from London clubs were checking him out. Word is getting around. With careful coaching and management he could have a great future, maybe even as an international. He's a great guy. Good to be part of his progress.'

Tom smiled. 'And he doesn't call you *sir* any more. Looks like school days have been left behind.'

Owen looked across at a table near the window where Chris and a group of rugby players and girlfriends were having lunch. They looked relaxed and happy with their lives. Two of the young women were sitting on either side of Chris and hanging on his every word.

'You're right, Tom,' said Owen thoughtfully. 'I'm just hoping he doesn't have too many extra-curricular activities.'

'Speaking of those,' said Tom with a smile, 'how's the nappy changing?'

'I'm pretty good,' said Owen with false modesty, 'although Sue does most of it. I help with bathtime and tell him bed-time stories.'

'Stories?'

'Yes, all the good ones about Wales stuffing the English.'

'I guessed as much. So how is Sue?'

'Fine. We're going out tonight. She's friendly with the woman next door and she's offered to babysit.'

'That's great. Where are you going?'

'The Odeon cinema. It's *Shirley Valentine*. Sue reckons it's brilliant and she's read that Pauline Collins and Tom Conti each deserve an Oscar.'

'Sounds good. Enjoy your night.'

'You ought to come as well. Bring Inger. I bet she would enjoy it.'

Tom shook his head. 'Not sure. She's been a bit reticent recently. Got a lot on her mind, I guess.'

'That's typical of women,' said Owen knowingly. 'They

play hard to get. I just use a bit of charm and after that they're putty in my hands.'

'So speaks God's gift to women.'

'Don't knock it, Englishman. If you've got it, flaunt it.'

Tom sighed. 'I'll think about it.'

Owen was on a roll. 'And, remember, don't hang around to buy tickets for New Year. Word has it they're going like hot cakes.'

Tom nodded. 'OK. Maybe I'll ask her before we leave tonight.'

It was afternoon break when Zeb called into Victor's study. She noticed he looked preoccupied and a little strained. 'Here are your tickets,' she said, 'and I'm hoping you and Pat can show us some of your dance moves this year.'

Victor gave a sad smile. 'I don't think our world is sufficiently liberated yet. Maybe another time.'

Zeb was insistent. 'We're almost into the 1990s. Attitudes are changing. It's only someone like the Vice Chancellor who would feel uncomfortable.'

'I know you're right, Zeb. Sorry if I'm not ready for such a leap of faith.'

'Well, you know best.' She studied her friend carefully. 'Shall I make you a coffee . . . and have you eaten? I didn't see you at lunch.'

'No, been a bit preoccupied. This has just come in.' He held up a paper headed 'Assessing Competency and Progression-Based Learning'. 'We've been asked to host a British Educational Research Association conference next spring.'

'But that's terrific,' said Zeb. 'Real status for Eboracum.'

'I agree,' said Victor with a sigh. 'It's just a great deal of work.'

Zeb sensed Victor had a lot on his mind. 'Look, I'll come back with a sandwich and I'll make you a coffee. Then maybe you could get off early and enjoy your weekend. We can work together planning this conference next week.'

Victor looked up at his loyal friend. 'Thanks, Zeb,' he said quietly. When she left he picked up the phone to call Pat. Then he replaced the receiver. He knew Pat would be working flat out on his recent canvas. There would be time to talk again this evening.

By four o'clock in York city centre the final rays of a winter sun had slipped behind the far horizon. Inside the city walls was a prestigious office with a brass plate outside its portico entrance. It read:

Keswick, Braithwaite & Meadows
SOLICITORS

In his spacious first-floor office forty-year-old Julian Meadows was staring out of the window, deep in thought. His affair with Rosie Tremaine had not developed in the way he had hoped. Unlike his previous relationships, this one was not a long-distance liaison. Her arrival in his office back in September had been unexpected and, lately, his wife had begun to question him about his late-night business meetings. There could be only one solution. He had to do something special for her. He lit a cigarette, sat down at his desk and rang home.

'Gillian Meadows speaking.'

'Hello, darling,' said Julian.

'What a lovely surprise,' said Gillian. 'To what do I owe this pleasure?'

'Well . . . I was thinking. It's about time I treated my beautiful wife to something she would enjoy.'

'How lovely. What had you in mind?'

'What about a weekend away? You've always wanted to visit Durham. Why don't we just do it?'

'Sounds wonderful but can you spare the time? You've been so busy of late.'

'For you, darling . . . anything.'

'In that case let's arrange it as soon as you're home.'

'We shall. Looking forward to it already.'

It was a smiling Julian Meadows who hung up and then proceeded to dial again.

'Good afternoon. Eboracum University,' said a brisk female voice.

'Extension 302, please.'

'Putting you through now.'

He heard the phone ring in study number two on Cloisters corridor, placed his cigarette in the ashtray on his desk and leaned back in his chair.

A telephone was also ringing in the science block. Richard Head had just finished his final tutorial and he picked up the receiver.

'Hi, Richard. It's Felicity here.'

'How nice to hear from you. Are you well?'

'Fine, thanks. It's been a good week and I've finished lectures for the day.'

'That's good. So have I.'

'I was just wondering what you were doing over the weekend.'

Richard smiled. 'Nothing special apart from keeping an eye on the close approach of the Moon and Venus tomorrow, but you will know about that.'

'Yes, they're in conjunction. Exciting, isn't it? So, Richard, I was thinking . . . shall I come over?'

'That would be wonderful and by pure coincidence I polished my telescope last night.'

'Excellent,' said Felicity. She paused for a moment. 'Then the only thing I have to decide is where I spend the night.'

'I have a spare bedroom, Felicity. You would love it. It has a painting of the Milky Way on the ceiling.'

Why doesn't that surprise me? she thought. 'That's perfect, Richard. Thank you so much.'

Inger had completed her final lectures and she climbed the stairs to Cloisters corridor and paused outside her study. She could hear the sound of someone sobbing and it was coming from Rosie's room. She tapped on the door and opened it slightly. 'Hello, can I come in?'

'Of course,' Rosie said and quickly wiped her eyes.

Inger walked in. 'Are you OK?'

'Yes, thanks, just something in my eye.' She stood up from the desk, regaining her composure. 'Shall I make a coffee?'

'That would be lovely,' said Inger. 'Very welcome. It's been a busy week.' There was a booklet about Durham Cathedral on the armchair. She picked it up and sat down. 'I love Durham. The cathedral is really special. Have you ever visited?'

Rosie paused as she spooned coffee into two china cups. 'No, I haven't. In fact I was due to go there this weekend with a friend but they had to cancel.'

Inger looked up, sensing what might have happened. 'Oh, that's a shame. Maybe another time.' Secretly she thought it might be a blessing in disguise.

For a while they sipped their drinks in silence. The chess set was on the coffee table. 'So, have you been practising your chess?' asked Inger. She leaned forward, admiring the intricately carved pieces.

'Yes, in fact Tom was in earlier and I taught him the Queen's Gambit.'

Inger smiled. 'I've heard of it. I used to play with my brother and I recall he mentioned it.'

Rosie nodded and put down her cup. 'It's one I tend to use. You lure your opponent into a false sense of security and then they lose.' She sighed and shook her head.

After that the conversation drifted along. They spoke of timetables, essays and the progress of Rosie's book about Oscar Wilde. By the time Inger returned to her study Rosie appeared settled.

It was nine o'clock on Saturday morning and Tom was eating a late breakfast of Crunchy Nut Cornflakes and listening to the radio. Lady Diana was in the news once again. She had attended a charity event and enjoyed the film *When Harry Met Sally* at the Leicester Square Odeon and met the co-stars, Meg Ryan and Billy Crystal. In a stunning red and gold dress she was the centre of attention and praised the Turning Point charity that had raised £50,000 for drink and drugs rehabilitation. Then, in complete contrast, it was reported that Vinnie Jones, the Leeds United hard man, had turned up for training with a black eye after a night-club fracas.

Tom stared out of the window at the frozen world outside as the disc jockey introduced Phil Collins singing 'Another Day In Paradise'. 'You have got to be joking,' Tom muttered as he carried his bowl to the sink. Just then his telephone rang. It was Inger.

'Hi, Tom.'

'Inger, this is a nice surprise. I came by your study last night but you weren't in.'

'It was probably when I was next door checking on Rosie.'

'How is she?'

'Fine, I think, but something happened yesterday. I was a bit concerned and thought I would share it with you.'

'What is it?'

'When I called in I'm pretty sure she had been crying.'

'Oh dear. What's the problem? Is it work?'

'No, it's not that. Apparently, she was preparing to go to Durham for the weekend with a friend but whoever it was pulled out.'

'Do you think it was the solicitor guy?'

'I don't know but it's very likely considering the state she was in.'

'We need to keep checking she's OK. It sounds like you've made good contact. That will help.'

'I guess that's all we can do for now but I thought I would let you know.'

'Thanks, Inger, I appreciate it.'

'Incidentally, there's something I forgot to mention. Owen called by yesterday during afternoon break. He said the tickets for New Year were going quickly and I had better get a move on before you were snapped up by another even more glamorous partner.'

'The cheeky sod!'

'Don't worry,' said Inger with a smile. 'He meant well. He's a good friend. So if the offer is still there I should love to come along with you. I've been a bit preoccupied lately. Sorry. There have been a few things on my mind.'

'You've nothing to apologize for and that's great news. I'll get some tickets on Monday.'

'Don't bother. Owen gave me two. He didn't want us to miss out.'

'Really?'

'Yes. Your little Welsh friend is very persuasive.'

'In that case I'll reimburse him on Monday.'

'No need. I offered to pay him and he refused. He said it was a gift, along with a few choice words about us two behaving like sulky teenagers.'

'Oh dear. He's not into subtlety, is he?'

'He's a dear friend, Tom – I don't mind. And I love how he is so proud of his family.'

'I know. Sue is brilliant and young Gareth is lucky to have two such loving parents.' Inger didn't reply, and after a moment Tom asked, 'What is it?'

'Just thinking back to Rosie. I think that's what she wants . . . a relationship just like that.'

'Too true.'

'I'm sad for her.'

'It was only yesterday she was teaching me one of her chess moves. She was so relaxed then.'

'Yes, she mentioned that . . . a Queen's Gambit.'

'Makes you think about what's important in life.' Again, there was no response for a while. 'Are you still there?'

'Sorry, Tom, just thinking.'

'OK. Thanks for ringing, Inger.'

'Good to talk. Bye for now.'

There was the buzz that ended the call and Tom replaced the receiver. *The Queen's Gambit is a bit like life,* he thought . . . *an initial sacrifice followed by a recovery.* When he looked out of the window the world didn't look quite so bleak any more.

Chapter Seven

Four Nativities and a Funeral

When Tom set off for Nether Bottom Church of England Primary School it occurred to him that it had not been blessed with the most sympathetic of names. As he crossed the bridge over the River Nether and descended into the valley beyond, he reflected on the events of the past days. It was Friday, 15 December, the last day of term, and his Primary Three students were completing their two-week school placement. Christmas had dominated the activities of the children and during the week he had already sat in on three nativity plays with a fourth expected this morning.

It was shortly before 9.00 a.m. when Tom arrived in the quaint North Yorkshire village and parked outside a Victorian school building. He followed a group of parents and children up the winding snow-covered path to the entrance porch. They were carrying various cast-off bed sheets, dressing gowns, a halo on a stick and a papier mâché donkey's head. A little girl was trundling behind them with her toy sheep on wheels.

The headteacher, Mrs Crossley, a cheerful, rosy-cheeked lady, was standing alongside a gaunt man in a clerical collar when Tom walked into the entrance hall.

'Good morning, Mr Frith,' said Mrs Crossley, 'and welcome to Nether Bottom. This is our Chair of Governors, the Reverend Jonah Grimshaw. He's called in to see our nativity play.'

'Yes, I attend every year,' announced the vicar in a commanding voice. 'In the past it has always gone like clockwork. I have provided the precise script and the children line up and recite one sentence each. It never fails.' He paused and gave Mrs Crossley a hard stare. 'However, Mrs Crossley has persuaded me this year to take an enforced sabbatical and permit your student to interpret the story of the birth of Our Lord.'

Tom noticed the hint of reticence in the voluble reverend's voice. 'That's very kind and I appreciate your support,' he said with a fixed smile.

Mrs Crossley looked up at the tall figure of the vicar. 'Perhaps, Jonah, you would care for a hot drink in the staffroom while we're getting prepared?' There was a note of determination in the question. She turned to Tom. 'Would you like to follow me, Mr Frith?' As they walked towards the school hall Mrs Crossley spoke quietly. 'Your student is like a breath of fresh air and this makes a welcome change. I love a real nativity play. It's as much a part of the festive season as mince pies and mistletoe.'

'I agree,' said Tom.

'I've no wish to speak out of turn but the vicar has always insisted on taking charge. It's the same every year. Weeks of practice with the same script and a noticeable lack of spirit.

The arrival of Miss Cassidy gave me the opportunity to bring our nativity up to date.'

'Well, I shall look forward to this one.' Tom smiled. 'Actually, it will be the fourth for me this week, all different of course – with the occasional disaster. Yesterday the little girl playing Mary refused to hold hands with Joseph and the previous day the Angel Gabriel had to go to the toilet in the middle of announcing the birth of Jesus. Before that, on Monday, there was a panic when the doll being used for baby Jesus couldn't be found and was replaced at the last minute with a Cabbage Patch doll.'

Mrs Crossley smiled. 'Oh dear . . . but that's what makes them so special. I saw yesterday's dress rehearsal and it was fine but no doubt today will be different again.'

Tom was encouraged by the news and Mrs Crossley's positive support. She clearly loved her village school. There were only sixty pupils on roll, divided into three classes, and Jodi Cassidy was working in Mrs Crossley's infant class with the five- and six-year-olds. She was surrounded by excited children while making last-minute preparations and gave Tom a cheerful wave.

Jodi was one of Tom's brightest student teachers, always eager and with an electric personality matched by her wild raven hair. She had ditched her acid-washed jeans for a black trouser suit with a short jacket and a red polo-neck jumper. In her pocket was her trademark headgear, a black beret which was a family heirloom that had been passed down from her grandfather. He had fought in the Royal Australian Armoured Corps in Egypt in 1942 and his photograph was always front and centre on the mantel-piece back in Whitby.

The room was heaving with activity and a few mothers were helping to dress the children. 'Thanks for coming,' called out Jodi. 'Exciting times.'

'I'll leave you to it,' said Mrs Crossley. 'I need to get all the parents settled in the hall.'

Tom looked at Jodi, who was repairing a cardboard crown. 'Is there anything I can do?'

'Yes please,' Jodi said and nodded towards the teacher's desk. 'Can you wrap the Kings' presents? There's some tissue and ribbon there.'

Not exactly gold, frankincense and myrrh, thought Tom as he wrapped a tin of tuna, a packet of Kellogg's Rice Krispies and an empty bottle of Old Spice aftershave.

Minutes later all was ready and Jodi prepared to lead the children into the hall.

'Good luck,' said Tom.

'Thanks,' said Jodi with a smile. 'Fingers crossed. We've been doing a lot of spontaneous drama with Zeb recently so I thought I would give it a try. Mrs Crossley seemed really keen. So there's no script.'

The hall was packed with parents and Tom found a chair next to the Christmas post box and began to write in his carbon-copy notebook. Word had got around the village that this year the nativity would be different and so it proved to be. It was a wonderful performance. After the children had waved to their parents and the donkey's ears had dropped off, the pupils acted out the timeless story. One of the Kings, after laying a tin of tuna at the foot of the wicker-basket manger, gave his tinfoil crown to his best friend who was dressed as a sheep. This prompted one of the shepherds to give his crook to the donkey. It all added to the innocence of the event and at the end there wasn't a dry eye in the house.

Following thunderous applause, Mrs Crossley stood up to thank everyone and declare the production a triumph. The vicar didn't stay for the coffee and mince pies.

It was just before eleven o'clock when Tom walked into reception. Perkins stood behind the counter and on the shelf behind him were dozens of Christmas cards. Perkins was a very popular man.

'Good morning, Dr Frith, another term completed for you. Pleased to hear it's gone so well.'

Tom was carrying a plastic bag containing a bottle of mulled wine and a Christmas card. He put the bag on the counter. 'Thanks, Perkins. This is for you. Merry Christmas and thanks again for all your support this year.'

Perkins looked in the bag and smiled. 'I'll share this with my Pauline and we'll think of you.' He leaned forward and shook Tom's hand. 'There's a card for you in your pigeonhole.'

Tom looked at his wristwatch. 'Must fly. I'm teaching in five minutes.'

Perkins watched him as he hurried away and looked thoughtful. Eboracum needed tutors like Tom Frith and he hoped one day he would find time to slow down and smell the roses.

Tom was just in time for his final tutorial with his Primary Two group before they went down for Christmas. It was a lively session and Tom highlighted the strengths and occasional weaknesses that had been experienced during their school placements. The discussion touched upon mixed-ability teaching and the huge difference sometimes to be found between the most and least able. Tom decided to include a session dedicated to this next term with a follow-up on identifying and supporting those children identified as *gifted*.

It was as he left and was walking back to the quad that Ellie MacBride caught up with Tom. 'Hi, Tom, thanks for your support this term. I should finish the first draft of my Jane Austen assignment by the New Year.'

'Good to hear,' said Tom. 'I'll look forward to reading it.' They had reached the quad. 'What are your plans for Christmas?'

Ellie paused and looked down at the frozen cobbles beneath her feet. 'The usual, I guess. Christmas with my parents and a couple of nights out with girlfriends. So, nothing special. What about you?'

Tom smiled. 'Similar to you. Christmas Day with my parents.'

'What about the staff New Year Dance in the Assembly Rooms? I guess you will be going to that.'

'Yes.'

'With Inger?'

'Probably.'

She looked at Tom. 'Oh well, best wishes for Christmas.'

'And to you, Ellie.'

He watched her walk away . . . still an enigma.

At lunchtime there was welcome hot food in the refectory and Tom saw Inger and Rosie sitting at a table well away from everyone else and deep in conversation. They had been regular companions during the past two weeks, which surprised him. Rosie had completed her tutorials on time and made all the school visits that were on her timetable. Meanwhile, Inger had been a frequent visitor to her study and they had enjoyed the occasional evening meal together in one of the city-centre restaurants.

Tom had no wish to disturb them and spotted Owen sitting alone in a far corner. He collected a plate of steaming hot stew and dumplings and sat down opposite his friend. 'So, any plans for Christmas?' he asked.

Owen was wolfing down his food. After two very physical sessions in the gym he was ready to refuel. 'We're going back to my home town in Wales to spend Christmas with my parents. They're thrilled about seeing young Gareth.'

'That's great,' said Tom.

'Yes, it took some sorting. Sue got hers to agree to alternate Christmases so I guess that's the pattern from now on.'

'Makes sense, I suppose,' said Tom. 'And the last game of the year tomorrow?'

'Yes, another big one and more scouts are beginning to gather to watch Chris Scully. His reputation is growing.'

'That's good, isn't it?' said Tom.

'Mixed feelings,' mused Owen. 'I would have liked to keep him for at least another season.' He put down his knife and fork. 'Not seen much of you this week.'

Tom grinned. 'I've had four nativities and a funeral.'

'I'd forgotten about the funeral. Last Tuesday, wasn't it? How did it go?'

'Eventful,' said Tom. 'It was my Uncle Maurice, one of my mum's elder brothers. Rarely met him. After the crematorium we all went to the wake in a pub in Leeds. It was the usual crowd of distant family members that you only meet at weddings and funerals. Everyone had a story about him. He was a milkman with a liking for the ladies.'

Owen grinned. 'Oh yes.'

'I was told Maurice had been visiting the local Sofa World store with his wife, Nora, in order to buy a new armchair. Apparently their Yorkshire Terrier, Bremner, had ripped their old one to shreds. Then, as he was about to sample the comfort of a high-backed imitation-leather chair, to his horror, across the room of soft furnishings, he spotted his most recent conquest, a barmaid known locally as Buxom Brenda.'

'I wonder why,' said Owen with a grin. 'Go on. This is a hell of a story.'

'Well, he panicked and flopped down into the chair and promptly suffered a heart attack.'

'Bloody hell!'

'That's not all,' said Tom. 'He and Nora had just returned from a fortnight in Lanzarote with a suntan so all the passing shoppers commented how well he looked for someone who had recently died.'

Owen shook his head. 'The poor sod. What a way to go.'

It was at that moment that Richard Head appeared, carrying a tray with a Scotch egg salad and a mug of tea. He was wearing a polo-neck jumper with a Christmas tree design on the front. In the science department it was festive jumper day. 'Hello, Tom; hello, Owen. May I join you?'

'Of course,' said Tom while Owen gave a perfunctory nod. 'We were just discussing Christmas. What are your plans?'

'I'm meeting up with Felicity. She knows a pub that does Christmas dinners. She's not into cooking.'

'Good decision,' said Tom.

Richard nodded and took great pains to cut his Scotch egg exactly in half. 'Better than being on my own. That's what it's always been in the past.'

'I'm pleased for you,' said Tom. 'It's good to have a friend for Christmas. She sounds a great companion – someone who shares your interests.'

He gave a shy smile. 'Yes, I suppose you're right. She's always full of news. A really up-to-date lady. Only yesterday she was telling me about the new eight-bit fourth-generation handheld game console.'

Owen put down his knife and fork. 'Pardon?'

'It's really topical,' said Richard eagerly. 'Felicity says it's the next big thing in new technology. It's been developed by Nintendo and was released in Japan earlier this year.'

Owen looked vacant. 'Released?'

Richard was animated. 'Yes, they sold their entire stock of three hundred thousand units within two weeks. It's called Game Boy.'

'Good name,' said Tom, 'but what does it do?'

'You play games with it,' said Richard.

'But why?' asked Owen. 'What's the point?'

'Modern entertainment,' said Richard.

Owen shook his head. 'Give me a game of rugby any day.' He had finished his meal and got up. 'Anyway, things to do. Catch you guys later.'

Richard watched him walk away. 'I don't think he's all that interested.'

'Owen enjoys *outdoor* sports,' said Tom.

'The thing is, Tom, one day he may be the only person on the planet who doesn't own one.'

Tom looked curiously at his studious friend. 'You really believe that, don't you?'

'It's simply the way society is developing.'

Tom shook his head. He had no desire to become a couch potato. 'Oh well, always good to talk, Richard.' He picked up his tray and strolled out, shaking his head while wondering if modern life was leaving him behind.

It was as he was leaving the refectory that Poppy Hartness, one of his Year Two students, caught him up. 'Tom, can I have a quick word?'

'Of course. What is it, Poppy?'

'It's something we mentioned to Zeb and thought had stopped but last night it happened again.'

'What did?'

'There's someone peeping in our windows at night. Not every night but it's getting uncomfortable. Some of the girls think it might be one of the rugby lads after a night on the beer.'

'OK. I'll check it out with Owen.'

'Thanks, Tom,' and she hurried away.

After his final lecture of the term with English One, Tom headed for the common room. He checked his pigeonhole and the bulging pile of Christmas cards. Ellie's distinctive handwriting featured on the top one. Victor and Zeb were enjoying a hot drink and Zeb waved for him to join them as he collected a mug of tea and a chocolate digestive.

'So, will you be there tomorrow evening?' she asked. 'It's a couple of years since Pat's last exhibition and this one is expected to be even more spectacular.'

Victor gave a gentle smile. 'Don't feel pressured, Tom, but

it would be lovely if you could join us.' He took from his pocket a beautifully illustrated postcard. It read:

'Breaking Chains – Studies in Modernity'
An exhibition by Patrick St John-Stevens
16ᵗʰ–17ᵗʰ December 1989

'I'll be there but I'm afraid I'm no art expert. It will be a first for me.'

'You will be most welcome, Tom.' He paused and raised his eyebrows. 'Although I have to warn you that most of the works are rather pricey.'

'Don't worry, Tom,' said Zeb. 'For us mere proles it's a case of look and learn.' She turned to Victor. 'And Inger said she would be there.'

'Yes, I thought she might.' He gave Tom a knowing look. 'Yet another incentive.'

Tom smiled. 'I guess it's a huge amount of work getting everything ready.'

'Definitely,' said Victor. 'I'll be busy this evening helping Pat complete the finishing touches. He's been working really hard arranging all the canvases in preparation for the opening. I'm excited for him. His work is remarkable, a huge talent. We simply need the usual buyers to turn up.'

It was late afternoon when Inger tapped on Tom's study door and walked in. He looked up expectantly.

'Tom, I'm going Christmas shopping in York tomorrow morning. I was wondering if you would like to come along.'

'Definitely,' enthused Tom. 'I can pick you up if you wish. What time?'

'Thanks. Is nine thirty OK?'

'Of course.'

'Zeb was saying the market is brilliant.'

'Then we must go,' said Tom.

'Also, she had a word about supporting Victor tomorrow evening. It's Pat's art exhibition in the city centre.'

Tom nodded. 'I've told Victor and Zeb that I'll be there. Owen mentioned it as well. He can't make it because he's busy with other rugby commitments.'

'OK,' Inger said and opened the door. 'I'll see you tomorrow.'

'Looking forward to it,' said Tom.

She left and Tom leaned back in his chair and smiled.

Half an hour later he was packing his satchel when there was another knock on the door. It was Rosie Tremaine.

'Hi, Rosie, this is a pleasant surprise. Inger mentioned you're travelling down to Cornwall tomorrow.'

'Yes, I'll be with my parents over Christmas but Inger encouraged me to be back up here for New Year.'

Tom looked at this slim, elegant woman. 'That's good. I'm pleased you've had the opportunity to spend time with her.'

'She's been brilliant. Anyway, I just wanted to wish you all the best for Christmas and here's a little something to say thanks.' It was a small parcel wrapped in red ribbon.

'That's very kind, Rosie.'

Then she surprised him by stepping forward and kissing him lightly on the cheek. 'I'm glad we had the chance to work together.' She smiled and walked out.

Tom opened the parcel. It was a leather-bound copy of *The Hobbit* by J.R.R. Tolkien. Inside was a dedication that read: 'To Tom, my buddy tutor, with thanks, Rosie'. Tom smiled and put it on his bookshelf alongside his copy of *The Fellowship of the Ring*, a gift from the late Professor Henry Oakenshaw the previous year.

On Saturday morning Tom awoke to a dawn of silence and light. A fresh carpet of snow covered the pantile roofs across the street and each windowpane was decorated with a curved stitching of frost. As he drank a mug of tea, Jill Dando was presenting a mixed bag of news on *BBC Breakfast*. The Tories were facing a revolt over allowing tens of thousands of refugees to enter the country from Hong Kong, while Fergie had asked doctors not to reveal the sex of her unborn baby due next March. She wanted it to be a surprise.

On Tom's drive into York the traffic was heavy and a low sun lit up the Minster as he navigated the busy streets. On the radio Jason Donovan was singing 'When You Come Back To Me' as Tom drove to the Knavesmire and parked outside Inger's home. As he walked up the path the door opened and she stood there smiling, wrapped in her warmest coat and scarf. Her blonde hair was tied back in a pony-tail and she added a bright red woollen hat as she stepped out and locked the door.

'Thanks, Tom,' she said. 'I could have driven in but the lift is welcome.'

He relaxed. It felt like old times. They were together again and Inger was animated. She loved shopping and it soon became clear there was something special she had in mind. Minutes later they had parked in the university car park and set off up Gillygate and towards the city centre. When they wandered into Coney Street Tom glanced in the window of

Boots. He recalled Inger preferred Dior perfume. It would make a perfect Christmas gift.

Finally they arrived at Dixons and stared at the window display.

'That's the one I'm keen on,' she said. 'Richard recommended it. He said it was a real bargain and my old one has seen better days.' The label read 'Sony Company Midi Hi-Fi System £199.99'.

They went in and were approached by an overzealous ginger-haired young man with a severe case of acne. He wore a badge on his striped shirt that read: 'Gavin Johnson, Technical Assistant'. 'Good morning, madam, ah'm Gavin,' he said with the smile of an expectant crocodile. 'Ah see you've spotted our Christmas bargain.'

Inger stepped back from his close attention and bad breath. 'I'm interested in this particular model,' she said neutrally.

'Well, you've come on t'perfec' day. Ah can do you a deal on t'finest portable CD player in t'UK . . . a bargain at £199.99.'

'I'll think about it,' said Inger.

Gavin was on a roll. 'Y'won't find nowt better, madam. It's a superb compact system wi' twin-cassette an' 'igh-speed dubbing.'

'Yes,' murmured Inger thoughtfully. 'Interesting.'

'Not t'mention FM stereo. It's got ever'thing y'need.'

'Really?' said Inger.

'Madam, it's gorra graphic equalizer an' an 'igh-speed edit.'

Inger looked at Tom. 'What do you think?'

Gavin didn't want to lose a sale and closed in on Tom. He

looked at Tom's well-worn jeans and slightly dishevelled appearance and came up with his pièce de résistance. 'Yer 'usband might like t'go for our one-off Christmas offer of £7.87 per month an' no deposit. Them's easy terms.'

Inger gave the young man a wide-eyed stare. 'This gentleman isn't my husband and I wouldn't want to pay monthly.'

Gavin wasn't Dixons' young salesman of the year for nothing. 'My apologies, madam, but yer looked t'perfec' couple an' can ah jus' mention it 'as a two-way speaker an' a semi-auto turntable. Yer lookin' at twenty-first-century technology ten years a'ead of its time.'

Inger stepped back, pursed her lips and nodded. 'I'll take it, please.'

'A wise choice, madam.' Gavin flashed his crocodile smile once again and thought of his commission.

After arranging delivery they wandered up to King's Square where a group of out-of-tune handbell ringers were playing 'We Wish You A Merry Christmas' and a stall was selling roast chestnuts. Nearby, at the top of the Shambles, they paused to take in the familiar view of the medieval street with its overhanging buildings and cobbled pathway. The sound of the nearby Christmas market could be heard and they joined the crowds around Bobby Dazzler's Toy Stall.

'No fancy London prices 'ere,' he was yelling while holding up a Disney Sno-Cone Castle. 'Ah've got all t'best-sellin' Christmas toys, Real Ghostbusters Table-Top Pinball, Polly Pocket an' a Batmobile wi' a rocket launcher. You name it, ah've gorrit.'

'That reminds me,' said Tom. 'I need to buy a gift for Owen's son.'

They walked on and next to a stall labelled 'Arnie Wainwright's Pork Pies' was Vinyl Pete's Records where there was a huge choice of LPs from Rock and Pop to Classical. On a stepladder was a loudspeaker and the odds-on favourite to be the Christmas number-one record was blasting out. It was Band Aid II with 'Do They Know It's Christmas?' featuring Kylie Minogue, Jason Donovan, Bros, Wet Wet Wet, Lisa Stansfield and Cliff Richard. The shoppers were singing along while Vinyl Pete was doing a roaring trade. In his baggy sheepskin coat, a roll-up cigarette hanging from his lips and with his long hair held back with a Stone Roses headband, he cut a distinctive figure.

'Come on,' shouted Vinyl Pete, 'let's be 'avin' you. Ah've got 'em all. Alice Cooper, Elvis, Madonna, Billy Joel, Iron Maiden. You name it an' ah'll find it.'

To Tom's surprise Inger gave a mischievous smile and raised her hand.

'Yes, luv,' yelled Pete. 'We 'ave a classy blonde lady 'ere what looks like 'er in ABBA. What d'you fancy, darlin'?'

Inger shouted out above the noise of the crowd. 'Have you got *A Classical Christmas* featuring Debussy, Vivaldi and Ravel?'

Vinyl Pete delved into a cardboard box labelled 'Classical' and pulled out the LP as if he was a magician. ''Ave ah gorrit, darlin'? O' course ah gorrit.' He gave her a wink. 'In fac' ah've got ever'thing you will ever need.' He looked up at the crowd and raised his voice. 'An' this lovely lady can 'ave it for a fiver.'

Inger produced a five-pound note from her purse.

'Come back any time,' said Pete as he slipped the disc into a brown paper bag.

As they walked away Pete put a new record on the turntable. It was 'I Don't Wanna Lose You' by Tina Turner and Inger smiled. 'Quite a character,' she said. 'I've been wanting this record for a while.'

'I bought one for you there last year. It was when you had your New Year party.'

'I remember, Tom. A kind thought and, speaking of kind thoughts, we ought to pay Owen for the tickets he bought for us.'

'I tried,' said Tom, 'but he refused point blank. He insisted it was a gift.'

Suddenly she held Tom's hand. 'I'm looking forward to it.'

Tom smiled. The Inger he once knew was back.

Shortly before seven o'clock Tom returned to Inger's apartment. She had changed into a long black leather coat and a fur hat. They drove into York, parked near Micklegate Bar and walked into the city centre where Pat had rented a large studio for four days.

A huge, illuminated poster in the window displayed one of his major works beneath the title of the exhibition. The doors had opened at seven and already an eager crowd of art enthusiasts and collectors had gathered.

Pat was wearing a classic ivory three-piece suit and white collarless shirt.

He looked a little pale and tired but was making every effort to be his usual ebullient self. Victor was at the door welcoming the new arrivals while Zeb was serving glasses of champagne and Hermione Frensham was sitting behind a desk recording sales. A glossy catalogue was available on a table at the side of the room and within minutes two of the works had a small circular red sticker attached to indicate they had been sold.

'This is remarkable,' said Inger as she stared at a canvas of magenta hues. The price in the catalogue was listed at £500 and it had already been snapped up by a London-based collector.

'What an experience,' said Tom. 'I'm so glad we came.'

The studio filled up and it was as if they were in a private cultural enclave. Conversation ebbed and flowed and Tom finished up chatting with Zeb while Inger found Victor standing alone. He was watching Pat in animated conversation with a group of connoisseurs of fine art.

'I love it when his talent is recognized,' said Victor.

'I can see that,' said Inger.

Victor turned to her and spoke quietly. 'Inger, make the most of your life. Don't lose a chance of happiness. Tom's a good man.' Then he squeezed her hand and walked away.

For a moment Inger held her breath. She had been close to revealing something of her past to the perceptive Victor.

Finally the evening drew to a close. There were heartfelt farewells and Christmas good wishes. Tom drove Inger back to her home and parked outside. They sat there in the darkness.

'Thanks for today,' said Tom.

Inger smiled and held his hand. 'Would you like to come in for a coffee?'

Chapter Eight

New Year Conversations

When Tom Frith drove out of Haxby on the last day of 1989, a frigid world of silence stretched out before him. Winter had closed over the land and the air was frozen. On this bleak morning it seemed as though the pale sunlight barely touched the earth. The sleeping city was waking to the iron fist of winter, an unforgiving monochrome of snow and sky. In the distance a church bell was tolling, mournful and muted. For some it was an omen of what was to come but for others it felt like a harbinger of hope and expectation. It was Sunday, 31 December, the final day before the dawn of the nineties and one that Tom would never forget.

He had arranged to meet Inger outside Bettys Café Tea Rooms in St Helen's Square at ten thirty but first he had a collection to make. As he drove into York the Christmas number one, Band Aid II and 'Do They Know It's Christmas?', was on the radio once again. He parked in the university car park and walked into the city centre.

He had ordered his outfit for the dinner dance from

Clarkson's, a gentleman's outfitter, and everything was ready for him on arrival. It included a smart tuxedo jacket, trousers with satin piping, a dress shirt with cufflinks and a black tie. The service was excellent and everything was neatly packed in a suit carrier with a shoulder strap. He agreed to return it the following Tuesday and hurried back to the university car park. After laying the carrier carefully on the back seat of his car he pulled his scarf a little tighter and trudged back on the icy footpaths to St Helen's Square. There was a queue outside the famous Bettys Café Tea Rooms and he waited patiently for Inger.

At ten thirty she arrived and kissed him on the cheek. 'Did you collect your suit?' she asked.

'Yes, it looks good. I'll look smart for a change.'

'About time too,' she said with a mischievous smile.

They were ushered inside by the maître d', past a display of inviting cakes and handmade chocolates and directed to a table for two next to a huge, curved window. Around them was an eclectic mix of traditional wood panelling and art deco mirrors. It was like going back in time.

'I love this place,' said Inger as a waitress in a 1930s cap and starched apron took their order. Soon they were enjoying a plate of fruity scones, known locally as fat rascals and filled with citrus peel, almonds and cherries. Inger poured tea from a silver teapot into the delicate china cups.

'All set for this evening?' asked Tom.

Inger nodded. 'Yes, should be fun and good to relax with colleagues at the end of a busy year.'

'How was your Christmas?' he asked. Inger had returned to Oslo to spend a few days with her parents, her brother Andreas and his girlfriend, Annika.

'It was wonderful. My parents are very traditional and Christmas is a special time. We call it *jul* and it's a time to celebrate. We always gather for a meal and presents on Christmas Eve. My father prepares his favourite dish of *ribbe*, roasted pork belly served with sauerkraut and boiled potatoes along with Christmas sausages, meatballs and gravy.'

'Sounds delicious,' said Tom.

'Then my mother always bakes her famous *småkaker*, seven different kinds of biscuits.'

'A bit different to my Christmas dinner,' said Tom. 'My mother does it all and Dad stays out of the way. She serves up a huge turkey with all the trimmings. After that at three o'clock we gather round the telly to watch the Queen and then put our feet up with a glass of mulled wine to watch the *Only Fools and Horses* Christmas special. This year it was *The Jolly Boys' Outing* to Margate. It was brilliant.'

'Jolly boys?'

'Just a men's day out.'

'Yes, we have those in Norway too. My father and brother go off walking after eating pickled herring for breakfast.'

Everyone to his own, thought Tom as he sat back contentedly and sipped his tea. He and Inger were an item again. Through the window they watched the crowds of shoppers hurry by while they ate their scones and chatted about life. Tom was relaxed. Little did he know it was destined to be a day of many conversations, occasional gossip and a tête-à-tête that would change lives.

Ten miles away Victor and Pat were in their kitchen drinking coffee. Pat was clearly unwell and lacking in energy. 'I'm simply not up to going out, Victor. I'm so sorry.'

'Then we shall have a quiet night in with a drink and the television.'

Pat shook his head. 'Victor, you're the Head of Faculty. You really ought to be there. It's important your colleagues see you at an event like this.'

Victor leaned forward and held Pat's hand. 'But I can't leave you on your own.'

'Of course you can. I'll wait up for you and we can celebrate the New Year together.'

Pat was in a determined mood and Victor knew it. 'I'm not sure,' he said quietly.

Pat stood up and paced the room. 'In fact, I have an idea. What about that young woman you appointed, Rosie Tremaine? I'm sure she would enjoy being your partner. Give her a call and see if she's free.'

In Wigginton, the telephone rang in Rosie's hallway.

'Rosie, it's Victor here. I'm ringing about the dinner dance in the Assembly Rooms this evening. I wondered if you had any plans. Pat is not up to going out. I was hoping you might be free to accompany me.'

'That's kind, Victor. Actually, I haven't a party to go to tonight.'

She'd had a long telephone conversation a week ago with Julian Meadows, who had explained he had to attend the company New Year Dinner in the Dean Court Hotel. She had been disappointed when he told her it was too soon to introduce her to his colleagues.

'In that case do come along. It's a black-tie event. It would be a special end to the year.'

Rosie made a decision. 'Thank you. I should love to come.'

'Wonderful. I'll pick you up at half six if that's OK with you.'

'I'll be ready, and thanks again, Victor.'

At six o'clock, Tom left home to drive through York, parking outside Inger's home on the Knavesmire. The warmth of her hallway was welcome as she put the finishing touches to her make-up and brushed her hair.

'You look beautiful,' he said.

Inger had selected her favourite classic off-the-shoulder black dress that she kept for special occasions. 'I'll need to carry my high heels in a bag,' she said. 'It's too far to walk in them from the university car park.'

'No need,' said Tom. 'I've booked a taxi. It will be here any minute now and it'll drop us right outside the door.'

'Perfect,' said Inger. She slipped on her shoes, picked up a shawl from the coat stand and wrapped it around her shoulders.

'That's it,' she said. 'I'm ready.'

'I'm a lucky man,' he said quietly as they heard the peep of a car horn outside.

The taxi pulled up in Blake Street outside the impressive Assembly Rooms and they stepped out under the soaring colonnade that supported the portico of grey stone. A door-man collected their tickets and pointed them towards the polished dance floor and the cloakrooms beyond. Beneath the sparkling chandeliers, hand in hand, they took in the warmth and light of this special place.

The disc jockey was already in party mood with his flashing lights and new turntable. Life was improving for

Groovy Kevin from Whitby. He had a fish stall in York market but his popularity as an entertainer was growing. He could adapt his dance music to any group and although he always smelled of fish, he was both cheap and cheerful. He surveyed his audience and decided it was more of an ABBA night than Johnny Rotten and the Sex Pistols.

While Inger walked to the cloakroom, Tom saw Owen and Sue at the bar. 'Hi, Sue. You look lovely and even Owen has made an effort.'

Sue grinned. 'Thanks, Tom. I told him he could stay at home with my mother if he didn't tidy himself up.'

'So not a difficult choice,' said Owen. 'Fancy a pint, Englishman?'

'Why not,' said Tom. 'I'll get them in. Inger will want a white wine. How about you, Sue?'

'Thanks, same for me, please.'

Inger appeared and immediately fell into conversation with Sue.

'Those two get on really well,' said Owen. 'I wonder what they find to talk about.'

They leaned against the bar and supped their pints while watching the arrivals.

'Wow! Take a look at Richard,' said Owen. 'She's done a makeover on our star-gazing friend.'

Richard and Felicity walked in hand in hand. Felicity had ordered a dinner suit for him while Richard had shaved off his goatee beard and had a haircut. He looked really smart, as did Felicity in a royal-blue dress with a matching shawl.

'Wonders never cease,' said Tom.

Meanwhile, the Vice Chancellor was moving from one couple to another doing his usual meet-and-greet but paused when he saw the next couple walk in. They caught everyone's attention.

'Hey, check this out,' said Owen.

'It's Gideon Chalk,' said Tom in surprise, 'and who's that with him? Is it his daughter?'

Gideon was wearing a white tuxedo and a red bow tie. His balding patch had been covered with brilliantine and a Bobby Charlton comb-over. A pair of shiny black shoes with two-inch raised heels had increased his height to five feet six inches. Alongside him was a shapely young woman in a tight-fitting red dress that left little to the imagination. Her carefully dyed blonde hair hung in ringlets above her high cheekbones and her four-inch stilettoes meant she towered over the diminutive bursar.

'It's not his daughter, Tom. I recognize her. She's local and a very highly paid escort. I've seen her at rugby dinners, always accompanied by a wealthy man.'

Their entrance had caused quite a stir and a red-faced Vice Chancellor walked over to meet them. It appeared to be an awkward introduction.

'Now that must be an interesting conversation,' said Tom with a grin.

Zeb walked over to them looking stunning in a black dress, with a silver headband holding back her flaming red hair. 'Well, I've seen it all now,' she said, shaking her head. 'Just look at the pompous little git.'

There was clearly no love lost between the Head of Drama and the self-important bursar.

'Good to see you, Zeb,' said Tom, looking around. 'Who are you with?'

She lit up a cigarette and pointed towards the far end of

the bar. 'I'm with Jonny. He's great fun.' Jonny Baglioni, the local Italian crooner, was Zeb's partner. 'By the way, Victor is here with Rosie. Apparently Pat is unwell. It's worrying because he's always the life and soul of a party but good to see that Victor has persuaded Rosie to join us.'

At the far end of the room Victor was sitting with Rosie. He was sipping a glass of red wine while she had an orange juice.

'I'm pleased she's here,' said Tom. 'When I spoke to her a while ago I had the impression she had other plans.'

It was not long before an announcement was made and they all took their places at one of the tables. The meal was magnificent and had a Christmas theme with pudding and brandy sauce for the sweet course. During coffee and mints everyone drifted off to meet up with other colleagues. Inger sought out Rosie while Victor crossed to the other side of the room to talk to the Vice Chancellor.

'Hi, Rosie. You look lovely,' said Inger.

'Thanks. Your dress is beautiful.'

'It's one I keep for concerts and events like this.'

'I see you're with Tom tonight?'

'Yes, he's over at the bar with Owen and Sue.'

'I've not met Sue.'

'She's terrific, a PE teacher. Owen's lucky to have her. They've got a baby son so life will be busy for her.'

Rosie looked wistfully in their direction.

Inger chose her words carefully. 'I'm so pleased you could make it.'

Rosie looked down for a moment. 'Yes, it was kind of Victor to invite me. I did have other plans but they didn't materialize.'

Inger could see the sadness in her eyes and guessed she was thinking of a certain solicitor. 'Oh well, you're here now and among friends.'

The music began again and Tom beckoned to Inger to join him.

'I'll catch up with you later,' said Inger and Rosie watched her join Tom on the dance floor.

It was then that a tall, cheerful-looking man in a somewhat ill-fitting dress suit appeared. 'Excuse me, Rosie. I'm Sam Greenwood from the science department. We were both appointed on the same day but I don't think we've spoken since. How are you getting on?'

'It's going well, thanks. I've had plenty of support. How about you?'

'Well, I'm working with Richard, who is simply brilliant. I've learned so much from him.'

Under his untidy mop of fair hair Sam had a rugged, weather-beaten face. He was a keen walker and loved the outdoor life.

'Say no if you wish but it looks like Victor is tied up with the Vice Chancellor and maybe one dance would be fun as it's New Year's Eve?'

'Why not?' said Rosie.

It was a slow waltz to Louis Armstrong singing 'What A Wonderful World'.

'I promise not to stand on your feet,' said Sam as he took her hand.

Rosie smiled up at him and for a short while she forgot her troubles as they danced slowly around the floor. 'So . . . how's life in the science department?' she asked.

'Good. Definitely good. I always remember the words of

Albert Einstein. He said that he never taught his pupils, he merely attempted to provide the conditions in which they could learn.'

'I suppose that's what I try to do,' said Rosie, 'but I've never really thought of it that way.'

The dance finished and he walked with Rosie back to her table. 'Thanks, Rosie. I enjoyed that. I don't get the chance very often.'

'A pleasure, kind sir,' replied Rosie with a smile.

He stood there for a moment. 'Rosie?'

'Yes?'

'I hope you don't think this is presumptuous but chess is one of my hobbies and I wondered if we could have a game some time?'

'Of course. It should be fun.'

'That's great. Thanks. Enjoy the rest of your evening.'

It was almost midnight when the DJ cut short 'Let's Party' by Jive Bunny and the Mastermixers and put 'Auld Lang Syne' on the turntable. Friends gathered round, linked hands and sang together. Tom had Inger on one side and Sue on the other. Opposite them was Victor with Rosie and Zeb. It was a happy end to the evening and balloons drifted down from the ceiling.

Eventually taxis arrived and everyone set off for home. 'See you next week,' said Victor to Rosie when they returned to Wigginton, 'and a Happy New Year.'

When he arrived back in Easingwold it was one o'clock and Pat had gone to bed, exhausted. His condition seemed to have deteriorated during the past week and he was constantly tired. Victor found himself standing by the lounge window staring out at the darkness beyond. The thought of losing his loved one was almost too much to comprehend.

His eyes were mirrors of a difficult past and an uncertain future. The equilibrium of his life had shifted on its axis. Everything comes to an end but he could not accept that his life with Pat might do so. On this bitter night, desperately seeking peace, Victor, the unbeliever, had resorted to the power of prayer. It was his final vestige of hope. Sadness swelled and beat like a hammer in his chest. His thoughts were in turmoil as he gazed at the blackness beyond the glass. Finally he crouched down on his knees but his words were lost in the night like dust on the breeze.

In Inger's apartment, Tom was drinking a hot chocolate while she sat opposite him on the sofa, her hands clasped as if in prayer.

'What is it?' asked Tom. 'You look pensive.'

'Tom . . . there's something I need to tell you. It's important and I don't want to start the New Year with secrets between us.'

'Secrets?'

'Yes.'

'That sounds serious,' said Tom. 'What's on your mind?'

'I know about *your* past but you don't know everything about mine.'

'I guess not. Growing up in Oslo for one.'

'It's something I've carried around with me for a long time.'

Tom placed his mug on the coffee table and sat back, the first hint of concern on his face. 'Go on.'

'It was back in Norway a few years ago. No one else knows.'

'What is it, Inger? Can I help?'

She took a deep breath and began to speak quietly and slowly. 'There was a guy called Kai Pedersen who came into my life. He was an engineer, smart, intelligent. At first we got on well but then I became unsure. There was something about him I didn't trust so I decided to end it. He had other ideas.'

She fell silent. 'I'm listening,' said Tom.

'There's a bridge in Norway, the Storseisundet.'

'I remember. We saw it last summer.'

'That's where it happened. He forced himself on me.'

Tom felt himself become tense. He clenched his fists and tried to remain calm.

'Since then I've felt unclean, withdrawn. I could never fully commit to anyone. Then I met you.'

'And no one else knows?'

'No, no one, but there were times when I thought my mother suspected something. She's very perceptive. If my brother found out he would kill him.'

That's how I feel, thought Tom.

'Tonight I felt safe with you. And Victor said something.'

'Really?'

'He said you were a good man.'

'That's kind.'

'I can't move into 1990 with this millstone hanging round my neck. It's been a burden for too long.'

Tom stood up and sat beside Inger. He held her while she sobbed. It felt as if it would never end. She was keening like a child who had lost all hope.

Thoughts were racing around Tom's head.

This man must be brought to account.

He might still be dangerous.
Should it be reported?
Is it too late?

'Inger, I'm so sorry. Thank you for sharing this with me. It must have been difficult.'

It was a long time before, hand in hand, they went upstairs and Tom knew this was a conversation he would never forget. As dawn broke on the first day of the 1990s Tom was still holding her. After many hours she had fallen asleep, safe in his arms.

Chapter Nine

White Noise

It was ten o'clock on a winter morning and the clarity of light was achingly pure. Diamond ice sparkled on the frozen windows of Tom's study and he smiled as he stared out at the scene below. There was a dusting of snow on the frozen grass and the stooped figures of members of the faculty were like a Lowry painting. He had spent the last three nights with Inger in her apartment and it felt good to be alive. Before him a new decade stretched out all the way to the millennium. It was Wednesday, 3 January 1990 and the new term was only a week away.

In the hallway of their house in Easingwold, Victor was putting on his coat and packing his shoulder bag. Pat was standing beside him and the mood was sombre.

'Ring me to let me know how it goes,' said Victor.

'I shall,' said Pat. He glanced at the clock. 'This is very late for you.'

'The faculty meeting isn't until eleven. I'm not needed

first thing and I wanted to make sure everything was in place for your first appointment.'

'I'll be fine.' He gave a wry smile. 'Apart from needing to pee all the time.'

'If you need anything,' said Victor, 'just call.' The anxiety was etched on his face.

'Don't worry. It's all been explained. Radiotherapy, five days a week for two months. I've been told I'll feel pretty tired.'

Victor held his hand. 'And then you will recover. You're still a young man. It's well known that four out of five men over eighty have some kind of cancerous prostate condition. Yours has been identified at an early stage.'

'I'm optimistic, Victor. Please don't worry. Now get off to your university and make your mark on the 1990s. This is your time.' He gave him a hug and watched him walk out to the driveway and scrape the ice from the windscreen of his Rover 2000.

So it begins, he thought.

Perkins was behind his counter when Victor arrived. 'Good morning, Professor, and a Happy New Year.'

'And to you, Perkins. How was your Christmas?'

'Wonderful, thanks. My Pauline sang beautifully at Midnight Mass, Christmas dinner was fit for a king and I was bankrupted by the grandkids at Monopoly.'

'Sounds perfect,' said Victor with a tired smile.

'Most have arrived for your faculty meeting, Professor. Dr Tremaine was in at the crack of dawn and the rest weren't far behind. Dr Larson and Dr Frith arrived together and just now Mr Llewellyn – how he stays on that bike of his in this weather is beyond me. Professor Head has shaved his beard and looks twenty years younger and his young apprentice, that nice man Dr Greenwood, gave me a torch as a present. I told him I knew light travelled five times faster than sound and he looked impressed.'

'Well done, Perkins,' said Victor. 'You don't miss a trick,' and he headed off for the quad.

Perkins called after him, 'Thank you, Professor. My mother used to say I slept in the knife box, I was so sharp.'

The door to Room 7 on Cloisters corridor opened and Owen walked in. He was wearing a fur-lined anorak, leather boots and his snow-flecked bobble hat had 'CYMRU' printed in red letters across the front.

'*Blwyddyn Newydd Dda*, Tom.'

'And a Happy New Year to you too.'

'I'm impressed,' he said with a smile. 'You're learning.'

'Any plans for today?' asked Tom.

'Yes. Prep for our field week. We leave on the twenty-sixth of March for the Brecon Beacons and I need to be well organized. It's always a special time for my final-year students.' Owen stroked his unshaven chin. 'Plus I've got a meeting first thing with Chalky.'

'Chalky?'

'Gideon Chalk. That's what Zeb calls him. The cocky little sod sent me a message requesting me to account for my field week costings. It's like being pulled up before the headteacher.'

'Well, good luck. You'll probably need it.'

'Zeb told me you're going to Harrogate this year.'

'Yes, there's a drama festival. We're taking Drama Four

and English Four on alternate days, Monday to Thursday. Should be a great experience.'

'Bit different to freezing in a bloody tent in Wales.' He pulled out a folder from his sports bag. 'OK, Tom, catch you later,' and he hurried downstairs.

At morning break Zeb was scribbling on a notepad when Tom walked into the common room.

'Hi, Zeb,' said Tom. 'Shall I get you a coffee?'

'Oh, hi, Tom.' She looked preoccupied. 'Yes, please. I need to get this done before the faculty meeting.'

Tom returned with two coffees and a couple of biscuits. 'You look busy.'

Zeb shook her head. 'It's that bloody bursar again. He wants us to reduce the budget for our visits to Harrogate.'

Tom frowned. 'Well, it's already cheaper than last year when we went to Stratford. There's no accommodation costs.'

'He's just playing silly buggers. A little man with a lot of power and he's using it to be top dog. He says the train fares are prohibitive.'

'Sounds like penny pinching.'

'Exactly.' She put down her pad, lit up a cigarette and puffed furiously.

'I had better tell Rosie,' said Tom. 'She's involved with the English Four visits.'

Owen arrived and sat down next to them. He had a face like thunder. 'Pompous little git,' he muttered.

'Don't tell me,' said Tom. 'You mean the bursar.'

'Asking me to redo the costings. How on earth did the governors appoint a guy like him? No class. No support. He lives in his own little world. Sadly it's not mine.'

'I heard he had a reputation as a top accountant,' said Tom. 'Some kind of financial entrepreneur.'

'That's the last thing we needed,' grumbled Zeb. 'We got the same. He was on to me about travel costs each day to Harrogate.'

'Hold on,' said Owen. 'Just a thought . . . Tom can drive buses.'

Zeb's eyes lit up. 'Is that right, Tom? Can you?'

'Yes, I've had a licence for ages. I got it years ago when I was a student. In fact, my parents' village has a minibus and I take my mum's Women's Institute ladies to various places. It's hilarious. You could write a book about their conversations.'

'Well, the uni has a twenty-seater minibus,' said Zeb. 'The caretaker, Charlie Cox, keeps it in a garage at the back of the science block. We can use that and you can drive.'

'Are you sure you can get it?' asked Tom.

Zeb smiled, leaned back and blew a smoke ring. 'Charlie fancies me so no problem.'

'Why are we not surprised?' said Tom. 'Bloody Mata Hari with leg warmers.'

'Cheeky bugger!' said Zeb. 'Anyway, there would be a bit of insurance to consider, I guess. Otherwise, it's sorted.' She glanced up at the clock. It was almost time for the faculty meeting. Colleagues were drifting in and sorting out the seating. Victor had arrived and was arranging some papers on a table at the front. He looked weary. 'Time to go,' she said and set off to join Victor.

Tom sat next to Inger on the back row and both took out notebooks. There was an air of expectancy in the room. Everyone sensed they were at the beginning of a new era.

Finally everyone settled and Victor got to his feet. As always he was smartly dressed in a crisp white shirt, blue bow tie, mustard-coloured waistcoat and neatly pressed blue jeans. His ponytail looked a little more grey than usual and there were dark rings under his eyes.

'Welcome back, everybody, and a Happy New Year.' There were cheerful responses. 'I do hope you've all had a restful break. Now, there is a lot of work ahead as we launch into the nineties.' He gestured towards the timetable on the huge noticeboard. 'Thanks for letting me have your amendments. They should all be in place now but please check before you leave. You will have spotted a new noticeboard next to the timetable. This one is specifically for school placements. It's become an even more demanding job with the influx of overseas students and our increasing numbers. Demands on local schools are considerable and we are having to establish links with more schools further afield. I should like to thank Tom for his work over Christmas to get this up and running. So please check this noticeboard from time to time when coordinating your own tutorials along with the new clubs and societies that are emerging. We don't want anything to clash.'

He held up a sheaf of papers. 'Now to the main issue of this meeting. I have here details of our forthcoming national conference, Assessing Competency and Progression-Based Learning. It follows the invitation from the British Educational Research Association to host this prestigious event and will take place over the weekend commencing Friday, the ninth of March. This is clearly an opportunity for Eboracum to be seen at its best.' He paused to emphasize the import of his words. 'We're expecting at least eighty delegates from various UK universities, plus a party of a dozen educationalists from Australia and New Zealand who will be visiting York as part of a fact-finding initiative. They have requested fitting our conference into their programme and I've agreed. I know you will make them welcome. I'll share more details before the event.'

He paused for a moment. 'Also, preparation is well advanced for field week and Zeb wants a brief word about this.'

Zeb stood up and smiled. 'Hi, everybody, good to see you've survived the New Year celebrations.' There were nods and knowing winks in her direction. 'I've spoken with the bursar and he wants an update on costings for our various field week activities. Apparently, money is a little tighter this year. So please will all heads of department check in with him before the start of term next Monday.'

She held up a poster. 'That apart, there's a welcome-back disco for students next weekend when they all return to halls and lodgings. Do come along if you wish. If nothing else it's an opportunity for you to get up to date with the current music scene.' There was general laughter around the room. 'So, that's all from me for now except to say best wishes for the new term and keep warm.'

At lunchtime Tom and Owen walked into the refectory and joined the queue behind Richard Head and Sam Greenwood. They collected hot servings of beef stew and found a table among the vast empty spaces.

'How's it going?' asked Tom.

Sam shook his head. 'Richard was getting some grief from the bursar this morning. We're going down to London during field week. There're a couple of lectures in the Science Museum. Should be a great trip and we didn't need any aggro.'

'He's a strange man,' said Richard. 'He's definitely got a few hang-ups . . . The personification of hubris.'

'It's just white noise,' said Sam. 'A distraction.'

Tom looked puzzled. 'White noise?'

'Yes,' said Sam, 'just the meaningless chatter of internal politics.'

'I'm not familiar with the term,' said Tom.

'It can be quite soothing,' said Sam. 'When I was a student back in Manchester my roommate used to listen to whale sounds. He said it helped him forget the stresses of the day.'

Owen looked at Tom. 'Don't even think about it, Englishman. It's bad enough you listening to Enya while you're marking papers.'

Tom had 'Orinoco Flow' on repeat on his cassette player. He had been a big Clannad fan in his university days. He smiled. 'Sounds like we all need a bit of white noise from time to time.'

'A Welsh choir singing "Land Of My Fathers" at Cardiff Arms Park is all I need, boyo,' said Owen.

'Everyone to his own,' said Sam. 'I'll stick to birdsong in the Lake District. That's my kind of white noise.'

Richard leaned forward, looking a little puzzled. 'However, *in scientific terms*, white noise is a random signal having equal intensity at different frequencies with a constant power spectral density.' He pushed back his horn-rimmed spectacles. 'It draws its name from white light, although light that generally appears white does not have a flat power spectral density over the visible band.'

Sam smiled at Tom and Owen raised his eyebrows. 'So now you know.'

'I think I prefer Sam's bloody birdsong,' said Owen.

'I agree,' said Tom.

Sam nodded. 'It can be good for you: gentle conversations that remove problems, wash away stress.'

I know who needs that, thought Tom.

It was mid-afternoon when the telephone rang in Rosie's study.

'Rosie, it's Julian.'

'Julian, this is a surprise. Lovely to hear your voice.'

'Something has just cropped up. I have a breakfast business meeting tomorrow in Thirsk. I'm staying in a local hotel overnight and I was hoping you might join me.'

'That would be wonderful.'

'In that case I'll meet you in Thirsk marketplace at seven. Can you be there?

'Of course. Are we dining somewhere?'

'We'll get room service.'

'I'll look forward to it.'

'See you soon, darling.'

The line went dead and she looked up at the clock. She needed to get home in good time and pack an overnight bag. It was a twenty-five-mile journey and she didn't want to be late. Then she smiled. She loved it when he called her *darling*.

During afternoon break Sam Greenwood was checking the mail in his pigeonhole when Rosie Tremaine appeared alongside him. She collected a pile of leaflets and letters and sifted through them.

'Hi, Rosie. I've just heard you won a chess tournament over Christmas.'

'Yes, down in Cornwall. I was the defending champion so I had to attend. It was good to meet up with the rest of the brood.'

'Brood?'

'A collective noun for us chess players.'

'Really?' said Sam. 'You learn something new every day. I used to be in the chess team back in my uni days in Manchester.'

'That's good,' said Rosie. 'It's always an exciting challenge. A real battle of wits. I love the game.'

'You're obviously in a different league to me. The hierarchy of chess is interesting. I've heard of Garry Kasparov and Bobby Fischer but I don't know any female players.'

'That's understandable,' said Rosie. 'It's men who have dominated as chess grandmasters but that might change. There's a brilliant young Hungarian called Judit Polgár, a teenage prodigy. A year ago she already had a world ranking of fifty-five. She could be the first woman grandmaster.'

'Wow! I didn't know that. Good luck to her.' He looked around the common room. Colleagues were relaxing, drinking tea, checking timetables and catching up on news. 'I've finished for the day. How about you?'

'I've just cleared my desk.'

'So . . . are you free now?' he asked. 'Maybe there's time for a quick game before you leave.'

'Sadly no, but it's good you're eager to play.'

Sam stood back and smiled. 'Speaking of eagerness, I wondered if you might care to join me for a drink this evening.' He paused, suddenly feeling nervous. 'I'll understand if you're too busy. I'm aware the workload is huge in your department.'

'That's kind, Sam, but I'm seeing someone tonight so maybe another time.'

'Can't blame a guy for trying,' he called after her as she hurried away to car park.

Gideon Chalk had an office in an annexe at the back of the Lodge. Each morning when he walked in he frowned as he passed Miss Frensham's desk. She had complained to Edward, the Vice Chancellor, about him smoking on the premises. But the Vice Chancellor had insisted Gideon was considered by the governors to be an excellent accountant. His bookkeeping was meticulous and there were suggestions of a healthy profit for the university.

'Occasionally,' he had said, 'we have to put personal opinions to one side for the good of the university.'

Time will tell, she thought.

Late in the afternoon, a group of four young men filed into the rear entrance of the Lodge and knocked on the door labelled 'Gideon Chalk, Bursar'.

'Come,' was the reply.

They entered the smoke-filled room where Gideon was seated behind his desk staring at the screen of his Apple Macintosh SE/30 computer. He was clearly irritated by the interruption and stubbed out his cigarette into an overflowing ashtray. 'Yes?'

Eighteen-year-old Bob Morton, a maths student, was the nervous spokesperson. 'Sorry to trouble you, Mr Chalk.'

'What is it?'

'We have a problem with our accommodation.'

'Which property?'

'The one up the Hull Road.'

'Go on.'

'There're eight of us and only four rooms.'

'Yes, eight men, I recall, so no problem with sharing. There're two single beds in each room, so perfectly adequate.'

'Plus it's freezing cold. The radiators don't work.'

'If they've been damaged you will be liable for the cost of repair. It's in your contract.'

'There's a tiny kitchen and the sink is blocked. We've tried to sort it out but it still won't drain.'

'Well try again. It can't be that difficult.'

'Also, the bathroom shower doesn't work and it's tough with only one toilet. Is there somewhere else we can rent?'

'You're signed up for the full academic year so there are no other options at present. Property is at a premium in York so you're fortunate to have a roof over your heads.' The four young men looked crestfallen. 'If that's all, I have work to do.'

After they walked out Gideon sat back and lit up another Benson & Hedges. His investments were going well and he smiled contentedly. During the summer he had taken on the lease of a large property with permission from the owner to sublet it to students. Gideon was never one to miss an opportunity. He could see how the house would accommodate far more students than would otherwise be possible with private tenants. Most students were unlikely to complain at being crammed in and if they did it was just hard luck. *Another nice little money earner,* he thought.

*

Tom was in his study when the telephone rang. It was Victor. 'Hi, Tom, glad I caught you. Can you call in tomorrow morning to check our current position regarding school placements?'

'Of course. What time?'

'Around nine should be fine. Before the start of term I'm keen to make sure we contact any headteachers who haven't got back to us.'

'OK, I'll see you then.'

'Thanks, Tom.'

'Victor, before you go, I'm aware Pat is unwell at present. Please pass on my best wishes for a speedy recovery.'

'That's kind, Tom. I just hope for the best as each day goes by. I guess it's simply fate. What will be will be. Buddhists call it karma. Who knows how this day will end. All we can do is hope and pray. Enjoy your evening and I'll see you tomorrow.'

At five o'clock Tom tidied his desk and packed his satchel. Owen had left an hour ago. He turned out the light and walked up the corridor to Inger's study. She was still busy at her desk when he stepped in.

'Hi, Tom. I've almost finished if you want to hang on.' She packed her shoulder bag and added a file of sheet music from the filing cabinet. 'I've got a lot to do tonight.'

He sat down in one of the armchairs. 'Before we leave can we have a chat? There's something on my mind.'

Inger looked curious. 'What is it?'

'Something is troubling me.'

She sat down. 'Go on.'

'I think we need to talk about what happened to you back in Norway.'

She gave him a sudden hard stare. 'Well, I don't. It's in the past now.'

'It's just that this guy is still roaming free. He might attack another woman.'

She shook her head. 'It's too long ago.'

'I'm not sure about that. I've never come across anything like this before but he needs to be stopped.'

'It's still too painful, Tom. Can we drop it, please?' There was a cold rhythm to her words that made him shiver.

Tom sighed. 'He hurt you, Inger. Now that I know, it's hard to let go.'

She clasped her hands and shook her head. 'I really don't want to hear this. I need to move on.'

'OK. I understand.'

'What brought this on?'

'I was talking to Sam earlier, the guy in the science department. He was telling me about white noise . . . words that can help a person who is feeling anxious, gentle conversation, a time to pause and reflect.'

'Whatever that is, Tom, I need to block it all out and move on with my life.'

'I suppose I was hoping for some sort of resolution.'

Inger stood up. She looked tense. 'I'm not sure white noise, or any sort of noise, can help. I'm surprised you brought it up again. You must know it's painful. I wouldn't have shared it with you if I'd known you would pursue it.'

'OK, I'm sorry. I thought it might help.'

She opened the door and stood there thinking. 'Look, Tom, I've got a huge amount of prep to do this week. I don't think I would be good company tonight so I'll catch up with you tomorrow.'

Tom sensed the determination in her voice. 'I understand,' he said quietly. For a moment he studied this complicated woman. The expression in her eyes revealed her soul and he realized no amount of white noise would heal the scars. He followed her downstairs to the quad. When he left reception he stepped out into a frigid world of Arctic air and his breath steamed in front of him. Frozen leaves, tinged with tiny ice crystals, swirled at his feet while the winter trees, like brooding guardians, watched over the monochrome panorama of the distant land.

With a heavy heart he drove home alone.

Chapter Ten

The Silence of Snow

It was an unforgiving morning when Tom walked out to his car on Monday, 22 January. During the night a bitter wind had scoured the countryside while creatures of the woodland found shelter. A silent shroud of snow covered the cottage and around him all sounds appeared to be suppressed. Beneath a wolf-grey sky, lazy trails of woodsmoke drifted into the air as the villagers stoked their fires.

When he drove south, the road ahead was a channel of blue glass and his windscreen wipers were slow to clear the berms of snow. Beyond the brittle hedgerows, hazel trees with lamb's-tails of catkins shivered in the breeze while millions of feather-light flakes landed fingertip-softly on the still, sepulchral land. It was a slow journey into York and a quilt of freshly fallen snow covered the university car park. The warmth of the reception area was welcome, as was Perkins's familiar smile.

'Good morning, Dr Frith, glad you have made it safely. You need to be Torvill and Dean out there with all that ice.'

'Hello, Perkins, yes, it was a difficult drive. How're things?'

As always Perkins was a fund of up-to-date news. 'Professor Grammaticus was in early. There's a lot of mail going out for the March conference. Dr Tremaine mentioned she's organizing a chess tournament for the students at the end of term and Mr Llewellyn was upset because Wales lost to France at rugby over the weekend.'

'And England trounced Ireland,' added Tom with a smile.

'I didn't mention that,' said Perkins. 'No point in adding to his misery.'

'Very wise.'

'That apart, and a bit unsettling to be honest . . . Charlie Cox said there's a report of some guy creeping round the women's accommodation during the evenings and peeping in the windows. He's going to check it out tonight.'

'Good news. That's exactly what we need.'

'Very true.'

'You'd think it was too cold for that sort of thing,' said Tom as he hurried towards the quad.

Perkins nodded sagely. 'As my mother used to say, there's nowt so funny as folk.'

In his study, Victor was on the phone to Pat. He wanted to check on the results of his latest appointment.

Pat sounded upbeat. 'Very encouraging, Victor. Dr Stern said it had gone well. They caught it early by all accounts.'

'That's good news.'

'He also mentioned that if your father or brother has it then you're twice as likely to develop it.'

'Yes, I've heard that.'

'And it did for my father but, thank goodness, treatment

has come on a lot in recent years. Anyway, I'll let you get on, you must be busy.'

'Yes, the conference is gathering momentum. There's lots of interest.'

'Well, good luck with all that. I'll make us something special for this evening's meal.'

'That will be most welcome. You're a saint.'

'Yes, but which one?'

'I should imagine St Macarius of Egypt. He's the patron saint of cooks, confectioners and pastry chefs.'

'Good Lord, Victor! How on earth do you know all this stuff?'

'I paid attention at school.'

'Ah, point taken. Anyway, you too are a saint.'

'Which one?'

'Sorry, no idea. I used to bunk off school to draw pictures.'

'Why doesn't that surprise me? I'll see you tonight. Get some rest.'

Victor smiled as he put down the phone. Einstein had once said that we should live for today but hope for tomorrow and that was how he was living his life.

At eight forty-five, Tom walked into his study to find Owen sorting out his lecture notes for his nine o'clock History of Physical Education session. 'You look busy,' he said.

Owen looked up. 'I've got a full timetable today plus rugby training in the gym tonight. Having said that, it's definitely worthwhile. This is probably the fittest squad I've had. Even so, no one is in the same league as Chris Scully. He's got one hell of an engine. Seems to be able to run for ever.'

'Takes me back,' reflected Tom. 'I was in the cross-country team at school.'

Owen was curious. 'So you didn't play rugby then?'

'Sadly, no. It was just football and cricket. I was centre half and a fast bowler. Mind you, in later years I was in the university swimming team but I've not really kept that up.'

'You ought to join in the rugby training, Tom. We've started doing it on Mondays and Thursdays. Come along if you fancy: it would do you good. It's just a circuit round the gym, running, press-ups, the usual stuff. Everyone goes at their own pace. A few of the staff join in occasionally. Sam Greenwood is a regular. We often go for a pint afterwards in the Keystones. He lives near me up the Hull Road so I get a lift.'

Tom shrugged. 'I'm working late tonight updating all the school practice placements.'

'Well, come on to the pub afterwards. Chicken in a basket and a pint.'

Tom thought of the empty fridge back in his cottage and came to a quick decision. 'Sounds good.'

'OK. If we don't catch up before, I'll see you in there around seven.'

He hurried away while Tom collected his notes about the novels of George Orwell for his lecture with English Two.

At morning break, Rosie was back in her study preparing for a series of tutorials with English Four. She was reflecting on her time in Thirsk with Julian and recalling his attention and affection. The fact they never visited one another's homes no longer concerned her. She had learned it was just Julian's way of doing things and she didn't want to press him for an explanation.

It was her firm belief that in the not-too-distant future he would propose and there was no doubt she would say yes. Valentine's Day was not far off and maybe that would be the time. Suddenly the telephone rang and disturbed her reverie.

'Hello.'

'It's me, darling.'

'What a coincidence. I was just thinking of you.'

'And I was just thinking ahead to Valentine's Day.'

'Wonderful. What had you in mind?'

'It falls during the middle of the week and, sadly, business gets in the way again. So I thought we could wait a few days and go away for the weekend to a nice hotel.'

'That's exciting. Where are we going?'

'It's a surprise.'

'Thank you, Julian. That sounds perfect.'

'OK. Talk to you later. A client has just arrived.'

There was a buzz on the line as the call ended and Rosie sat back and smiled. She had guessed the surprise hotel was the Waldorf in London. She had seen a letter when she was last in his car confirming a reservation for Saturday, 17 February. A weekend in one of London's best hotels was perfect. Perhaps it was time to go shopping for a new dress.

Meanwhile, outside the lecture block, Tom's English Two group were heading for a warm drink in the refectory. Ellie MacBride had something on her mind and it wasn't the fact that some animals were more equal than others in *Animal Farm*.

'Tom, a few of the girls in the group are a bit worried, particularly those with rooms on the ground floor.' She pointed towards Amy Fieldhouse, a cheerful, hardworking nineteen-year-old from Oldham who was chatting with her friend, Liz Colby. 'Amy told me she thought she saw a face at her window last night. Apparently those blinds they've got in the accommodation block don't always give full privacy. I've told the caretaker. Maybe you can raise it with Zeb or the bursar. It needs sorting.'

'I'll do my best. I heard Charlie Cox will be out tonight trying to apprehend the culprit.'

'That's good. Whoever it is needs catching and putting away.'

'I agree. Let's hope it's sooner rather than later.'

'And ideally before he meets me. I did self-defence in Barnsley. If he comes close enough I'll kick him where it hurts.'

Tom winced at the thought as Ellie caught up with the rest of the group.

In the common room, Zeb was in the far corner looking through her mail while drinking coffee and smoking a cigarette. She beckoned to Tom, who had just approached the counter where the imposing figure of Mavis Shuttlebottom was serving hot drinks and rock-hard slices of her famous flapjack, and he sat down next to Zeb.

'Victor looked happier this morning,' she said. 'I gather Pat's appointment went well.'

Tom sipped his coffee and made an unsuccessful attempt to bite into the dense flapjack. 'That's good to hear. It's been a worry for him.'

'Plus he's up to his ears in prep for the conference. I'm calling in for a late session with him tonight.'

'If there's anything I can do, let me know.'

'Maybe you can. I know he wants a few colleagues to give a brief summary of their course content. Richard and Inger are both definites for Science and Music and maybe you and Rosie could do a double act for English.'

'Yes. Happy to help. I'll see what she thinks.'

'Anyway, must fly. Drama Four in ten minutes.' She stubbed out her cigarette and stood up. 'By the way, you may have heard. There's a peeping Tom out there.' She looked down at Tom and grinned. 'Present company excluded, of course.'

'Yes, I've heard. Charlie Cox will be on the prowl tonight.'

'I told him to do me a favour and castrate the little pervert or I'll do it for him.'

Once again Tom winced at the thought. He finished his coffee and stared at the adamantine flapjack. *A tougher punishment might be to get the poor sod to eat this,* he thought.

At lunchtime, Sam Greenwood and Rosie Tremaine were sitting together in the refectory and enjoying bowls of hot soup and crusty bread. They had found time to play chess during the previous week: three games that each lasted barely a few minutes. Rosie had won them all but was gracious with her praise. 'You definitely have potential, Sam. It's just down to practice and maybe curbing your eagerness.'

Sam shrugged. 'Thanks, Rosie.'

She cast around for some encouragement. 'In the last match you had a great chance to cause me problems by castling. You'll recall it's the only move that allows two pieces to move simultaneously. Also, there must be no pieces between the king and the rook and neither of those pieces can have moved prior to castling. I'll show you next time we play.'

Sam remained calm. 'I'll keep trying.' There was something special about this remarkable woman but he found it difficult to say exactly what he felt. He could have comfortably shared his thoughts on quantum mechanics theory or palaeomagnetism, but understanding women was beyond him.

At afternoon break Tom called into Rosie's study. She was busy at her desk, marking assignments.

'Hi, Rosie, sorry to disturb you but Zeb mentioned something this morning about the conference.'

She put down her pen. 'Yes. It sounds as if it's going to be really special. I know Victor is putting a lot of work in. Last I heard we may have anything up to a hundred delegates.'

'Victor is looking for input from a few faculty members describing the nature of our courses. Sam is doing a brief fifteen-minute overview of the Science curriculum and Inger something similar for Music. He was wondering if you and I could share a similar presentation regarding how we structure our English courses and plan teaching practice.'

Rosie gave a confident smile. 'Fine by me. How about you?'

'I'm happy to do it and we've both got some decent slides for visuals.'

'In that case let's meet up and make sure we're word-perfect and the timings are exact.'

'Thanks. I'll pass on our acceptance to Zeb and Victor and they can fit us into the programme.' He paused at the door. 'Perkins mentioned you're organizing a chess tournament for the end of term?'

'Yes. I thought it would add a bit of interest after everyone has returned from field week and before we go down for Easter. I'm offering the occasional chess workshop during the term. Apparently there're at least a dozen club players among the students and someone suggested it might be fun for me to play against them all simultaneously.'

'That sounds very demanding. How on earth can you do that?'

'I've done it before down in Cornwall. It's fairly common as an exhibition at the end of a tournament and a great thrill for an individual in the group who might beat you.'

'Has that ever happened to you?'

She smiled and shook her head. 'Happily, no, but I was only up against club players at best.'

Tom shook his head in wonderment. 'So you won't need advice from your buddy tutor.'

She raised her eyebrows in mock disbelief. 'Not this time, Tom.'

It was late afternoon when Inger called in to see Rosie. They had become firm friends in recent weeks and Inger had visited Rosie's home to share a few evening meals. Rosie had also requested that Inger become a keyholder in case anything cropped up. They were relaxed in each other's company.

'How's your Oscar Wilde book progressing?' asked Inger.

'Really well. I had to smile last night when I was writing about his quirky beliefs. He said that nothing that is worth knowing can be taught.'

Inger smiled. 'Makes you wonder why we're here.'

'Exactly.'

'My students have mentioned Sam Greenwood. They seem to think he likes you. He's a lovely man, a bit shy but seriously bright.'

'Ah, Inger . . . I tend to ignore student gossip.'

'Touché,' said Inger. 'I deserved that.'

Rosie stood up and began to fill the kettle. 'I've got some lemon and ginger herbal tea here. How about it?'

'Great,' Inger said and settled into one of the armchairs.

At six forty-five Tom was alone in his study. He closed his school placement file with a sigh and sat back. It had been a long stint. Slowly he began to tidy his desk and pack his satchel. He had only spoken briefly to Inger that day. She seemed to be spending more time with Rosie and it was clear they had formed a friendship. His thoughts were occasionally troubled when he recalled the conversation with Inger about the incident involving Kai Pedersen. Anger would bubble up inside and he found it difficult to control his emotions. He had not handled it well. His initial thoughts had concerned retribution rather than what might be best for Inger.

Meanwhile, there were frost patterns on the leaded windows and icicles hung like frozen daggers from the eaves. Far below, a few figures trudged slowly across the icy cobblestones.

Ricky Barraclough was a disturbed young man. He stood on the Ouse Bridge and stared down at the icy waters with eyes of black glass. The river flowed past while around him ghostly shadows formed a haunting, malevolent presence. He was a creature of the night and liked to prowl, to spy, to steal. Peering in the windows of his unsuspecting victims made him feel powerful. The streets of York were his playground and with drug-induced bravado he set furtively off into the darkness.

Dressed entirely in black, he felt invisible as he stepped lightly through the snow towards the back gate of the university. He knew the best places. The shrubbery that nestled against the walls of the women's accommodation blocks provided ideal cover. He knew which windows to select and where bright light shone through the gaps in the blinds. In his corrupted mind he thought the forces of darkness were his to control.

At seven o'clock Tom walked down the frozen pavements of Lord Mayor's Walk to the Keystones pub at Monk Bar. It was a relief to get out of the cold and into the lounge bar. Sam and Owen waved a greeting and ordered three pints of Tetley's Bitter and the 'special': namely, chicken and chips in a basket. They settled at a table by the window to enjoy the welcome feast surrounded by the chatter of a dozen conversations and the clinking of glasses. In the far corner a television was on and Terry Wogan was sharing his Irish wit.

As always, Tom missed Inger's company but he gradually relaxed and began to enjoy the warmth, the hot food and the company. The conversation was wide-ranging to say the least. Sam described in detail his excitement concerning the forthcoming launch of the Hubble Space Telescope; Tom wondered what the response would be next month to Sky's first pay channel; while Owen merely grumbled his way through the problems of the Welsh rugby team and how he would solve them if he was their coach. It was a happy end to a busy day and the three of them were in good spirits when, shortly before eight thirty, they stepped out into the cold and set off for the university car park.

At that same moment Amy Fieldhouse was in her room sitting on her bed and chatting with her friend Liz Colby about her new boyfriend. They were on the ground floor of D Block, a three-storey, pebble-dashed edifice that housed thirty-six students. Amy loved her room. It was her own personal space with a bed, a wardrobe, a bookshelf and a bedside lamp with an orange lightbulb. Above the desk and in front of the window was an ill-fitting blind. At the end of the corridor was a shared bathroom and a small kitchen. Amy and Liz were both approaching their twentieth birthdays and, although they didn't know it then, were destined to be friends for life.

Above the bed the wall was filled with pictures of Amy's favourite men: George Michael, David Bowie, Bruce Springsteen and her special favourite (surprisingly), Davy Jones, lead singer of the sixties supergroup the Monkees. They were relaxed, sipping hot chocolate and, on her Sharp cassette player, Simon and Garfunkel were singing 'Bridge Over Troubled Water'.

Suddenly Liz screamed. 'There's a face at the window!' she cried. She'd caught a brief glimpse of a man peering through a gap in the blind but in an instant he was gone.

Outside Charlie Cox was on the prowl. A huge, blunt-spoken Yorkshireman, he was proud of his job as caretaker at Eboracum. Hard as nails, he barely noticed the bitterly cold weather as he patrolled the university campus. When he spotted a furtive figure in a black anorak creeping along the side of D Block he burst into action. In his younger days he had played rugby league and his tackling skills had never been forgotten.

'Oy! You! Come 'ere,' Charlie yelled and he set off in pursuit, but the intruder was clearly a fleet-footed younger man who skidded across the frozen snow like a frightened deer. Charlie was determined, though, and the chase was on.

At that moment Tom, Sam and Owen were crunching through the snow-covered car park towards Sam's distinctive Citroën 2CV, or 'Tin Snail' as he called it with its bug-eyes. It was a wonder how it stayed on the road in these icy conditions but Sam loved the bungy suspension and roll-back sunroof.

'Thanks,' said Tom. 'I've enjoyed this evening.'

'Well, come next time,' said Owen, 'but bring your sports gear and join in.'

'Will do,' said Tom. He looked at Sam's car dubiously. 'And a safe journey home.'

As he turned towards his Ford Escort there was a loud cry. They all looked in alarm to see Charlie Cox chasing a young man who was running as if the hounds of hell were after him.

'Stop him!' cried Charlie. 'Stop that guy! He's the fuckin' peepin' Tom.'

It was Owen who reacted first, quickly followed by Sam and Tom. They all broke into a run. Under the sodium lights at the far side of the car park was a line of bushes and that's where the chase ended. Owen turned back the years to when he played rugby for his village 1st XV in Wales and launched himself in the air to make a perfect tackle. Owen and the man tumbled together into the bushes, then Tom and Sam grabbed him and dragged him out. They pinned him face down in the snow.

'Let's get the bastard into reception,' gasped Charlie, 'and the night porter can ring for the police.'

Ricky Barraclough, winded and defeated, was carried like a rag doll back into the university. A call was made and the police arrived. The four men watched on as he was whisked away in a police van.

'Thanks a lot,' said Charlie. 'Ah never would 'ave caught 'im. 'E were too quick.' He looked at Owen. 'Great tackle, Mr Llewellyn. You ain't lost it.'

Owen looked down at the torn knees of his trousers. 'God knows what Sue will say when she sees these.'

'Don't worry,' said Sam. He patted Owen on the back and smiled. 'I'll tell her that you're a hero and you've been catching criminals. Come on, let's get you home. Goodnight, Tom. See you tomorrow.'

They walked back to the car park and Tom watched them drive away.

'Thanks, Dr Frith,' said Charlie. 'I'll report to t'Vice Chancellor in t'morning.' He shook hands with Tom. 'Safe journey 'ome.'

Tom got into his car and as he drove out of York it began to snow again; the world beyond his windscreen became opaque.

Back in his cottage he telephoned Zeb to pass on the events of the evening.

She sounded relieved. 'Thanks for the call, Tom. I'll talk to the students concerned tomorrow. They will be pleased to hear the news. Let's hope they lock him up and throw away the key.'

Much later, Tom stood by his bedroom window and stared out. The street was now a place of calm and everything was still under the star-studded sky. The moonlight on the cold unforgiving land was harsh and there was a stillness as if the earth was in slumber. Only the prints of a midnight fox disturbed the smooth patterns of frost, soon to be covered again beneath the silent snow.

Chapter Eleven

A Different Valentine

Rosie Tremaine received the telephone call that was destined to change her life during afternoon break on Friday, 16 February.

She was sitting at her desk, staring out of the window and dreaming of the weekend that lay in store with Julian. Outside a weak sun was sinking over the rooftops and the cold weather seemed endless. Snowflakes drifted like confetti against the windowpanes and the world outside looked like the everlasting winter of Narnia. Wind rattled the leaded windows and beneath her the quad was still as a stone under a new fall of snow.

Then the telephone rang.

Julian sounded harassed. 'I'm so sorry, darling, and I know it's short notice but I have to cancel our weekend away. Something has come up at work . . . an important client conference that I can't miss. These things happen from time to time. I shall make it up to you, of course. I'll reschedule. I do hope you understand.'

'Oh no, Julian! I was so looking forward to it . . . but I understand the demands of your work . . .' Rosie could not hide the disappointment in her voice.

'So, apologies once again but must get on. I'll ring you early next week. Don't worry, I'll have a new proposal,' and the call ended.

A new proposal? thought Rosie hopefully. She sat back and reflected on their relationship. Julian was a highly successful solicitor and a partner in a powerful company. She presumed that when they were together permanently his work would be something she would have to accommodate. Meanwhile, an empty weekend stretched out in front of her – and she had bought a new dress.

Julian was facing a dilemma. His wife had become increasingly concerned about his late-night business meetings. She had made her feelings clear the previous evening. 'I feel neglected at times, Julian,' she had said. He looked at the Waldorf Hotel reservation letter. It was made out to Mr and Mrs Meadows. He made a decision.

In the common room, Inger and Tom were drinking tea and catching up on the news of the day. They had spent the night of Valentine's Day together after a meal at the Dean Court Hotel and Tom was happy because Inger appeared more relaxed. He had avoided mentioning her past troubles in Norway and, once again, they were enjoying each other's company. The weekend beckoned and they were going to spend it together.

'I've arranged to meet Rosie on Monday to begin planning our presentation to the conference,' said Tom. 'How is yours going?'

'Fine. I've done it,' said Inger confidently. 'It was quite straightforward. I've arranged for one of my students to operate the carousel slide projector and include a few slides that show the range of music and the progression of work with the choir. The rest is simply some words from me. This is a good opportunity, Tom. There will be some influential delegates in the audience and I'm hoping to establish a few new links with other institutions.'

'Well done,' Tom said but secretly felt a little deflated. He had still to negotiate with Rosie over the content and structure of their talk, which might be challenging.

It was then that an animated Zeb came over to join them. 'Guess what?' she said excitedly. 'I think I've found my new home.'

'Brilliant,' said Inger. 'Tell us more.'

'It's a barn conversion north of here, up in the village of Crayke, and a bit quirky, all beams and big spaces, which is probably why I love it. Best of all, it's within budget.'

'That's great,' said Tom.

'I'm checking it out tomorrow morning. Victor is taking me.'

Inger smiled. Zeb's enthusiasm was obvious. 'I hope it works out for you.'

'And if you need a lift any time,' said Tom, 'simply ask.'

Zeb leaned back and looked thoughtful. 'That's another thing. I'll have to buy a car so life will be different. My apartment in York is lovely and I can walk to work but you can't swing a cat in there. The barn looks brilliant, great for entertaining.'

'Sounds a wonderful opportunity,' said Inger. 'Likewise, if you want some company some time we could drive up there together.'

'Thanks, I'll take you up on that. Anyway, must dash. Enjoy your weekend,' and she hurried away.

'I hope this will be right for her,' said Inger. 'Buying a property can be difficult sometimes and I presume she will have to put her apartment on the market first.'

'Her flat's an attractive proposition,' said Tom. 'A city-centre home within walking distance of coffee shops and theatres and museums sounds perfect. Somebody out there will love it.'

'Maybe even you,' said Inger with a whimsical smile.

In Room 2 on Cloisters corridor, Rosie had begun to pack her shoulder bag with work for the weekend but then stopped suddenly. *Be adventurous,* she thought. *Life is too short to waste an opportunity.* She walked out to the car park deep in thought. It was during her slow journey out of York that an idea began to form and by the time she drove into Wigginton village she had made a decision. She had put some money aside for the anticipated visit to London and there was nothing to stop her going on her own. On impulse she sat down at her dining table and checked through one of her copious spiral-bound notebooks.

There was a boutique hotel in Bloomsbury where she had stayed before and it was within budget. It would be ideal. She picked up her notepad and sat down in her hallway next to the telephone and began to write. Minutes later she had booked the hotel, checked the times of the early-morning trains from York to King's Cross and booked a taxi. There was no point in feeling miserable at home. The weekend stretched out before her and she intended to enjoy herself. It was a confident and liberated Rosie that began to pack an overnight bag.

*

Tom and Inger crunched through the frozen quad and into reception where Perkins was behind his counter.

'Goodnight, Dr Larson, Dr Frith. Have a good weekend.'

'Thanks, Perkins,' said Tom.

'Have you any plans?' asked Inger.

'Dancing,' said Perkins. 'My Pauline has joined a ballroom-dancing class and they're having a tea dance in the Assembly Rooms tomorrow.'

'Sounds wonderful,' said Inger.

'So, are you a dancer?' asked Tom.

'My Pauline says I've got two left feet but it's never too late to learn something new. She's really keen and our silver wedding is coming up. It's the least I can do after everything she's given me.'

'Well, good luck,' said Tom.

Perkins watched them walk out together and smiled. *Young love,* he thought, *I remember it well.*

'He's a lovely man,' said Inger as Tom unlocked his car. 'Maybe you could learn to dance.'

Tom climbed in the driver's seat and shook his head. A teenage girlfriend had once likened his dance moves to a drunken giraffe. His ballroom technique had gone downhill since. 'I suppose anything is possible,' he replied cautiously.

'Only joking,' said Inger with a smile. *If nothing,* she thought, *I am a realist.*

Rosie boarded the train for King's Cross very early on Saturday morning. As the miles flew by she thought of Julian and wished he could be beside her. She stared out at a bleak landscape and the bare limbs of the trees etched against a grey sky. The world seemed dormant now, waiting silently for the trigger of warmth and light while the stillness of winter lay heavy on the countryside.

It was with a sense of excitement that she arrived in the capital and made her way to Russell Square. She loved Bloomsbury with its cafés, bookstores, trees and museums, a historic home for artists and academics. London was alive and bustling with activity and by eleven o'clock she had checked in to her hotel and left her overnight bag at reception. The city stretched out before her and she headed south until she reached Covent Garden. She strolled around the market and bought a guide to London museums and a silk scarf from one of the smart shops in the piazza. Then she had an idea. She had missed out on staying at the Waldorf Hotel but there was nothing to stop her calling in to see what it was like. It was only a short distance away so she walked purposefully towards Aldwych.

A smart doorman in a bowler hat welcomed her and ushered her into the elegant reception area where a waiter was serving refreshments. There was a table within earshot of the reception desk but hidden behind a huge areca palm tree. She sat down and ordered a pot of Earl Grey tea and a toasted sandwich. It was good to relax and people-watch. As she sipped her tea from a china cup she marvelled at the huge amount of luggage that accompanied many of the arrivals, particularly the American visitors, and enjoyed catching snippets of conversation.

Suddenly she heard a familiar voice and froze. Surprised, she peered through the tall fronds of the palm tree. There, at the reception desk, stood Julian with an attractive lady. They had their backs to her but she could hear the conversation clearly. She stood up, confused and alarmed.

'I should like to check in,' Julian said and handed his reservation letter to the receptionist.

The young man in his made-to-measure three-piece suit smiled graciously and checked the printed note before him. 'Ah yes, good afternoon, Mr Meadows. Welcome to the Waldorf.'

Julian gave a cursory nod of acknowledgement. 'Is our room ready?'

'Not quite,' he said and glanced up at the clock. 'If you would like to wait in the reception area I can arrange for tea or coffee to be served and then have your luggage taken up to your room as soon as it becomes available.'

'And how long will that be?' asked Julian.

'No more than twenty minutes, sir. It's being prepared as we speak.'

The woman stepped forward. 'In that case is there a telephone I can use?'

'Yes, Mrs Meadows. The concierge will assist.'

'Why do you need a telephone?' queried Julian.

'I want to check on the children.'

Julian gave her an enigmatic smile. 'But they're always fine with your mother.'

'I know but I want to make sure,' said the woman firmly and she walked away in search of a phone.

At that moment Julian turned, glanced around him and stared aghast at the sight of Rosie. 'What . . .?' he began to say.

Rosie stepped back in confusion and stumbled against the table. Crockery crashed to the floor.

A waiter hurried to assist her. 'Don't worry, madam, I can deal with this and then bring you a fresh pot of tea.'

Rosie was transfixed. She simply stood there, staring at

Julian in disbelief. He took a hesitant step towards her but then stopped. He looked nervously towards his wife, who was talking on the phone, and then back at Rosie. His dilemma was obvious. They stood there facing each other, a tableau of deceit.

Rosie pressed her clenched fists against the tabletop. She knew in that moment with a shattering realization that it was over between them. Then, with tears in her eyes, she strode out of the hotel, a stunned Julian staring after her. On the pavement she stopped and her breath steamed in front of her, but there was ice in her veins. In a cloud of self-condemnation she set off back to Bloomsbury and the sanctuary of her hotel room.

Gillian Meadows returned to reception. 'The children are fine,' she said with a smile. Then she noticed Julian looked pale. He was leaning against the counter as if in shock. 'Are you OK?'

'Just a little tired,' he said quickly.

'You've been working too hard. Come on. Let's sit down and have a coffee, then you'll feel better.'

With a perfunctory nod he followed her to an empty table near the window. Outside, shoppers and theatre-goers hurried by while Gillian ordered a cafetière of coffee and two Danish pastries. Meanwhile, Julian was process-ing the events of the last few minutes with a sinking heart. This was an impossible – and unexpected – situation and he would need all his professional composure to deal with the outcome.

'This is wonderful, Julian,' said Gillian as she relaxed with her cup of coffee. 'I love surprises.'

*

Back in her hotel room Rosie lay on the bed and wept. She had been betrayed. She was heartbroken to think Julian could have been so deceitful. Everything gradually fell into place: the cancelled meetings, the furtive calls, the private hotel rooms. She stared in the mirror, then ripped off her rowan pendant and threw it on the floor. It couldn't protect her any more. As the hours went by she reassessed her life and felt a deep sense of shame. Her dreams had been shattered in an instant. The life she had envisaged was over.

On Sunday morning, following a tearful night, she rang reception and asked if she could stay on for another night. Her life had been turned upside down and Eboracum could wait.

Early on Monday, Tom and Inger left her apartment and walked outside as a thin light bathed the frozen land. Above them rooks squawked in the high elms while on the fence a solitary robin gave a mournful stare as its feathers ruffled in the breeze. A new week lay ahead and Tom had an early meeting with Rosie.

Following a cheerful welcome by Perkins in reception they hurried upstairs to Cloisters corridor where they parted. Tom tapped on Rosie's study door but there was no answer so he set off for the lecture block. Just before nine o'clock, when Tom was welcoming English Two for his first session of the day, Zeb called in. She looked concerned and spoke quietly.

'Excuse me, Tom. Have you seen Rosie? A couple of the students from English Four have just had a word to say she's not in her study for their tutorial. I told them to go and work in the library until she showed up.'

'That's strange,' said Tom. 'We were supposed to meet this morning before lectures but she didn't appear. I guess she's held up somewhere.'

'Or may be unwell,' said Zeb, 'except she would have called in. I'll leave a message with Perkins. He might know something.'

Tom's lecture on famous female writers ended shortly after ten o'clock. Once again, there had been lively discussion on the various merits of Mary Shelley, Charlotte Brontë, Emily Brontë and Doris Lessing. He returned to reception where Perkins was sorting the morning mail.

'Hello, Perkins. I was wondering if you had seen Dr Tremaine this morning.'

'Sorry, no sign of her. She's not passed me.'

'In that case, could you contact me when she arrives?'

'Will do.' He gave a mock salute and returned to checking the post.

Tom set off for the common room where Zeb was talking to Inger and he walked over to join them.

'Any sign?' asked Zeb.

Tom shook his head. 'It's a mystery. In the meantime I can double up on her tutorials for the rest of the morning.'

Inger stood up. 'Let me check her study, then I'll ring her home. I'm concerned. This isn't like her.'

Room 2 was empty when Inger walked in. The room was tidy as always. Nothing was out of place. There were no clues. Inger returned to her study and opened her telephone index. She rang Rosie's home number but there was no reply. After a few attempts she returned to the common room. Zeb and Tom looked up expectantly and Inger shook her head.

'This is a worry,' said Zeb. 'I had better let Victor know.'

'Before you do,' said Inger, 'I've got a key for her home in Wigginton. If she hasn't called in by lunchtime Tom and I could drive out there. She may be unwell.'

'Or had an accident,' said Tom.

'My God!' said Zeb. 'I hope not.'

After the lunchtime bell rang Tom and Inger drove up the A19 to Wigginton. Rosie's home was a rented cottage in a quiet cul-de-sac. Her car was parked in the drive. 'She must still be here,' said Tom, pointing to the car.

Inger pressed the doorbell and waited. There was no response so she tried again, then took out a Yale key and opened the door. She called out, 'Rosie, it's me . . . Inger. Are you home?' There was only silence and they stepped into the hallway. 'Tom, have a quick look around down here while I go upstairs.' It was soon obvious the cottage was empty.

Inger was a familiar visitor, whereas it was the first time Tom had been there. Everything was as he expected: uncluttered and well organized. The lounge looked like an extension of Rosie's study: books, trophies in a cabinet, watercolour paintings of Cornwall and a chess set on a coffee table. In the hallway was a telephone on a small semi-circular table with a carver chair next to it. On the table was a spiral-bound pad.

Tom picked it up and called upstairs. 'Hey, Inger, look at this.' He scanned the notes listing a London hotel, a telephone number and a list of train times. 'Looks like she's gone to London.'

Inger came downstairs and looked at Rosie's familiar neat

cursive writing. 'Maybe she's still there.' Inger copied the hotel number on to another sheet, tore it off and put it in her pocket. They left quickly, locked the door and returned to Eboracum. Inger went into her study and rang the number she had written on the piece of paper. She adopted her authoritative tone of voice. 'Hello, I'm Dr Larson, a friend of Dr Rosie Tremaine. Could you put me through to her room, please?'

'Of course, ringing now.'

A quiet voice spoke. 'Hello.'

'Rosie, it's Inger here. How are you? I was a little worried when I didn't see you this morning.'

There was a long pause. 'Inger . . . I've been stupid.'

'Why is that, Rosie?'

'It's complicated.'

'I'm your friend. Please tell me what's happening.'

There was a long sigh. Rosie sat up on the bed and stared out of the window. 'It's the man I've been seeing . . .' Her voice trailed off.

'I'm listening.'

'I was supposed to be with him this weekend. He had booked a room at the Waldorf here in London but then cancelled at the last minute because of his business commitments.'

'Yes,' said Inger. She could guess what they might be. 'So why did you go down there?'

'It was a spur-of-the-moment decision. I thought I would come anyway and enjoy a break.'

'So, what happened?'

'I decided to call into the Waldorf just to see what it was like. Then it happened.'

'Go on.'

'I saw him checking in. He was with his wife.'

Inger began to realize the enormity of the situation. 'Oh dear. I'm so sorry.' She was aware that Rosie still hadn't mentioned his name.

'That's not all. They have children. I hate him for what he's done.' She spoke softly but with menace like the whisper of thunder. 'I've just been in my room since then. I stayed an extra night. Please tell Tom and Victor I'm sorry.'

'Don't worry. Victor is not aware you're absent and Tom has covered for you so far. So we're getting through the day.'

There was a pause. 'Thank you,' she said. 'I've let you all down.'

'No, you haven't. It's *you* that's been let down.'

'I've been so naive.'

'This isn't the time for self-recrimination, Rosie. You've been badly misled. Your true friends are here so do come home and we can sort all this out.'

'It's just that losing someone hurts so much.'

Inger could hear the melancholy in her voice. It was heartbreaking. Rosie had discovered love and lost it again in an instant. 'I understand. It's been a painful experience for you. Sometimes the world is dangerous.'

'And so is truth. It's a strange feeling – like the end of my world as I knew it. C. S. Lewis lived in the Shadowlands and now I know what he means. It's the simple things I will miss – the touch of his hand, his footsteps walking beside me.'

'We can talk about this, Rosie.' There was a long silence. 'Are you still there?'

'Yes, sorry.'

'What are your plans? If you come back today I could meet you at the station and then you could stay at mine if you wish.'

Rosie stared at her suitcase lying open on the floor. Her new dress was still neatly packed away. She took a deep breath. It was time to get hold of her life again. 'Very well,' she said. 'I'll ring you from King's Cross.'

It was mid-afternoon when Victor popped his head around Tom's door. 'Hi, Tom. I heard Rosie was absent.'

'Yes, a bit under the weather. She's spoken to Inger and she'll be back tomorrow. I covered for her today so no problem.'

'OK, thanks. I'll look out for her tomorrow morning. I don't want her coming back too soon if she's unwell.'

'I'm sure she'll be fine.'

'How's the prep for your presentation coming along?'

'I'm meeting Rosie this week and we'll be well prepared.'

Victor nodded. 'Thanks. I'm sure you will. Hermione in the Vice Chancellor's office is coordinating the programme so I'll just need a title and a one-liner from you at some stage.' He glanced at the clock on the mantelpiece. 'In fact, I'm due there now. The VC wants a progress report.' He gave a tired smile and closed the door behind him.

That evening Inger met Rosie in York station. She gave her a hug. 'Welcome back.'

'Thanks, Inger. I'm really grateful.'

'Let's get you to my place, have a restful evening and then see how you feel in the morning. There's no rush to get back. Tom can cover for you and we can set work for some of your groups. It's normal. If you were unwell this would happen.'

'I must get back to my students,' she said quietly.

'OK,' said Inger and they linked arms as they walked out into the night. 'It will be fine. This will all be over soon and you can make a fresh start.'

'Perhaps,' said Rosie.

'Time is a great healer, Rosie. Believe me, I know. All good things come to those who wait.'

For Rosie Tremaine one door had closed but another was about to open.

Chapter Twelve

A Penny for Your Thoughts

When Tom awoke on the morning of Friday, 9 March he was full of anticipation. It was the first day of the Eboracum Conference and he and Rosie had prepared well for their fifteen minutes of fame the following morning. He packed his satchel with his lecture notes and locked the door behind him as he stepped outside. The snow had gone, a few snowdrops shivered in the bitter wind and winter jasmine clung to the wall. Blue-grey bullet heads of daffodils speared through the grassy banks to announce the first signs of spring. The season was changing and, as he drove into York, a fitful sun pierced the iron-grey clouds.

The car park was busier than usual and four coachloads of delegates had arrived from their hotel on the outskirts of the city. A queue of academics stood in reception and Perkins was directing them towards the common room for checking in. A huge banner in the quad read:

British Educational Research Association
'Assessing Competency and Progression-Based Learning'

The common room was full of activity with an eclectic gamut of academics. Many were reacquainting themselves with old friends while newcomers were seeking out like-minded colleagues. Inger found Rosie, who was collecting a coffee from the counter. 'Hi, Rosie,' she said, 'love the new dress.'

Rosie smiled. 'Thanks. Bought it last weekend. Thought I would treat myself.'

Inger studied her friend. She seemed more relaxed these days. She and Rosie were spending more time together and Inger had become a trusted confidante for the Cornish chess champion.

In the days after the split with Julian Meadows Rosie had opened her heart. 'I cry a lot these days,' she had said. She had confided that she had been doing a lot of soul search-ing, seeking to understand how she could find peace and serenity in her life once more. Inger had been by her side through it all.

'All this is very exciting,' said Rosie. 'There are some high-flyers speaking today.'

Inger smiled. 'And our turn tomorrow morning. How has it gone with Tom?'

'Fine. We've been through it a few times. I'm doing English and he's explaining how our teaching practices are organized.'

'Well, good luck.' There was movement at the far end of the room. 'Looks like we're beginning.'

A microphone had been set up in the corner on a raised

platform and Zeb stepped up wearing a stylish black trouser suit.

'Good morning, everybody. I'm Zeb Peacock, Deputy Head of Faculty.'

There was a sudden silence as everyone turned towards this striking figure with the flaming-red hair.

'Welcome to our conference. It's an honour to be your host over the weekend. I'm sure you will enjoy our hospitality. This is our staff common room where refreshments will be available. Also, a large area in the refectory has been reserved for lunch from twelve fifteen onwards, where you will find a wide choice on the menu.' She glanced up at the clock. 'The plenary address will commence in thirty minutes at nine forty-five a.m. in the main lecture theatre, and will be presented by Professor Desmond Montague from Oxford.' She gestured towards a line of students all wearing Eboracum sweatshirts. 'We have some of our final-year students to act as your guides. In the meantime, please ensure you collect your name badges before you leave.' At that moment the sun broke through the clouds and streamed in through the high-arched windows. Zeb smiled. 'The city of York is a wonderful place to live and work and I do hope you will take the opportunity to sample its rich history. Thank you.'

Immediately there was a hubbub of conversation as delegates signed in, collected name badges and gradually filed out towards the quad and through the archway to the teaching blocks.

The Ayckbourn Lecture Theatre was a new state-of-the-art building and a recent addition to the campus. There was comfortable tiered seating for an audience of up to five hundred in a semi-circular configuration wrapped around a stage. A huge television screen on the back wall behind the lectern featured the guest speaker. In the spacious foyer was a ticket desk, a coffee bar and a display of enlarged photographs celebrating the work of the university. It couldn't but fail to impress.

As the delegates walked in, each was issued with a glossy A4 folder containing the conference programme and a mini-guide to York. Two flights of stairs led up to the first floor where there was an office, a comfortable seating area and various vending machines. On the stage, Inger's students were playing Debussy's String Quartet in G Minor. It set the scene beautifully.

At nine forty-five, Victor strode confidently on to the stage wearing a new charcoal-grey three-piece suit, a white shirt and a navy-blue bow tie. The toecaps of his black leather boots reflected the footlights. A hush descended as he stopped at the lectern. He looked out at the sea of expectant faces and wished Pat could have shared this moment with him.

'Good morning and welcome. It is indeed an honour for our university to have been selected for such a prestigious conference and I thank the members of the British Educational Research Association for choosing Eboracum. The programme for today and tomorrow is very full as you can see and includes mainstream lectures, department presentations and small group seminars. Sunday is clear for social activities and any follow-up meetings you may wish to organize among yourselves. You will all be aware we are in the midst of huge educational change. The demands we face in this decade before the onset of the new millennium are considerable. With this in mind, I have great pleasure in introducing our plenary speaker. Please welcome Professor Desmond Montague from Oxford.'

There was a ripple of polite applause as a tall, sombre and studious-looking man approached the lectern. His was almost a serene presence. He spoke with quiet authority and his address was wide-ranging. The focus was on those young people of whom others might have low expectations, the need for a change in workforce demographics and the concern of multimedia approaches that were beginning to transcend the printed word. After forty-five minutes there was huge applause and, at the side of the stage, Victor sighed with relief. It was a good start.

Everyone was back in the common room where Tom and Owen were drinking coffee. A tall, dark-haired, athletic man in his mid-forties approached them. He had a craggy face and, at some stage in his earlier life, had suffered a broken nose. He tapped the badge on his lapel.

'Hello, I'm John Penny, headmaster of Christchurch Boys School in New Zealand. Victor mentioned you had volunteered to take our party around York on Sunday.'

Tom immediately took a liking to this engaging man with his distinctive New Zealand accent. 'Pleased to meet you, John. I'm Tom Frith. I teach English and teacher training. This is my colleague, Owen, from the physical education department. And, yes, we're your guides on Sunday.'

They shook hands. 'I'm very grateful. There's a dozen of us. We're a mixed bunch. Some Aussies but mostly Kiwis. A day out with you guys sounds great.'

'Maybe we could catch up at lunchtime to see what you might fancy doing,' said Owen. 'There's plenty to see: the Minster, a boat trip, even a different pub for every day of the year within the city walls.'

John Penny stared at Owen. 'Hey, a Welshman. Are you keen on rugby?' He touched his nose and smiled. 'I used to play.'

Owen grinned. 'It's my religion. We have a great team here. I'm the coach.'

'That's good to hear. My school has a proud tradition for rugby. Some of our pupils go on to become All Blacks.'

'Hate to say it,' said Owen, 'but you've got the best team in the world. We're playing catch-up in the UK.'

John smiled. 'You'll get there one day. You've got all the resources here.'

'Maybe,' said Owen.

'OK,' said John. 'Pleased to have met you. We can catch up at lunchtime.'

They watched him walk away. 'A good guy,' said Owen, 'a headteacher and an ex-rugby player. Good combination.'

Rosie and Inger were at the far side of the common room and looking at the swarm of delegates. 'Come on,' said Inger. 'Let's circulate.' They spotted a young fair-haired woman wearing jeans and a black tracksuit top with a white fern emblem. Her badge read 'KIRSTY MULLIGAN, Music Teacher, Auckland' and they walked over to meet her.

'Hello, Kirsty. I'm Inger. I teach music as well. This is my colleague, Rosie, in the English department.'

Kirsty smiled. 'Good to meet you.' She had a distinctive accent, a soft and cheerful tone that rose at the end of a sentence.

'Shall we get some coffee?' asked Rosie.

'Yes, please.'

They found a relatively quiet space near the pigeonholes and immediately discovered they enjoyed each other's company. Kirsty told them that she had watched her sister compete in the recent Commonwealth Games in Auckland. 'Then we all listened to your Queen Elizabeth at the closing ceremony. It was really special.'

'So, what's it like working in Auckland?' asked Inger.

'Brilliant,' said Kirsty. 'I teach music in a girls' school. What about you?'

'My work is mainly orchestra and voice,' said Inger. 'It's my passion.'

'Loved the string section this morning,' said Kirsty. She glanced at Rosie's badge. 'And what about you, Rosie?'

'I teach English literature and work in Education training teachers. It's a fulfilling life supporting the next generation.'

Kirsty looked thoughtful. 'Trying to place the accent. Different to everyone else I've spoken to.'

'I'm from Cornwall.'

'I've seen it on the telly. Spectacular beaches. Pounding seas. I go surfing at home. I guess I would be right at home there.'

Rosie smiled. 'I'm sure you would, and we'd serve you up some Cornish pasties and cream teas.'

'Perfect,' said Kirsty.

'What's Auckland like?' asked Inger.

'It's a great place to live. Very cosmopolitan. You'd love it. Our schools are very different to the ones we've seen over here. It's a great experience sampling another culture. You ought to visit some time. We would make you most welcome.' She smiled. 'I could even take you paddleboarding at Takapuna on the North Shore.'

A bell rang to announce the next lecture was about to begin. The time for caffeine and conversation was over.

'No rest for the wicked,' said Kirsty. 'Great to talk to you two. See you later,' and she walked away to join the rest of her party.

'Auckland sounds good,' mused Rosie. 'I'd like to visit.'

At eleven o'clock the next keynote lecture featured Victor, who gave an overview of the challenges in higher education. The audience was kept spellbound by this learned academic. He didn't use any visuals and merely captivated everyone with his calm manner and his cognizance of a complex subject. It was followed by a lively Q & A until a bell rang for lunchtime.

Tom and Owen were in the queue in the refectory when John Penny approached them. He pointed to the far corner where the Antipodean contingent was gathered. 'Come and join us,' he said. Around their table Rosie and Inger were chatting with Kirsty Mulligan while Sam Greenwood was deep in conversation with two young science teachers from New South Wales. It was a lively union of different cultures.

Tom and Owen collected their trays of food and joined John Penny at the end of the table. Inger and Rosie looked up and waved.

'We really appreciate you accommodating us,' said John. 'It's proving a valuable experience. Thanks for making us welcome.'

'A pleasure, John,' said Tom. 'It goes both ways. We can learn so much from you as well.'

'Especially rugby,' quipped Owen.

Tom looked across at Inger and the perceptive John recognized the deep-felt appreciation.

'I admire your colleagues,' said John. 'There's a lot of talent here. I wish I had a music teacher like Dr Larson. She clearly inspires her students. I spoke with the string quartet this morning. They were full of praise for her.'

'That's good to hear. Yes, Inger is special,' said Tom quietly and John smiled.

The final lecture of the day, Globalization and Education, was delivered by Professor Justin Geoghegan from Cambridge. Tom sat on the back row with Inger and Rosie. He noticed how they had become even closer in recent weeks. Even so, when he enquired what it was they found to talk about at such length Inger's responses were always bland and evasive. 'Just women's talk,' was her cryptic reply.

Back in their study he mentioned it to Owen. His blunt Welsh friend merely shrugged and said, 'Don't bother, Tom. Women are different. Understanding them is like trying to comprehend the offside rule in football. Bloody impossible!'

Following those words of wisdom, Tom walked up the Cloisters corridor and tapped on Rosie's study door.

'Just checking arrangements for tomorrow morning. Are we meeting up for a final run-through or are you happy as we are?'

Rosie smiled. 'Why don't we meet in the common room nice and early, say, eight fifteen a.m., and check we're OK?'

'Sounds good. Are you working late?'

She looked at the clock on the mantelpiece. 'No, I'm going for a drink with Inger.'

'OK. See you tomorrow.' As he walked back to his study it struck him that he hadn't been invited. *Owen was right,* he thought. *Impossible to comprehend!*

Tom returned to his Haxby cottage after picking up his favourite Friday night fish-and-chip supper and sat down in the kitchen. He switched on the small portable television on the worktop and smiled. It was *Carry On Teacher* with Kenneth Williams and Hattie Jacques, which seemed appropriate. Later he settled in the lounge to go through his notes for the morning presentation. He knew Rosie would be word-perfect and he intended to be the same.

Suddenly the telephone rang. It was Inger.

'Hi, Tom. Rosie and I have arranged to meet up with a few of the Australians and New Zealanders tomorrow evening in the Black Swan. We could make a night of it if you like.'

'Yes. Great idea. They're an interesting bunch, aren't they?'

'I made good contact with a music teacher from Auckland, Kirsty Mulligan. You would like her. She's a surfer. Loves the outdoors. Rosie was even talking about travelling there.'

'How is she?'

'Much better now. Sorry I've neglected you recently but she really needed a friend these past weeks.'

'I understand.'

'It's been quite revealing. She said she trusted me because I gave but expected nothing back.'

'Interesting,' said Tom quietly.

'She's pleased you'll be with her tomorrow morning. She said you're a reassuring presence.'

'Is that what I am?'

'Yes, Tom, you are . . . and lots more.'

By mid evening Tom had relaxed with the BBC comedy *'Allo 'Allo!* in which General von Klinkerhoffen was having troubles with his invasion plans. Tom decided to leave him to it before switching off and returning to his presentation notes. It was late and sleep seemed far away when he turned on the television once again. The classic western *High Noon* was on with Gary Cooper and Grace Kelly. The haunting song that accompanied the film, 'Do Not Forsake Me, Oh, My Darling', was on his mind as he finally climbed the stairs to bed.

On Saturday morning warmth and light had spread over the countryside and Rosie was waiting for Tom when he walked into reception. She was talking to Perkins.

'Hope it goes well for you both this morning,' he said. 'I've seen the programme and you're kicking off a busy day.'

Tom gave a smile. 'Thanks, Perkins. I'm sure it will be fine.'

'We're well rehearsed,' said Rosie confidently.

'Well, I must say, you both look very smart,' said Perkins approvingly.

Tom was wearing his best grey suit, the one reserved for weddings, funerals and interviews. Rosie was wearing a two-piece pinstriped business suit and had subtle high-lights in her hair. Also, she had begun to wear lipstick and eye shadow.

Just before 9.45 a.m. they were in the Ayckbourn Lecture

Theatre standing at the side of the stage with Victor. There were three short presentations before morning coffee. They were on first to be followed by Inger with her overview of the Music curriculum and then Sam Greenwood representing Science. Victor had persuaded Richard that it would be good experience for Sam without suggesting this engaging Lancastrian was a far better communicator.

Victor had whimsically described the audience as a procrastination of professors, a doctrine of doctors and an abstraction of academics. He had always loved his collective nouns. He whispered, 'Good luck,' as Rosie and Tom approached the lectern. A sea of faces rose up before them.

Rosie went first. Behind her was a slide of the four-year programme for English Literature. Shakespeare, Dickens, Woolf and luminaries of twentieth-century American literature figured prominently. She spoke with clarity and then stood to one side while Tom described the strategies for developing teachers with appropriate classroom-management skills along with the capacity to cope with the evolving National Curriculum. It went well and there was polite and sustained applause when they had concluded.

They passed Inger as she took her turn at the lectern. It was Tom's turn to whisper, 'Good luck.' Then he smiled at Rosie: 'Well done.'

At the side of the stage Victor was delighted. 'Excellent,' he said with enthusiasm. 'Short, sweet and to the point. A great start to the day. Many thanks.'

After giving a thumbs up to Sam Greenwood, Tom and Rosie hurried through the fire door, dashed up the stairs and crept back in. They found seats on the back row and settled down to listen to Inger and then Sam. Both were

outstanding, particularly Inger, who was used to address-
ing large audiences. At the end of her contribution she took
time to congratulate the members of the string section of
her orchestra. Then Sam spoke: he was impressive with an
easy, casual humour. 'There's more to him than meets the
eye,' said Rosie.

By ten thirty the talks had finished and a hum of conversation rose as everyone departed for the common room. Owen
caught up with Tom and patted him on the back. 'Well done,
mate. That was bloody good. Even *I* was interested.'

Tom grinned. 'Thanks, partner. Just pleased it's over.'

'Good luck for the rest of the day,' said Owen. 'Our
transport will be here soon. This afternoon's game is in
Wakefield.' He wandered off to the students' common room
where the rugby team had assembled and Chris Scully was
looking annoyed.

'What's wrong, Chris?' asked Owen.

'It's the bursar again. We give him legitimate complaints
about overcrowding in our accommodation and all the
problems with gas and electrics but nothing is ever done.
A lot of the guys are really fed up.'

Owen had his own opinion of the self-important bursar.
'I'll see what I can do,' he said.

After lunch, John Penny sought out Tom following a lengthy
conversation with Victor. There was half an hour before the
afternoon programme commenced. It was much less formal
with an assortment of group discussions. John tapped Tom
on the shoulder. 'Where's your Welsh friend going? I just
saw him hurrying to the car park.'

'He's off to Wakefield with the rugby team,' said Tom. 'It

will be late when they get back but he'll be around tomorrow morning for our walk around York.'

'Shame we can't go and watch the rugby,' said John wistfully.

They collected a mug of tea and found a quiet corner.

'So what's life like for you, Tom, here in the UK?'

'Fine. I enjoy my work. Victor is an excellent boss and I have good colleagues, particularly Owen.'

John nodded. 'I could do with a guy like him at my school. My physical education teacher has just got married and moved to South Africa.'

'Owen's wife, Sue, is a local PE teacher as well. They have a young son.'

John put down his mug and stared thoughtfully at Tom. 'So, if you don't mind me asking, are you married?'

'No.' He nodded towards Inger, who was deep in conversation with Kirsty Mulligan on the other side of the room. 'Inger and I spend time together.'

'Kirsty was telling me what a talented woman she is.'

'That's right, and she loves her work.'

'And where do you see your career developing, Tom?'

'Well . . . here for the time being.'

'Not back in school?'

'Maybe one day.'

'There're lots of opportunities out there for a guy like you. I was about your age when I became a deputy headteacher. I learned a lot. It was good preparation for the job I do now.'

'I can understand that,' said Tom. 'I feel as though I've moved on in my career since coming to Eboracum.'

'Yes, Victor speaks highly of you.'

'Good to hear,' said Tom, while curious to know why they had been discussing him.

'Anyway,' said John. 'I'm a group leader for this afternoon in one of the lecture rooms so I need to be prepared. I'm told by Kirsty we're meeting in a local pub tonight so no doubt I'll see you later.'

'Yes, the Black Swan. Great place. It's been there since the fifteenth century.'

John nodded in appreciation. 'Probably a couple of hundred years before the Dutch guy, Abel Tasman, landed on the South Island and met some of the local Maori people. I guess our history is a little different to yours,' and he wandered off.

The afternoon of group discussions went well and after a meal in the refectory Tom and Inger led John Penny and Kirsty Mulligan through the streets of York. They were followed by Rosie and Sam and two science teachers, Jess Johnson and Mia Stewart from Sydney. The two women had struck up a great rapport with Sam and it was a relaxed group that arrived outside the wattle-and-daub walls of the Black Swan. They found a table in the wood-panelled room under a coffered ceiling and John bought the first round to kick off a convivial and relaxed evening of lively banter. Tom found himself sitting next to John and developing a great respect for this positive and articulate headteacher. They shared stories of their backgrounds, growing up on opposite sides of the globe, and formed a bond of trust as the evening progressed.

It was after ten o'clock when they walked back to the university car park and everyone said goodnight to Rosie and Inger. Sam drove Jess and Mia back to their hotel and

Tom followed on with John and Kirsty. They agreed they would meet again at ten thirty the following morning for their guided tour of York.

Sunday morning dawned bright and clear and Tom and Owen had planned a varied day for their guests. All twelve members of John Penny's party were there. They were in awe of the morning service when they visited York Minster and were fascinated by the Jorvik Centre. They had lunch in one of the riverside pubs followed by an afternoon boat trip. Finally, back at the university, they gathered for afternoon tea in the refectory and waited for their coach to return them to the hotel.

John Penny took Tom to one side and they walked out to the quad. He did not waste words. 'Tom, I'll be straight with you. You have a great CV and you're approaching your mid-thirties. It's clear to me you already have a lot of varied experience. My deputy head is nearly sixty and will be retiring later this year. This means I'm on the lookout for someone to take his place. I think you would be ideal.' He handed over an A5 brochure. 'This is our school prospectus. It's a big school and you would be on a decent salary. Give it some thought.'

'This is unexpected,' said Tom, bemused. 'I appreciate the confidence you have in me.' He looked down at the glossy prospectus. 'It's a lot to take in.'

'I understand. Think of it as an opportunity.'

'I shall,' said Tom.

'Our school terms are different to yours so I would want you to fly out during your summer holiday. You could be in post by late September.'

'It's all very sudden.'

'Tom, this is a serious offer and a chance for your career to develop down under. In the meantime, you have a decision to make and I would need to know by Easter.'

'Thanks, John. I'll do that.'

He paused and smiled. 'And there's something else.'

'Yes?'

'Bring Inger as well.'

Chapter Thirteen

Rainbow's End

When Tom left his cottage on Friday, 30 March the scent of wallflowers was in the air. It was a morning when the first breath of spring was tantalizingly close. Winter days had gone and the promise of light and colour stretched out before him. Beneath the sharp buds of the hawthorn hedgerows, sunny primroses on the grassy banks were a salve to the soul. The mist was lifting as he drove towards Eboracum with the promise of a new day. Snowdrops brightened the new grass and sticky buds on the horse chestnut trees were bursting open. However, the beauty of nature was not uppermost in his mind. It was a time of new life and Tom wondered if he would be sharing it with Inger. A decision about the teaching post in New Zealand had to be made. The deadline was fast approaching and a difficult conversation awaited him. As he pulled up in the car park Lisa Stansfield was on the radio singing 'Live Together'.

It had been a busy week. The Harrogate Drama Festival had been the perfect choice for field week. Tom had driven the minibus to and from the university to Harrogate and Zeb and Rosie had accompanied him on alternate days. It had been a special experience for the English and drama students in their final year. Meanwhile, Owen was due to return later in the morning following a cold but rain-free week under canvas in the Brecon Beacons. Tom had missed his friendly camaraderie with the Welshman. When he walked into reception, Perkins was putting up a poster for next week's chess competition.

'Good morning, Dr Frith. Good to see you back after all that bus driving to Harrogate.'

'Thanks, Perkins. Yes, it was quite an experience.'

'Well, field week seems to have gone well this year. The history students enjoyed Blenheim Palace and Professor Head said the Science Museum in London was simply perfect. He arrived this morning with that lecturer who came for interview last year. I remembered her . . . blonde lady with a Filofax. Says she works in Sheffield now and she's got a long weekend in York.'

Tom smiled. As always, Perkins was a fund of knowledge. He was also aware that Dr Felicity Capstick, Richard's fellow astrophile, had been a frequent visitor of late and they had spent many an evening staring up at the stars together. He set off for the quad.

'Your post is in your pigeonhole,' Perkins called out after him. 'I noticed one with a New Zealand stamp.'

Tom smiled. Perkins didn't miss a trick.

At nine o'clock, Tom's first tutorial was a follow-up to the drama festival with English Four. Many of the students had a keen interest in writing screenplays and Tom used some of the step-by-step exercises from Syd Field's *The Screenwriter's Workbook* to explore essential narrative structure. All went well until Pam Salter, a twenty-two-year-old from Basingstoke, said, 'Tom, can we have a word about next term's final exams? A few of us are concerned.'

Tom had anticipated this and he distributed copies of old examination papers which tended to ease the fears. By ten o'clock these had been discussed and it was a relaxed group that finally walked out into the quad.

He headed for the common room where Inger was sitting alone and drinking coffee. She was sifting through a folder of music manuscripts. Tom collected a hot chocolate and walked over to her. 'Inger, can we meet up later today? There's something I want to discuss with you.'

She looked curious. 'That sounds intriguing. What's it about?'

Tom looked left and right and sat down beside her. There was no one within earshot. 'I've had a letter from New Zealand. John Penny says they need a decision by the end of next week.'

Inger frowned. 'The deputy headship? I presumed you had decided not to go ahead.'

'It's a big decision and it's been on my mind a lot these last few days. I can't put it off any longer.'

At that moment Rosie arrived. 'Hi, you two.' She appeared animated. 'Guess what, Inger? I've finally taken your advice.'

Inger looked up. 'Go on, I can't wait.'

'Impulsive, I know, but I'm hoping you're both free to come to my place for drinks and nibbles tomorrow evening. It's a bit short notice but I thought it would be good to wind down after field week. I'm just going round now inviting a few friends. It occurred to me as I was driving in.'

'Lovely idea,' said Inger. 'I'll be there.'

'Thanks, count me in,' said Tom.

Rosie sat back and sipped her coffee. She looked relaxed in her blue jeans and cream blouse. 'I've not hosted a party since I've been here. I thought it was about time.'

'Can I help set up?' asked Inger.

'Yes, please. Come along whenever you can.' She spotted Zeb at the counter talking to Sam Greenwood, put down her coffee cup and jumped up. 'Excuse me.'

Inger watched Rosie chatting with Zeb and Sam. They seemed to be sharing a joke. 'Good to see her looking happy again.'

'It is,' said Tom, 'and you've been a good friend to her.'

Inger closed her manuscript folder and stared at Tom. 'So . . . this job in New Zealand. Are you saying you're considering it?'

'It just sounds like a great opportunity.'

'And what have you decided?'

'That I would talk to you first.'

'I see,' Inger said and looked curiously at Tom. This had come as a surprise. Just then Rosie reappeared with Zeb at her side.

'Looks like we're partying tomorrow night,' said Zeb cheerily, 'and soon we'll be having one at my new place. I can't wait for you to see it. It's the one on the outskirts of Crayke village. I've just told Victor that my offer has been accepted. He's taking me out there again tomorrow morning.'

'That's great news,' said Tom.

'What about your apartment?' asked Inger.

Zeb tapped the side of her nose with her forefinger and smiled. 'No problem . . . a private sale is imminent. They descended like vultures when the word got out.'

Inger looked at Tom. 'I told you it was a great location. Perfect for working here.'

The conversation continued on Zeb's exciting news. She was clearly thrilled about the prospect of her barn conversion. Tom sat back while the three women chatted happily. He knew Crayke well. He had made teaching-practice visits to the pretty village with its fifteenth-century castle set in the beautiful countryside of the Howardian Hills. It was renowned for being a peaceful village, and Tom wondered if it would stay that way when the dynamic Zeb finally made her entrance.

After break Tom had his final session with English Two. They discussed the highs and lows of the last term and before the lunchtime bell Tom asked about their plans for the Easter holiday. Most appeared to be going back home for a rest, a soft bed and three meals a day. Others had planned holiday jobs. Amy Fieldhouse and Liz Colby were returning to Bridlington to sell ice creams from a seafront kiosk, Tommy Birkenshaw was going to work in a bookmaker's in Liverpool and Ellie MacBride would be selling fruit and veg once again on Barnsley Market. There were also some surprises among the incongruous range of temporary occupations. They included carrying frozen meat in a factory, a slipper-bath cleaner, varnishing ornamental gourds and even a chicken-plucker, which caused amusement. Tom smiled at the range of life experiences that lay before them.

Meanwhile, Poppy Hartness, a twenty-year-old from Brentford, was in high spirits telling everyone about an Orbital rave in London. Her friend had written to say she had spotted a smiley face logo in a local telephone box advertising the event. Tom took her to one side and urged caution. An acid house party with access to Ecstasy was always fraught with danger.

'As if, Tom!' said Poppy with a smile. 'No problem. I'm too safe for words.'

Tom watched her walk away with the confidence of youth.

Ellie MacBride came to stand next to Tom. 'Bit of a wild one,' she said quietly. 'By all accounts she hangs out with a crazy bunch down in London.'

'Only young once,' said Tom.

'Too true,' mused Ellie, pushing her long black hair back from her face and looking up at Tom.

'So, are you taking a holiday or just helping out on the market stall?'

'At the minute it's just the stall,' said Ellie. 'Dave Hardisty, the history student, asked me to go to Filey with him for a couple of days.'

'And?'

'I turned him down. Not my type.' She smiled. 'Enjoy your holiday, Tom, and see you next term.'

He watched her walk away . . . always a conundrum.

When Tom left the lecture block he spotted Owen outside the refectory, looking weather-beaten after his time in the Brecon Beacons. He was in conversation with Gideon Chalk and it didn't seem to be going well.

'But surely something can be done,' said Owen. 'The

students were waiting for me when I got off the bus. They need you to respond to their grievances.'

'I already have,' replied Gideon curtly.

Owen frowned. 'But word has it you now own half a dozen properties. Do you deal with all the occupants in this off-hand manner?'

'I *sublet* them,' said Gideon with a scowl. 'There is a difference but I don't expect you to understand.'

Owen fumed. He had suffered this type of condescending arrogance all his professional life. As a tutor of physical education an elitist few assumed he wasn't as bright as the professorial luminaries in the faculty. 'I can assure you, boyo, that I do understand.' He leaned forward and glared at the diminutive bursar. 'So are you going to help these students or not?'

Gideon Chalk gave him a look of pure contempt. 'Contracts have been signed. There's nothing I can do and, if you'll excuse me, I have work to get on with.' It was becoming clear there wasn't a compassionate bone in his body. He turned and strutted away.

'You've not heard the last of this,' muttered Owen.

Tom arrived by his side. 'Welcome back.' He nodded towards the retreating figure of the bursar. 'Trouble?'

'Sadly, yes,' said Owen. 'He won't give the guys in my rugby team a fair deal.' He shook his head. 'They need support.'

'I doubt you'll get it from him,' said Tom.

'He's just an arrogant little bastard. One day he'll get his comeuppance.'

'Come on,' said Tom. 'It's lunchtime. Let's get something to eat and you can tell me about living in a tent in Wales.'

Tom was glad to have his friend back at Eboracum and they took their meals of fish pie and mushy peas to a quiet table. Owen had clearly loved going back to the stunning scenery of the Brecon Beacons mountain range in South Wales.

'It was great, Tom. We climbed up Pen y Fan and sang songs in the local pubs. It's always good to watch friendships being forged that will last a lifetime.' He wolfed down his food and then looked up at Tom. 'So, what about you? How did yours go?'

'Fine. I'm now known as the university's bus driver. Everything went well. Zeb's organization was perfect as always and Rosie enjoyed it. She's invited us to her place for drinks tomorrow evening. It's to celebrate the end of field week. You and Sue must come if you can get a babysitter.'

'Sounds good,' said Owen.

'There's something else,' added Tom hesitantly.

'Let's hear it then,' said Owen. He pushed away his plate and stared curiously at Tom. 'What is it? You look worried.'

Tom reached into his pocket and took out a creased envelope. It had a New Zealand stamp. 'It's this.' He took out the letter and passed it to Owen. 'John Penny has been in touch. He wants an answer about the job.'

Owen scanned the letter. 'By next week. Bloody hell, Tom!' He studied Tom's expression. 'You're thinking about saying yes, aren't you?'

'Not sure. I'm talking to Inger later. John Penny wants her to go as well.'

Owen was quiet for a moment. 'And what happens if she says no? She's happy here, Tom.'

'I know . . . but I have to discuss it with her further. It concerns her as much as me.'

'I guess so.' He handed the letter back to Tom. 'Does Victor know?'

'Yes, I've spoken to him. He said it's up to me.'

Owen nodded. 'He wouldn't stand in your way.'

'So, what do you think?'

'It's a hell of a decision. Do you really want to go to Christchurch? I thought you were happy here. You've made good friends.'

'I know. And I *am* happy here. But I was intrigued by the offer.'

'I'd be sad to see you go. So . . . if Inger says yes will you leave?'

Tom stared out of the window and didn't reply.

Owen stood up and patted Tom on the shoulder. 'Think hard, my friend. This is a big call. Whatever you decide, I'll support you,' and he walked away.

Following his tutorial with Primary Three concerning next term's teaching practice, Tom walked through the quad to the common room. Inger was with a group of students heading for the music room. She waved. 'Catch you later,' she said and hurried away.

Tom collected a mug of tea and sat down next to Zeb and Rosie. Zeb was telling Rosie that Margaret Thatcher was having a hard time in the Commons with the opposition to her poll tax and that Nelson Mandela had refused an invitation to meet her. Rosie, another Liberal, nodded in agreement.

Rosie looked up at Tom and smiled. 'Everybody I've invited is coming,' she said enthusiastically, 'and even Selina Morton said yes.' Sadistic Selina, the man-hater, was Richard Head's colleague in the science department.

'That should be interesting,' said Tom. 'Apparently her U3A course on "Euthanasia in a Future World" is going well. Get her talking about that or her proposal to have all men neutered and you'll be fine.'

'Oh dear,' said Rosie.

'Ignore your buddy tutor's attempt at banter, Rosie,' said Zeb. 'Selina is an acquired taste.'

'What would you like me to bring for the party?' asked Tom.

'A bottle of wine would be fine,' said Rosie. 'The food is pretty well sorted.'

'OK,' said Tom. 'What time?'

'Seven onwards,' said Rosie as she and Zeb got up to leave. 'See you then.'

Tom watched them walk away and wondered what they might think if they knew of his dilemma.

By 4.30 p.m. Tom had spent two troubled hours marking essays before walking up Cloisters corridor towards Inger's study. She was standing by her door talking to her star soprano, Arabella Esposito. 'Thanks, Inger,' said Arabella and she headed for the stairs, clutching a folder.

Inger smiled. 'Hi, Tom.'

'Are you free now?' he asked.

'Yes, that was my last tutorial. Come on in.'

As they sat down Inger noticed that Tom appeared anxious. 'What is it?' she asked.

He took the envelope from his pocket and placed it on the coffee table. 'This arrived in the post. You might want to look at it.'

Inger began to read. After a few moments she sat back but said nothing.

'You can see why I wanted to share it with you,' said Tom.
'Go on.'

'Well . . . the last time I spoke with John Penny he said
something significant. It concerned you.'

'Really?'

'Yes. He said, "Bring Inger."'

'I see.'

'He made it clear he held you in high esteem.'

'That's good to hear. The feeling was mutual. He came
over as a dedicated educationalist and it sounded like he
runs a good school.'

'I agree,' said Tom. 'He's a great guy.' There was a long
pause. 'So . . . what do you think?'

Inger leaned forward and gave Tom a level stare. 'About
what, Tom? Are you simply talking about this post or are
you considering moving to the other side of the world?'

'It's a completely unexpected opportunity. I need to know
your feelings about it.'

Inger shook her head. 'I would be sad to see you go, Tom.
So would Owen and Zeb.'

This wasn't the way he anticipated the conversation
would progress. 'I was hoping you might come with me.'
There was a long pause. 'I've spoken to Victor and told him
of the offer.'

'And what was his response?'

'Supportive, as you would expect. He said he would
never stand in the way of a colleague seeking promotion.'

'Yes, Victor would say that. You could learn so much
from him.'

Tom frowned. 'I already have.'

'And what about loyalty? The only reason you're here

today is because of his belief in you as a good professional. We're all indebted to him.'

'I know that, Inger, but if I go I want you to come with me.'

'My work is here, Tom. I've built something special in the music department. I can't just fly off.'

Tom was beginning to feel anxious and disappointed. 'I just thought it was a chance for us to start a new life together.'

'No, Tom. Life doesn't work like that for me. I can't give up everything I've created here. I love working at Eboracum. Surely you must see that.'

'I do . . . but you could create something equally special in New Zealand.'

She sighed and sat back in her chair. 'It's for you to decide, Tom. Go away and think about it. I wouldn't stand in your way.'

Suddenly he felt drained of energy. He stood up and walked to the door. 'OK. I'm glad we've spoken about it. I'll see you tomorrow night at Rosie's.'

As he drove home he tried to reassess what was important in his life, while back in her study Inger was doing the same.

On Saturday evening Tom collected a bottle of Chardonnay and drove to Wigginton. There were lots of cars parked in the cul-de-sac outside Rosie's home. It was Sam Greenwood who opened the door and Elaine Paige's *Cinema* LP was on the record player. She was singing 'The Way We Were' as Tom walked into the lounge.

The dining table had been pushed up against the wall and Inger, Rosie and Zeb were arranging food. The table setting looked very grand. There were Wedgwood plates and a silver service given to her by her parents on the occasion of her twenty-first birthday. The assortment of party food included ham sandwiches, cheese and pineapple on sticks, sausage rolls, potato croquettes and Turkey Twizzlers. Inger had brought a tray of ham and cheese hot pockets and Zeb had arrived with one of her specialities: tomato-stuffed mushrooms. For a dessert, Rosie had baked some strudels. It was a veritable feast.

Tom looked at the three women. Zeb, unorthodox as always, was wearing an off-the-shoulder sweatshirt and Jane Fonda leggings. Inger looked elegant in a floral dress and with her blonde hair in a French plait. Rosie was wearing a white blouse and blue jeans. She appeared happy again. All of them moved with the confidence of liberated women.

Around him his friends and colleagues were huddled in groups, enjoying a drink and relaxed conversation. Owen was chatting with Sam Greenwood about outward-bound activities in the Lake District while Felicity Capstick and Selina Morton were discussing the merits of the Hubble Space Telescope. Meanwhile, Victor and a much-recovered Pat were studying the watercolour paintings by Cornish artists that filled the walls. On a more topical note, Sue Llewellyn was telling Inger that she had read Fergie couldn't agree with Andrew on a name for their week-old baby. 'For my part I didn't have much choice,' she complained. 'Owen made it clear it was always going to be a true Welsh name,' and Inger smiled.

Tom poured himself a glass of pale ale and walked into the small conservatory at the back of the cottage where

Richard Head was staring up at the stars, a glass of tonic water in his hand.

'Hi, Richard. You look deep in thought.'

'Hello, Tom. Yes, just admiring the view. Did you know the distance to the Pole Star is somewhere between three and four hundred light years?'

'No, I didn't.'

Richard nodded. 'That's around ninety-nine to one hundred and thirty-three parsecs.'

'Yes, I suppose it is,' said Tom, bewildered. 'I imagine you enjoy studying the stars with Felicity.'

'Yes, we do it frequently now. In fact she's just decided we should get married.'

'Pardon?' Tom put down his beer.

'Yes, she's proposed marriage.'

'Oh, well . . . congratulations, that's wonderful news,' and Tom shook Richard's hand. Then he paused. 'Did you say it was *Felicity* who had decided? What about you? How do you feel about it?'

'I explained to her I was used to living alone and liked order. She said she didn't mind me triple-locking the doors and having essential routines in my life.'

'That sounds positive,' said Tom without conviction. He was aware the cerebral professor had an obsessive-compulsive disorder as well as being a perfectionist in his work. His repetitive actions were also well known, not least regular handwashing owing to his fear of germs.

'Yes,' said Richard, looking up once again at the firmament. 'Felicity thought it was for the best. So she suggested it. We have similar interests and at the moment we're both living single lives.'

'So . . . is it companionship you're looking for, Richard?'

The quirky scientist pondered this for a moment. 'Yes, I think so. For example, only last week we did a spectrometry experiment together concerning a measured decrease in density, and that seemed to work well.'

'Good to hear,' said Tom dubiously. Knowing Richard as he did, there were a few concerns. The relationship he described was more than a meeting of minds: it was a collision of the inexplicable, a paradox of utter confusion. At first, it made no sense.

'Well, I wish you luck, whatever the future holds.'

'Thank you, Tom. I've thought hard about it and I'm sure it will work.'

Tom nodded in agreement. As a renowned scientist, Richard's analytical abilities were second to none. Tom wandered back into the lounge and left his star-gazing friend looking up into the darkness at stars that twinkled like fireflies.

Owen caught sight of Tom and ushered him into the hallway. 'Go on then. What did Inger say?'

'She wasn't keen. Said Eboracum was more important.'

'That's understandable,' said Owen. 'So are you going to kick this job into touch?'

'I guess so.'

'Is that a yes?'

'Maybe.'

Owen shook his head. 'Surely you've told Inger it's a no-go. If you haven't you'll lose her.'

'It was all undecided when we last spoke. She didn't sound pleased.'

'In that case, Englishman, get your arse in gear and tell her tonight you're not going anywhere without her.'

'It might be too late. I've handled it badly.'

'Then do something about it.' He glanced across to the conservatory where Richard was still staring up at the stars. 'Were you sharing this with Richard?'

Tom shook his head. 'No. Guess what? He's just told me that he and Felicity intend to get married.'

'Bloody hell! Does she know what she's taking on?'

'I presume so.'

'Did he say when?'

'No. Apparently that will be for Felicity to decide. She's making the running with this.'

'Well, good luck to them both. Let's hope he doesn't wear his identity lanyard when he walks down the aisle.'

Meanwhile, Victor had approached Inger in the kitchen. 'A lovely party,' he said. 'I'm pleased for Rosie. You've obviously been a great help to her.'

'She needed to escape the clutches of a manipulative man. I was simply there to help her through it.'

'Well, you've done a great job. I was concerned for her.' He glanced around him and spoke quietly. 'Incidentally, Tom has told me about the letter from New Zealand and mentioned that he has spoken to you.'

'Yes, it sounded to be an attractive proposition,' said Inger guardedly. 'He said the headteacher wanted me to go as well.'

Victor gave a wry smile. 'That's right. John Penny knows a good thing when he sees it. Two for the price of one.'

'Victor, I made it clear to Tom that I don't want to leave Eboracum. I love working here.'

'And what about Tom? How would you feel if he left?'

She put down her drink and folded her arms. 'It would demonstrate his priorities,' she said pointedly.

Victor gave her an enigmatic smile. 'Good luck,' he whispered and walked back into the lounge.

As everyone was leaving, Tom walked with Inger back to her car.

'I'm sorry to have caused confusion,' he said. 'I saw a chance for you and me to share a new life together.'

She unlocked her car and stood there thoughtfully. 'My future was always here. I value the chance to work at Eboracum. Victor knows how I feel.'

'I know that now.'

'It's for you to decide, Tom. At the moment you seem to be looking for a pot of gold at the end of a rainbow.'

'Maybe it appeared like that. I just saw it as a chance to be with you.'

'Perhaps you don't know me well enough.' She climbed in her car and drove away.

On the way home Tom stared out into the darkness. Sinéad O'Connor was on the radio. She was singing 'Nothing Compares 2 U'.

Chapter Fourteen

Gifted

Alexandra Jane Bisset was different. It was something she had realized aged nine at primary school in the village of Pity Me in County Durham. When her teacher said, 'What are we going to do with you, Alex? You know all the answers,' she understood she didn't fit in.

At that point she made a decision not to stand out from the crowd. From then on she made friends and coasted along in her academic subjects without drawing attention to herself. No one suspected how easily mathematics came to her, or how remarkable her memory was. In the world she created she became one of the invisible children.

It was only later that she would realize she was gifted.

Now a slightly built, brown-haired twenty-two-year-old in her final year at Eboracum, she had continued her pretence of being a good student and nothing more. Her main subject was mathematics with Victor and she had worked steadily, handed in assignments on time and made sure not to stand out. Her alter ego was unremarkable. And as a voracious reader, she was probably one of the few students who knew that it was Cicero who had coined the term 'alter ego' as part of his philosophical construct in first-century Rome. It was a fraction of her vast knowledge that she didn't share with the other women in her accommodation, who seemed to fill the air with aimless chatter.

Now, in the final week of term before the Easter holiday, she stood quietly in reception and stared up at the poster advertising the chess tournament.

'Good morning, Miss Bisset,' said Perkins.

'Hello, Perkins,' said Alexandra. She pointed to the poster. 'Sorry to trouble you but I've been told the tournament has been moved to the music room.'

'That's right. There's been so much interest it was decided to find a bigger space. It starts at ten thirty. I'm told Dr Tremaine has never lost a group challenge such as this. How on earth she can play so many games at once is beyond me.'

'I'm one of the ten students who will be challenging her,' said Alexandra. 'I thought I would give it a try.'

'Well, best of luck.'

Alexandra merely nodded. She loved chess. This would make a change from sitting alone with her chess set and always playing against herself while replicating the games of grandmasters. 'Thank you, Perkins,' she said and walked away.

A gentle soul, thought Perkins as he watched her step briskly towards the quad. *I wonder what will become of her.*

Moments later Rosie entered reception and Perkins smiled up at her. 'Good morning, Dr Tremaine,' he said cheerfully. 'A lot of mail for you today.'

'Thank you, Perkins,' said Rosie. 'I'll collect it now if I may.'

'Of course.' He lifted a pile of a dozen letters from behind the counter and passed them over. As he did so he noticed the top one had been franked with the name of a local solicitor.

Rosie put them in her shoulder bag and smiled at the friendly figure of the head porter. 'Thank you for all your support this term.'

Perkins beamed. 'Always a pleasure.'

'Will you be taking an Easter holiday?'

'Yes. I'm taking my Pauline to Filey for a couple of days. In the meantime I'm training up young Albert, my new junior porter, to look after things here in reception.'

'He's a lucky man to have a teacher such as yourself.'

'Those are kind words, Dr Tremaine, and if I may be so bold, good luck today with your chess tournament. Even though I expect you won't need it.'

'That's kind of you to say. Yes, I'm looking forward to it.'

Perkins was pleased she looked happier these days and wondered why.

At 8.30 a.m. Tom was unpacking his satchel when Owen walked into their study. 'Morning,' said Tom. 'You OK?' His Welsh friend looked distinctly tired.

'Up with Gareth in the night. Poor little sod has got a cold.'

'Sorry to hear that. How's Sue?'

'The same . . . just a bit tired. She never complains.'

Tom nodded in agreement. Owen was a lucky man to have such a partner. He took an envelope from his satchel and placed it on the desk. 'I'm posting this today.' It was addressed to John Penny in New Zealand.

Owen looked up at his friend. 'Go on then. What have you decided?'

'I'm turning the job down.'

'Bloody good decision. Who else is there to keep this study tidy?' He stepped forward and shook Tom's hand. '*Croeso nôl*, my friend . . . welcome back.'

'Thanks,' said Tom.

'So, have you told the lovely Inger?'

'I rang her last night. She was disappointed I had considered it in the first place, so I got a cool response.'

'In that case you need to use some of my Welsh charm. Take her out for a meal and while you're about it apologize for being a gullible Englishman.'

'For once, I agree,' said Tom.

Shortly after ten o'clock, Sam Greenwood was collecting his coffee in the common room and Tom joined him at the counter. 'Are you going to watch Rosie play chess?' he asked.

'Definitely,' said Sam. 'I've rearranged my tutorials this morning and put back my meeting with Richard and Selina until the end of the day.'

'I've done something similar,' said Tom. He looked at his watch. 'It kicks off at ten thirty. Have you been to one before? Apparently she's playing ten people at once. Sounds impossible.'

Sam shook his head. 'Not for Rosie. I've played her a few times and she literally wiped the board with me. It's as if she goes into a zone and shuts everything out. It's formidable. So hell will freeze over before a student can beat her.'

They drank their coffee while Sam, a member of the Labour Party, complained about the poll tax. 'Maggie's bitten off more than she can chew this time,' he grumbled. 'A quarter of a million were demonstrating in London last weekend.'

Tom sighed. It had dominated the recent news. The Prime Minister's Community Charge, commonly known as the poll tax, had led to riots countrywide. 'Owen told me he's going to join something called 3D.'

'What's that?' asked Sam.

'Don't Register, Don't Pay, Don't Collect.'

'Makes sense. It's the less well-off that get stuffed every time.'

Tom smiled. He had grown to appreciate this generally unassuming Mancunian scientist.

At precisely ten thirty in the music room, Victor stood up to introduce the chess tournament. On the stage, arranged in a large circle, there were ten students all seated at a table on each of which there was a chess set. Rosie was standing in the centre of the circle. In a smart linen trouser suit, she looked composed.

Victor turned to face the large audience. 'Good morning, everyone, and welcome to what is a first for the university.' He gestured towards Rosie. 'We're privileged to have an outstanding chess player in the faculty, Dr Rosie Tremaine. In recent times she has returned to her native Cornwall and won the South of England Chess Championship. Today, Dr Tremaine will be playing a simultaneous exhibition match against ten students. For your information in chess circles this is known as a *simul*.'

On the back row, Tom smiled. Victor was always a fount of knowledge.

Victor took an embossed postcard from his pocket and held it up. 'Some interesting news . . . I've been informed that the Vice Chancellor has booked a table for lunch today at Bettys in York for Dr Tremaine and the last player remaining in the competition.' There was applause from the audience and expectant looks from some of the players. 'So now I shall pass over to Dr Tremaine to explain the rules.'

Rosie spoke in a clear, confident voice. 'Good morning, everybody, and welcome to our chess tournament. I'm delighted we have a thriving chess club here in Eboracum and today ten of our best players will be playing against me. The rules are simple for an exhibition such as this. No clocks will be used although time is limited. Each player will be expected to have made their move by the time I arrive in front of them. Then I shall make my move in as brief a time as possible. As games are finished off that opponent will leave the circle and join the audience. I shall play white in all the games.'

She paused and looked at the ten students; a few stared back in trepidation. 'Some advice for all of you. Take special care with your opening. This will make it more difficult for me. If, after twenty moves, you are still in the game, you can propose a draw but keep in mind it is unlikely I would accept. Also, do not be afraid to exchange pieces, it will make the endgame more interesting. Finally, there is no talking and nothing must be done that irritates your opponent. We must always demonstrate good manners. Good luck to you all and play well.'

You could hear a pin drop as the tournament began. The

music room had never been so quiet. At first there was a flurry of moves as Rosie stepped swiftly from one table to the next. It was as if she required no thought. The first player was eliminated after four moves, the next two after eight and one more after ten. Then it got more interesting. The audience was spellbound. After thirty minutes, only Alexandra Bisset remained and it was noticeable that Rosie was taking more time over her moves.

The tension was almost unbearable. Alexandra's eyes never left the board. On one occasion she removed her spectacles and polished them slowly with her handkerchief. That apart, there was no movement, only complete concentration. Finally, the twelve o'clock bell rang for lunch and Rosie looked enquiringly at Alexandra. It was as if they had both reached an impasse. Alexandra looked up and gave a shy smile.

Rosie gave a brief nod. 'A draw?' she enquired.

'A draw,' replied Alexandra.

They both stood up and shook hands while the audience of students and staff erupted into sustained applause.

Rosie smiled at Alexandra. 'A celebratory lunch beckons.'

'Looking forward to it,' said Alexandra. 'I've only ever been to Bettys when my parents have treated me.'

'Well, this is on the Vice Chancellor and he can definitely afford it. Come on. You've earned it.'

Perkins gave them a cheery wave as they walked out of reception and up the winding path to Lord Mayor's Walk. Soon new shoots of lime and ash would burst into life. Rooks cawed loudly in the elm-tops and the first primroses brightened the new swards of grass, while early-April forsythia lifted the spirits.

*

Inger had arrived in the car park and was appreciating the onset of springtime. She enjoyed her long walks in the countryside or by the river. A car pulled up beside her. It was Tom.

He jumped out and looked expectantly at Inger. 'Truce?' he said.

Inger paused and looked at the dishevelled figure before her with his crumpled suit and long hair. For a moment Tom was unsure how she would respond but then she gave a hopeful smile. 'Truce,' she replied. She leaned back against her car and looked up at him. 'Tom . . . I'm glad you decided to stay. Eboracum is a great place to work and you have only just started your career here . . . and, besides, you would be missed.'

'That's kind of you to say.'

She laughed. 'I mean, who would put up with Owen and what would your students do without you?'

'And what about you?'

Inger paused. 'Well, I suppose I would miss you . . . a bit.' Tom looked concerned. 'I'm only teasing,' she said. 'Of course I would. I didn't want you to leave me but I had to know that, given the choice, you wouldn't. And now I know.'

Tom smiled and felt a weight fall from his shoulders. 'So, are you free for a drink tonight?'

She raised her eyebrows. 'I think I can fit you in.'

Tom stepped forward and held her hand. 'How about the Black Swan? I can pick you up at seven.'

Together they walked into reception.

Rosie and Alexandra were seated in the famous Bettys Tea Rooms and being served by a waitress dressed in the traditional 1930s cap and apron.

'That's the first time I've ever failed to win a game in an exhibition,' said Rosie. 'So well done.'

'Oh dear. I'm sorry,' said Alexandra. 'I'm sure it's because you were fatigued after playing against so many simultaneously.'

'Not at all,' said Rosie, 'I'm used to it. However, one thing did puzzle me. You paused on move thirty-six. A more decisive move at that point could possibly have beaten me.'

'I know.'

Rosie looked at this young woman with new interest. 'Are you saying you held back?' Alexandra looked down at her meal and was silent. 'I'm intrigued,' said Rosie. 'I've not met another player like you. Tell me truthfully: could you have won that game?'

'Possibly,' said Alexandra quietly.

'Then why didn't you?'

'Habit, I suppose. It's what I've done all my life.'

'But why?'

Alexandra sighed deeply. 'I don't want to be different. It's my choice and I choose *normal*.'

'You're one of Victor's maths students, aren't you?'

'Yes.'

'Are you anticipating getting a first?'

'Probably . . . but that will only be to please Victor and my parents. It would mean a lot to them.'

Rosie leaned forward and spoke softly. 'What did you mean when you said you choose *normal*?'

Alexandra realized here was someone she could trust. It was time to open Pandora's box. 'I made that decision when I was at primary school. It was obvious I was different to everyone else. The work that was set for me was too easy. I didn't want to be a freak.'

'My God! You're not that, Alexandra. You have a special talent.'

'But it's been a millstone around my neck since I was young so I chose a quiet middle road.'

Suddenly Rosie picked up a napkin and spread it on the table. With a pen she drew two axes shaped like a right angle. On them she drew a bell curve. 'Let me share something with you. An IQ is a standard score, based on the normal curve where one hundred is the average.' She drew a straight line from the top of the curve to the base line and then pointed to the lip of the curve on the right. 'The top 2.4 per cent is generally regarded as indicative of mental giftedness. The problem today is that gifted students with very superior reasoning abilities can become bored in classrooms. They find the work too limiting and are not challenged. That was you, Alexandra.' She paused. 'And it was also me.'

Alexandra stared wide-eyed at this revelation while Rosie pressed on. 'The work of the American psychologists Getzels and Jackson back in the 1960s was significant. They explored creativity and intelligence in gifted children. I was one of those children – taken out of school at a young age and subjected to a wide range of tests, everything from solving geometric patterns to more creative ones such as how you would weigh an elephant. It was a strange time in my life. So I made the same decision as you. I did well enough but no more. It was a difficult and frustrating journey.'

Alexandra smiled. 'Thank you, Rosie. This is probably the first time I haven't felt alone.'

They sat back, ordered more tea and relaxed in each other's company.

As they walked back to Eboracum, Alexandra grinned. 'So . . . how did you weigh an elephant?'

'Simple, really,' said Rosie. 'I lured the elephant on to a huge weighing platform by placing its favourite food just within reach.'

'I think I would have done the same,' said Alexandra with a smile.

When Rosie returned to her study she sat at her desk and began to open her mail which comprised the usual invitations to conferences and updated book lists. Then she spotted the letter from Julian and immediately felt a sickness in her stomach. She was tempted to tear it up and throw it away. However, curiosity got the better of her so she opened it and began to read.

My darling Rosie,

What can I say? How can I ever apologize for what I have put you through?

I am so very sorry that you had to witness me with another woman when you were at the Waldorf. You quite rightly left immediately.

I was so distressed to know how much pain I had caused you and so it has taken me some time to gather the strength I needed to write to you and beg your forgiveness.

I know that you may decide to throw this letter away and if you do, I would understand. But if you have got this far, I beg you to carry on reading.

I did not tell you that I was married because I was afraid that I would lose you. You are too precious to me to risk that and so I unwisely let you think that I was free. I am not happy in my marriage and that is why, when I met you, I knew that I had found the perfect companion and wanted to see you again and again. This is no excuse for my behaviour, but I hope that it will in some way explain my actions.

If it is possible to see you once more I should be so happy. I shall be in the Old White Swan in Goodramgate at 7.00 p.m. on Wednesday, 4 April and the next two evenings. Please come so that we can talk this through. If you do not turn up, I will know that I have lost you for ever and my heart will be broken.

With all my love,
Julian

As Rosie read she wondered if he could be telling the truth. She felt both sick and excited. Inger was next door but, for the moment, this wasn't something she could share. She drove home quickly, laid out a smart dress and shoes and took time with her hair. There was a sense of anticipation when she drove back into the university car park and set off for Goodramgate.

Rosie walked to the entrance of the Old White Swan Inn and opened the door. When she peered inside, there at a table in the far corner was Julian Meadows. He was reading a newspaper. She stood there transfixed. She recalled the picture of Julian and his wife in the Waldorf and the look on his face when he saw her. Almost as a reflex she took a step back, turned round and walked back out of the door. 'What a bastard,' she muttered as she made her way back through the streets of York. She didn't need a cheat like him in her life. She had seen him for what he really was and felt sad for his wife, shackled to such a man. With a feeling of freedom she strode back to the university car park.

Sam Greenwood had finished his meetings and was walking to his car when he saw Rosie. 'Hey,' he said, 'this is a nice surprise. You look great. Are you going somewhere?'

Rosie smiled. 'Actually I was but changed my mind.'

For Sam it was now or never. 'In that case' – he looked down at his jeans and scuffed boots – 'although I'm not as well dressed as you, can I buy you a drink? We could celebrate your success.'

'Why not?' said Rosie.

'Great. Any preference?'

Rosie didn't hesitate. 'How about the Old White Swan in Goodramgate? That's not far.'

'Perfect, I know it,' said Sam, enthused by his good fortune.

As they walked, Rosie's mind was racing. She had been presented with an opportunity too good to miss.

When they walked into the pub Rosie saw Julian stand up and smile. Then he saw Sam and looked confused.

'Does this guy know you?' asked Sam.

'He does,' said Rosie.

They approached his table. 'Hello, Julian. Let me introduce you to my colleague, Sam.'

'Good evening, Sam,' said Julian formally. 'I'm pleased to meet you.'

Sam murmured a greeting.

'I'm so pleased I bumped into you, Julian. You sent me a letter.' She took it from her shoulder bag. 'Now I can pass it back to you. The contents are irrelevant, as you can see.' She nodded towards Sam.

The colour drained from his face. He took the letter from her in astonishment and with a grim expression he walked out.

'So who is he?' asked Sam.

'Julian is my solicitor . . . or rather he was.' She smiled as they ordered drinks at the bar.

They were soon settled at a table.

'The chess tournament was remarkable,' said Sam. 'To play against so many at one time must take huge concentration.'

'It's fun. I enjoy the challenge.'

'Who was the student at the end?'

'Alexandra Bisset, final-year Maths. One of Victor's high-flyers.'

'She did well to last that long. I guess you ran out of time.'

'Actually we agreed on a draw. She was a terrific opponent.'

'Impressive. She must be pretty bright.'

Rosie looked down at her glass of wine and gave an enigmatic smile. 'Sam, Alexandra is much more than that . . . she's gifted.'

Chapter Fifteen

The Kite Flyer

Tom stopped in the dappled shade under the avenue of horse chestnut trees and stared up at the sign on one of the stone pillars. It read:

**RAGLEY & MORTON CHURCH OF
ENGLAND PRIMARY SCHOOL
North Yorkshire County Council
Headteacher: Emma Hartley B.Ed**

He had visited many village schools. This one was a tall red-brick Victorian building with a grey-slate roof and an incongruous bell tower. It was Friday, 27 April, the end of the first week of the summer term, and the Primary One students were all out on teaching practice. Chris Scully had been placed with a third-year junior class and Tom was looking forward to catching up with the young rugby player.

Tom had jumped in his car shortly before ten o'clock and

driven up the A19 to the pretty village of Ragley-on-the-Forest. He had passed a parade of shops on the high street and turned right at the village green and parked his car. When he stepped out he breathed in the clean air and took in the view. Outside the Royal Oak was a duck pond and a lady with chestnut hair – now turning grey – was sitting on a bench and looking at the school. She was humming the tune to 'Edelweiss' from *The Sound of Music* and appeared content in her world. Near by stood a weeping willow tree whose branches caressed the new grass beneath like gentle swordplay between respected friends. Outside the post office was a red telephone box and two ladies with shopping bags were sharing their news. It was a familiar village scene.

Tom walked into the entrance hall where a petite and polite young woman introduced herself.

'Good morning, I'm the school secretary. I was told to expect you.'

'Yes, I'm Tom Frith from the university, here to see Mr Scully.'

'The headteacher, Miss Hartley, said if you arrived during morning assembly you should simply go straight into the hall.'

'Thank you, I shall.'

When he pushed open the double doors he saw Chris Scully on the other side next to a tall woman with a blonde ponytail. Over a hundred children were sitting cross-legged on the wood-block floor listening to a thin, angular figure with a clerical collar who was standing at the front. He was talking about the importance of going to heaven.

Three other teachers were sitting at the back of the hall: a short, stocky man flanked by two ladies. One had ginger hair and a freckled face. She looked distinctive in her baggy flared cords, mint-green blouse and hand-stitched waistcoat. The other lady was much more traditional in a smart dress and cardigan.

The headteacher stood up and whispered in Tom's ear, 'Welcome to Ragley. I'm the headteacher, Emma Hartley. We can talk after assembly. It's almost over.' Tom sat on the empty chair next to her.

The vicar ended his talk with a relieved look on his face. Emma stood up. 'Thank you, Mr Evans. That was very interesting. Has anyone got a question?' A few children raised their hands. Emma pointed to a ruddy-faced ten-year-old. 'Madonna Fazackerly, you go first.'

'Mr Evans, will there be horses in heaven?'

The vicar looked flustered. 'I'm sure there will.'

'But what will they run on if there's only clouds?'

This clearly stumped the poor cleric. 'God will find a way,' he replied.

Eleven-year-old Patience Crapper was the next with a question. 'Will I meet my grandad in heaven?'

'Probably,' said Joseph Evans with a beatific smile.

'That's good,' said Patience. 'I'll tell him when I get home.'

'Just one more before the bell for morning break,' said Emma.

Two hands went up simultaneously. It was a pair of identical twins.

'Hermione, you go first,' said Emma.

'Will I stay the same age in heaven?'

Before Joseph could respond her sister, Honeysuckle, called out, 'And will I always be with my sister?'

'Yes, for eternity.'

The two girls knew what eternity meant and frowned. 'Oh no,' they muttered in perfect unison.

Emma brought everything to a close and thanked the vicar once again. The children went outside for their fifteen minutes of freedom while the staff sauntered into the staffroom. Emma Hartley was a slim, forty-year-old woman with a short bob of brown hair and she smiled up at Tom. 'Let's have a coffee in the office.'

Tom walked into an L-shaped room with two desks and a filing cabinet. On the walls were rows of school photographs, showing generations of smiling children. The secretary arrived with two coffees and a plate of biscuits and Tom settled back in the visitor's chair.

Emma began: 'I'm pleased to say that Mr Scully has made an excellent start. He's well prepared and his meteorology project is going well. The children have all made kites and they're going to fly them after break. He's done a huge amount of science and mathematics, plus stories about balloon flights. His teacher, Pat Brookside, is thrilled with his contribution.' She was clearly impressed.

'That's most encouraging. Thank you for the update. Incidentally, this is my first visit to your school and I must say, the artwork and writing on display in the entrance hall is exceptional, some of the best I've seen.'

'That's kind of you to say. We have five classes and I have a wonderful staff. My deputy, Anne Grainger, has been here for very many years and provides the youngest children with the best of starts. Sally Pringle is a talented artist and musician, Marcus Potts is a wizard with computers and Pat Brookside is an outstanding sportswoman. So we have a diverse range of talent. I teach the oldest children full time.'

'Have you been here long?'

'This is my second year. I took over from Jack Sheffield who moved into Higher Education at the college in York. You may have come across him.'

'Yes, I've met Jack occasionally at education seminars. He's doing the same job as me, training the next generation of teachers.'

'He was enormously helpful when I arrived from my deputy headship in Skipton.'

'That's good to hear. Of course now you've got the National Curriculum ahead of you.'

Emma sipped her coffee and looked thoughtful. 'Yes, a new era in education. It's certainly a challenge but we're coping.'

When the bell rang for the end of morning break, Emma led Tom to Pat Brookside's classroom and introduced him to the class teacher. She was wearing a tracksuit prior to an inter-school netball tournament later in the day.

'Pleased to meet you,' she said. At six feet tall, she gave Tom a level stare and liked what she saw.

'Many thanks for your support,' said Tom. He gestured towards the displays. 'Love the cross-curricular work.' The walls were full of the children's writing and diagrams of kite construction.

'Hope you can stay for the kite flying.' She grinned. 'When we knew you were coming Mr Scully made one for you.'

There was a buzz of activity among the eight- and nine-year-olds as each child collected their kite from the washing line that stretched across the windows. Every kite had a long, colourful tail and a child's name printed on the bamboo canes. Tom looked at all the names: Zach Eccles,

Walter Popple, Kylie Ogden, Dylan Fazackerly, Dallas Sue-Ellen Earnshaw, Suzi-Quatro Ricketts, Alfie Spraggon, Emily Snodgrass and many more. The one on the end was a bright blue kite and labelled 'Dr Frith'.

Chris Scully held it up and called out, 'Shall we give this to our visitor?' and everyone cried, 'Yes.'

Tom smiled. 'Well done.'

'Come on,' said Chris, 'you're now officially a kite flyer.'

Pat Brookside led the children out on to the school field and Chris and Tom followed on.

'She's brilliant,' said Chris. 'A great teacher and a county-standard netball player. I'm learning so much.'

No one knows what the future might bring but the scene Tom witnessed on that field became an image that he would always remember: young Chris Scully flying his kite in the breeze, surrounded by excited children. It was a happy tableau: primary education at its best. Tom recalled the old Chinese proverb that he had been told when he was a student: 'I hear and I forget, I see and I remember, I do and I understand.' The children in the class were learning so much from this first-hand experience on that sunlit morning.

So it was that Tom flew his kite, wrote a positive critique in his carbon-copy notebook and thanked the headteacher before he left. As he drove out of the school gates the lady on the bench was still there, staring up at the school and looking at peace with the world. She smiled and gave him a wave. As he left Ragley village he wound down his window. The sun shone through a powder-blue sky and the distant hills were rimed with golden fire as a gentle breeze caressed the land.

*

At lunchtime in the refectory Zeb, Inger and Rosie were in conversation. 'We've started rehearsals for *The Importance of Being Earnest*,' said Zeb. 'So, Rosie, I'm keen for you to be involved, particularly as you're our resident expert on Oscar Wilde.'

'Thanks. Yes, happy to help. One of his famous quotes was "Be yourself . . . everyone else is taken." So I'm here and I'll do my best.'

'Excellent,' said Inger.

'I've got a copy of the script here,' said Zeb. She passed it over to Rosie. 'Check it out and let me know what you think. We may decide to cut it a little. I would prefer the running time to be no more that two hours ten minutes. It was twenty minutes longer than that when I last saw it in London.' She glanced up at the clock. 'Anyway, must fly. Victor wants a word about Royce Channing. God knows why.'

As Zeb hurried away Inger turned to Rosie. 'Royce organizes the set for us. He's also our artistic director.'

'And you look after the music.'

'Yes. There was a musical adaptation of the play back in 1984 at the Ambassadors Theatre. I've got the CD so I'm working on that.'

They finished their meals and Inger looked expectantly at Rosie. 'Herbal tea in my study?'

'Yes, please,' said Rosie. She guessed why.

Zeb had made her way to Victor's study and found the professor looking grave.

'Thanks for calling in,' he said. 'Take a seat.'

'Bloody hell, Victor. Will I need one?'

'Maybe.' He sat down facing her. 'I've just had a long chat with Siobhan Malone. Her baby is due at the end of term.'

'That's good, isn't it?' said Zeb. 'She will have completed her degree.'

'Yes, that's a blessing. It's just that I now know who the father is.'

'Go on.'

'It's Royce Channing.'

It took a moment for Zeb to process this. 'Have you spoken to him?'

'He's with Edward now.'

'The VC will not be pleased.'

'Siobhan says they want to get married. She's twenty-five; he's forty-five. They're both single.'

Zeb gave Victor a knowing look. 'Royce has been around the block a few times. I hope she knows what she's taking on. He even propositioned me a few years ago.'

Victor looked thoughtful. 'Tutor–student relationships are still frowned upon but, by the sound of it, they're both consenting adults.'

Zeb smiled. 'In that case I wish them the best of luck.'

'I agree.'

'OK, Victor, thanks for letting me know. In the meantime, I'm looking forward to seeing both you and Pat at my house-warming party tomorrow evening. How is he these days?'

The relief was obvious on Victor's face. 'He's fine. It's a slow, steady recovery. We'll be there. Looking forward to it.'

Unexpectedly Zeb jumped up and gave Victor a kiss on the cheek. 'You're a good man, Victor Grammaticus.' She hurried away, leaving a blushing Head of Faculty behind her.

*

Inger and Rosie were enjoying a cup of camomile tea in Inger's study. 'So,' said Inger. 'How are you doing now?'

'Relieved. It's a new start. I can't believe I was manipulated in such a way.'

'We all make mistakes, Rosie. You're not the first and you won't be the last. The good thing is that it's behind you.'

'Strange, isn't it? It affected all my life . . . my work, my health, my relationships with colleagues.'

'You have some great friends here. We support each other.'

Rosie sipped her tea and sat back in her chair. 'Tom has been there when I've needed him. Maybe the VC's buddy-tutor idea was a good one after all.'

'I've heard Zeb has invited the VC to her housewarming party.'

'In that case I'll be careful what I say to him. Tom warned me a long time ago that he misses nothing.'

'Very true.'

Rosie smiled. 'So, how's it going with Tom?'

'Fine. We give each other space when it's needed. I'm getting a lift with him tomorrow evening. We could pick you up en route if you wish.'

'That's kind. Yes, please. I'm guessing it will be a late night.'

'Definitely. There's some entertainment as well. She's asked for my string quartet and has invited Arabella Esposito to sing for us.'

'Sounds great.'

'And Sam Greenwood will be there as well,' added Inger with a mischievous smile.

'A lovely man,' Rosie said neutrally and continued to drink her tea.

*

As Tom drove home, Depeche Mode's 'Enjoy The Silence' was on the radio and he reflected on the day. He was pleased he had made the decision to remain at Eboracum. His work was varied, from training teachers to travelling around the villages of North Yorkshire with its stunning scenery. He had even flown a kite today surrounded by happy children. These were special times and, of course, there was also Inger.

After his supper he settled down with a bottle of Theakston's to watch Nicole Kidman in *Bangkok Hilton*. The movie star was clearly having a tough time in prison when the phone rang and he switched off the sound. It was Inger.

'Hi,' she said. 'What are you doing?'

'Thinking of you,' he said quickly while averting his gaze from the screen.

'I told Rosie we could pick her up on our way to Zeb's tomorrow evening if that's OK with you.'

'Yes, that's fine. How is she?'

'I think she might be interested in Sam and there's no doubt he's keen on her.'

'So . . . she's moving on then.'

'Definitely, unlike you who is staying where you are.'

'That's good, isn't it?'

There was a pause. She smiled. 'So . . . shall we say six thirty here?'

'See you then.'

'Bye,' and the call was ended.

He stayed up late to watch Cyndi Lauper at Stevie Wonder's birthday celebration singing 'Girls Just Want To Have Fun' and, once again, Tom wished he understood women.

*

On Saturday evening Tom collected Inger and Rosie on his way towards Crayke village. It was only two miles east of Victor's home in the market town of Easingwold and the countryside was beautiful. The lambing season had begun, swifts and swallows were returning to their nesting places and curlews were flying over the distant moors. Tom drove up the steep Castle Hill and turned off on a side road that led to Zeb's barn conversion. It was easy to see why she had chosen her new home. It was a large Yorkshire-stone building on a quarter-acre site with a south-facing walled garden.

When they walked in, the members of Inger's string quartet were playing Prokofiev's *Peter and the Wolf* beneath the vaulted beam ceiling while in the open-plan kitchen Victor and Pat were serving drinks. In the far corner a baby grand piano was covered with greetings cards and a scattering of sheet music. Next to the patio window a creaking trestle table covered in a white cloth was filled with plates of chicken legs, ham sandwiches and sausage rolls.

Everyone had contributed. Sam had brought a Manchester tart; Rosie had made crispy pancakes; Pat had spent all afternoon preparing a sumptuous peach Melba roulade and a lemon and elderflower traybake. Victor had carried in twelve bottles of wine and Sue Llewellyn had made some Welsh cakes; Inger had prepared Norwegian meatballs and Tom and Owen had each brought a crate of beer.

Wisely, Zeb had invited her immediate neighbours and they were clearly intrigued with the way Zeb had given the property an individual style. There were African wall hangings, a film poster of Patrick Swayze and Jennifer Grey in

Dirty Dancing, a dramatic charcoal line drawing of Olivia Newton-John and John Travolta in *Grease,* and a beautiful black-and-white photograph of Rudolf Nureyev.

The Vice Chancellor had arrived with a bottle of his favourite sherry and immediately took Victor to one side. It was clear that he wished to share his news.

'So, Edward, what was the outcome?' asked Victor. 'I heard it was a lengthy meeting.'

Edward sipped his sherry thoughtfully while pondering his reply. 'You're right, it was. We had a long talk. Quite frankly at times it was a labyrinthine tale and hard to believe. The bottom line is that Royce admitted he had become infatuated by a much younger woman. According to Hermione, who understands these things, Miss Malone was simply love-struck, besotted with a charismatic man. We've both seen it before, Victor, and I suspect we shall see it again. For my part I have to protect the reputation of Eboracum.'

'What will happen next?' asked Victor.

'Marriage in the late summer has been discussed and Royce intends to purchase a new home . . . where, I have no idea. He may intend to move away and seek employment in another university.'

'That would be a great loss to Eboracum,' said Victor.

'I agree.' He shook his head. 'Shakespeare said there is a tide in the affairs of men.'

Victor smiled. 'And George Bernard Shaw said that the perfect love affair is conducted entirely by post.'

'I wish it were so,' said Edward. 'Now to more important matters: how is Patrick?'

They both looked across the room and smiled. Pat was back to his expressive self. Now in full flow, he was engaging Zeb's neighbours with tales of the theatre.

Tom had caught up with Owen who was working his way through the crate of beer. 'I saw Chris Scully yesterday. He's doing really well in school.'

Owen nodded. 'That's good news – and you should have seen him this afternoon. Last game of the season and he was brilliant. Predictably, scouts were hovering again, yet again. He may not be playing for us next season.'

Zeb suddenly appeared next to them. In a skintight leotard and a baggy linen shirt she looked both striking and relaxed in her new home. 'So what do you think?' she said, gesturing towards the assembled throng.

'A great party and a perfect home,' said Tom. 'I'm so pleased for you.'

'And what about your degenerate friend?'

Owen grinned and looked around. 'It would be perfect for our annual rugby dinner.'

'Bollocks to that!' said Zeb.

'Seriously, though,' said Owen, 'you've done well. You've worked hard and you deserve all this.'

She leaned forward and gave him a kiss on his stubbly cheek. 'I knew there was a soft spot in there somewhere. Anyway, I have a proposition for you.'

Owen grinned. 'With my charm and rugged good looks it was inevitable.'

'Well, you're certainly rugged but it's your handsome mate who has the good looks.'

Owen shook his head. 'Like you said . . . bollocks!'

'No, seriously, Owen. I've had an idea. Should be great for student–tutor relationships and a bit of fun as well.'

'Go on.'

'There's a pram race a fortnight today – during Rag Week. So how about it, my Welsh friend? It's open to staff and students. Good for morale, I guess.'

'Who's pushing who?' asked Owen with a grin.

'Well, you've got the muscles and I'm a lightweight.'

'What's in it for me?'

'The glory of winning? But the winner does get a firkin of beer too . . .'

'Bloody hell, that's nine gallons.'

'Exactly.'

Owen grinned. 'Count me in.'

Zeb smiled and as she walked away she called out, 'And we have to dress up.'

'Shit!' muttered Owen.

Tom clinked his friend's glass. 'Can't wait.'

On the other side of the room the Vice Chancellor approached Rosie and smiled. 'You're looking well.'

Rosie, mindful of his reputation, replied cautiously, 'Thank you, Vice Chancellor.'

'Edward, please. We're off duty this evening.'

'Thank you, Edward.'

'You appear to be very busy these days.'

'Yes, it's a full programme with lectures and school visits.'

'I hear from Elizabeth that you have agreed to help with the Oscar Wilde play.'

'Yes, I told Zeb . . . Elizabeth that I would check through the script for her.'

'That's splendid. What a remarkable playwright he was. I loved it when he said, "Always forgive your enemies; nothing annoys them so much."'

'Just so,' said Rosie quietly. She had learned from past experience to approach these cryptic conversations with circumspection and she wondered just how much he knew about Julian Meadows.

'Well, enjoy your evening, Rosemary, and, of course, Victor speaks highly of you.' He wandered away to discuss with Sam Greenwood the fact that Labour now had a twenty-three-point lead over the Conservatives according to the latest MORI poll while Rosie stared after him.

Eventually there was a natural pause in the proceedings. Food had been enjoyed, conversations shared and Zeb's fridge was gradually emptying of bottles of white wine. Then Inger stood by the piano and Zeb tapped a spoon on a wine glass. 'Please find a chair, everybody, and let us enjoy a musical break. Inger will accompany the wonderfully gifted first-year soprano, Arabella Esposito, on the piano. We thought this was a good opportunity to use you as guinea pigs and sample a few of the songs that will be included in *The Importance of Being Earnest* to be performed later this term.' There was a ripple of applause as everyone settled to enjoy a selection including 'One Love', 'Every Flower In The Garden' and 'I Need Someone To Rescue Me'. It added a touch of class to a special evening. Meanwhile, Tom simply looked at Inger's grace and composure at the piano and fell a little more in love with this beautiful woman.

*

Later in the evening Sam Greenwood plucked up the courage to approach Rosie. 'Can I get you another drink . . . a fruit juice perhaps?'

Rosie smiled. 'Yes, please, a lime cordial.'

They had found a quiet space at a coffee table next to two huge bookcases and Sam studied the new Rosie who sat before him. There had been a time when it seemed as though her zest for life had gone. He recalled days when a soporific lassitude had settled on her shoulders like a cloak of sadness. Now that was all behind her. Rosie looked relaxed in the company of this gentle, unassuming man.

'I was thinking,' said Sam. 'Is there any point in asking you for another game of chess or would it be too boring for you?'

'Why don't I give you a book on intermediate chess? Then we could discuss it over coffee some time.'

'Or maybe even dinner at the Dean Court Hotel,' said Sam, taking the plunge.

Rosie raised her glass. 'Checkmate,' she said with a smile.

It was late when Tom drove Rosie back to Wigginton and then into York where he parked outside Inger's apartment.

'That was a really successful evening,' she said.

'I loved the music and singing,' said Tom. 'In fact, everybody did, including Zeb's new neighbours.'

'Thanks. I was happy to do it – I think it made it special for Zeb.'

'This might be a strange question, Inger, but have you ever flown a kite?'

'Probably, a long time ago when I was a child in Norway.'

Tom pointed to the vast grassy acres of the Knavesmire

across the road. 'It's just that I've got a kite in the boot. It's huge. I was given it yesterday on one of my school visits. So why don't we give it a try tomorrow morning?'

Inger smiled. 'You're very persuasive, Tom.'

'It could be fun.'

'Did you say tomorrow morning?'

'Yes.'

Inger leaned forward and kissed him softly. 'In that case bring it inside and you can teach me how to fly it.'

Chapter Sixteen

Nearly Nineteen

Bright sunlight caressed the distant hills as Tom drove towards York and, beyond the hedgerows, a woodland carpet of bluebells spread out beneath the tall limes. It was a relaxing start to a new day.

When he arrived at the university he found the car park had been transformed. Students were busy cordoning off a wide lane around the perimeter in preparation for the final and most widely anticipated event of Rag Week: namely, the pram race.

It was mid-morning on Saturday, 12 May and the end of a hectic few days of student activities. There had been a pub quiz, a bingo night, a Prohibition Murder Mystery Evening in 1920s costume, a raft procession on the river and an egg-and-spoon race around the quad. However, it was this morning's pram race that had created most interest.

As Tom walked along the winding path towards reception he was enveloped in the sweet smell of spring flowers. Almond trees were in blossom and darting swallows had returned to their nesting places. The air was soft and balmy and the bronze, red and yellow cups of tulips swayed in the gentle breeze. Tom smiled as he entered reception where Perkins was, as ever, behind his counter.

'Good morning, Dr Frith,' he said. 'I've seen some interesting sights coming through here this morning – including Mr Llewellyn. He didn't look happy in his dress.'

'I'm not surprised,' said Tom with a grin. 'I don't think the colour suits him!' He had been there yesterday when Zeb had delivered a dress and a blonde wig to their study. 'He certainly took some persuading to wear it but it's all in a good cause.'

'That's what Miss Peacock said. She was wearing a striped flannel nightie and a pink bonnet. They've both gone to the common room for a coffee before the eleven o'clock start. Albert, my junior porter, is excited. He's been given the honour of holding the chequered flag.'

'Good to hear,' Tom said and set off for the quad where Ellie MacBride and her photographer friend were hurrying towards the start of the race. She smiled and held up her notebook. An article for the *Eboracum Echo* beckoned.

'Perfect weather for the race,' she called out.

Tom waved a greeting. Ellie's enthusiasm always made him smile.

Meanwhile, the bursar, Gideon Chalk, was checking the profit column of his accounts for his various properties. It was looking healthy. The only nagging doubt was the fact that on two occasions during the previous week groups of students had expressed their grievances. A particularly vociferous female student had told him in no uncertain terms she intended to issue a written complaint to her friend, Ellie MacBride, for inclusion in the next issue of the *Eboracum Echo*.

From his window he spotted Ellie, who had become well known to him since his arrival. She had spoken to him on a number of occasions and with each conversation his dislike for this confident and forceful woman had grown. She was deep in conversation with a young man carrying a camera. No doubt they were about to cover the ridiculously noisy and juvenile pram race.

He hurried from his office and stepped out on to the path. 'Miss MacBride,' he called out.

Ellie stopped in surprise. She saw the bursar striding towards her. 'Yes?'

'A word, please.'

'Go on.'

'I'll press on, Ellie. Don't want to miss anything!' said the photographer.

Gideon glared after him, then spoke. 'It's come to my attention that you may be considering writing an article regarding matters of accommodation.'

Ellie gave him a glare. 'Your point being?'

'I'm recommending you use caution. There is much you don't understand about the finances of the university. It's a complex operation.'

'I'm sure it is.'

'So take this simply as helpful advice. Any negative comment will be unpicked with great precision.'

'Are you threatening me, Mr Chalk?'

Gideon Chalk gave Ellie a look of pure malice, turned and walked away.

*

In a corner of the common room, Zeb was smoking a cigarette and adjusting her bonnet while Inger and Rosie were offering friendly support.

'You look great,' said Inger. 'Perhaps we should have entered as well.'

'Sorry,' said Rosie. 'I recall Sam mentioned it to me but it's been a busy week and it slipped my mind.'

'That's OK,' said Zeb. 'You've all done your bit. Sam did the quiz, Tom was the bingo caller and you two made up the numbers in the egg-and-spoon race.'

'Well, best of luck,' said Rosie, 'and stay safe.'

'Yes!' added Inger. 'Hold on tight. Owen won't be holding back against all those young men in his rugby team.'

'Either way we can celebrate tonight,' said Zeb. 'Victor has invited us all to join him for a drink outside the Kings Arms at Ouse Bridge. We're meeting by the river at seven.' She glanced over to the serving counter where Owen had ordered coffee. 'Meanwhile, I'll definitely be buying a pint for my little Welsh pram-pusher. God knows how I persuaded him to dress up.'

Owen was collecting a tray of coffee when Tom arrived by his side. 'Let me assist you, madam,' said Tom with a grin.

'Piss off, Englishman.'

'All in a good cause,' said Tom. 'Zeb was thrilled you volunteered.'

'Volunteered to push, yes.' He pushed his blonde wig out of his eyes. 'Wear fancy bloody dress, no.'

Tom stared out of the window. 'Everybody seems to have bought into it. Even your rugby team.'

'You're right. They've opened a book on me versus Chris

Scully. Problem is they've made him favourite. Only consolation is that he's pushing a great lump of a scrum half around the course while I've got Zeb.'

'Isn't it just for fun? Taking part is good enough.'

'No chance,' grumbled Owen through gritted teeth. 'I'm here to win.'

At ten forty-five Owen and Zeb had finished their coffee and set off to collect their pram and head for the start. There was applause and a few cries of 'Good luck' from other faculty members as they walked through the quad and out towards the car park. Zeb had chalked 'Dirty Dancing' on the side of their pram and lit up another cigarette as she climbed in. Around them there was laughter and high spirits and even Owen's mood softened as he saw the happy young faces around him.

Chris Scully waved in Owen's direction. He was dressed as Fred Flintstone in a caveman outfit with the muscular scrum half, Rod Parfitt, sitting in the pram wearing leopard-print underpants. 'See you at the finish,' he shouted.

'I'll wait for you there,' replied Owen.

Back in the common room, Sam had arrived and sat down next to Tom, Inger and Rosie. 'Hell of a crowd out there,' he said, 'and a guy from the *York Post* has arrived to take photos.'

'We'd better warn Owen,' said Tom. 'Not sure he will want to have his picture plastered all over the local paper looking like rugby's answer to Rapunzel.'

'Some of the sights are incredible,' said Sam. 'A couple of my science students have entered dressed in *Star Trek* costumes in a pram that looks like a rocket ship.'

'By the way,' said Inger. 'Zeb said that Victor has invited us all for a drink at seven tonight at the Kings Arms down by the river at the Ouse Bridge.'

'Great venue,' said Sam, 'but I heard it floods four times a year.'

'Not today,' said Rosie with a smile. She was beginning to enjoy the easy camaraderie with the tall, sandy-haired science lecturer.

By the time they all wandered outside, the pram race was about to start. Owen was leaning on a battered old pram and still grumbling. 'I look friggin' stupid.'

'It's only a dress and a wig,' said Zeb. 'Look at the state of me. I've got a pink bonnet and psyche-bloody-delic pyjamas.'

There were around twenty pairs of competitors lining up and everyone was in some form of fancy dress. There were students dressed in lacy nighties along with some incongruous 'babies', including a few members of the rugby team, huge men sucking dummies and wearing knotted tea towels. It was also an eclectic mix of transport. There were old prams and pushchairs along with an adapted porter's barrow and a couple of supermarket trolleys covered in flags.

'I'm guessing you didn't do this in Norway,' said Tom.

Inger smiled. 'It's a definite first for me.'

'Who do you think might win?' asked Rosie. 'It's a long way around the car park.'

'And some of the so-called babies look quite substantial,' said Sam.

'My money's on Owen. He's really fit and Zeb weighs nothing.'

'What about Chris Scully?' said Sam. 'Younger and even

fitter and he's only got the scrum half to shove around the course.'

'Maybe,' said Tom, 'except Owen won't want to lose to an Englishman.'

It was a colourful scene as Dawn Jenkins, the President of the Students' Union, picked up her megaphone and welcomed everyone. 'This is it, everyone. The event you've all been waiting for. It's one anti-clockwise circuit of the car park and please be careful on the corners. We don't want any injuries. When you arrive back here turn right towards the finish under the archway where Albert will wave his chequered flag. The presentation of a firkin of beer to the winner will take place in the quad immediately after everyone has finished. So good luck' – she waved at Owen – 'and you all look delightful.' Then she raised her starter's pistol and with a loud crack the race began.

The start was frantic. Chris Scully powered into an immediate lead while Owen was balked by a supermarket trolley and a couple of female maths students whose pram lost a wheel after only ten metres. There was cheering as the contestants reached the first bend and the prams began to stretch out with the young men of the rugby team leading the way. Out in front was Chris Scully with an apparently effortless and metronomic stride pattern. Already, the leading group of four prams had left the rest behind. Then came Zeb, now kneeling up and doing a good impression of a modern-day Boudica. She was yelling at the top of her voice as Owen gradually increased his pace. After the second corner and along the far straight the gap reduced between Chris Scully and Owen. A group of young women began chanting 'Scully, Scully.'

By the third corner it was clear it was a race between Owen and Chris Scully. After the last bend and down the final straight they were neck and neck. Chris had never changed his stride whereas Owen pushed the pram to the limits of his endurance. Zeb was screaming encouragement as Owen took the lead and, on two wheels, turned into the archway. Albert waved his chequered flag as Owen and Zeb hurtled past him with Chris Scully in second place. Behind them it was chaos as prams collided and teams jostled for position.

In the quad Zeb leapt lightly out of the pram and gave the exhausted Owen a big kiss on his stubbly face. 'Well done,' she cried, 'we won,' and went off to congratulate the other competitors.

Owen leaned forward, fighting for breath, and rested his hands on his knees. 'I'm knackered,' he said.

Chris Scully came over. 'A good race, Owen. Well done.' The young man was barely breathing hard and he grinned. 'How about going round again – or maybe the best of three?'

'Bugger off, you cocky sod.'

'Seriously though,' said Chris, 'that was a hell of a finish.'

'Just experience,' gasped Owen. 'You'll have it one day.'

Chris offered his hand. 'Thanks, Owen, for all you've done for me with the rugby. It's been great.'

They shook hands and Owen gave a gentle smile. 'Here's to next season.'

'Looking forward to it,' said Chris. 'Maybe you might join us for a drink later. I'm going to a few pubs with all the lads. We're celebrating.'

'Celebrating?'

'It's my birthday. I'm nineteen today.' He paused and

smiled. 'Although, to be precise, not until just before mid-night. That's when my mum said I was born.'

'Bloody hell! Why didn't you say?' Owen thought for a moment. 'Chris, we're going to the Kings Arms later. If you're passing, call in and I'll buy you a pint.'

'Will do.' They spoke for a few moments more and then, with another smile, Chris walked away.

The quad was filled with staff and students as Dawn Jenkins announced through her megaphone that Owen and Zeb had won the pram race and Rag Week was officially over. The barrel of beer was on the table beside her. Owen whispered in her ear. 'I've just been told,' said Dawn, 'that the winners have kindly donated the firkin of beer to the Students' Union.'

This was greeted with a huge cheer and Owen and Zeb were photographed, still in costume, next to the prize. Meanwhile, Ellie MacBride was scribbling in her notebook.

Tom walked up to her. 'If that photo goes in the *Echo*, God knows what Owen will say.'

Ellie smiled up at Tom. 'Don't worry, I'll clear it with him first.'

'Thanks. Makes sense.'

'By the way, I've completed my Jane Austen study so shall I hand it in next week?'

'Yes, do that.'

'There's something else, Tom.'

'Yes?'

'I've been threatened by the bursar.'

'Go on.'

'He said if I published anything about his dealings it

would be the worse for me. He'd heard that I intended to list all the student grievances in the next issue of the *Echo*. He was absolutely furious. Sadly, I guess it's only my word against his. There were no witnesses to the conversation.'

Tom looked concerned. 'Leave it with me.'

Ellie touched his sleeve lightly. 'I'm grateful.'

Victor had called in to the peace and quiet of the Lodge at the request of the Vice Chancellor.

'Well, it's official now, Victor,' said Edward. 'Royce Channing has an interview next week in Cardiff.'

'He will be a very strong candidate,' said Victor. 'I'll be surprised if he's not appointed. His CV is outstanding.'

'He came to see me this morning and told me about his application, but assured me he will still do his best to support our Oscar Wilde production next month.'

'That will be a relief to Zeb. Meanwhile, what about Siobhan Malone?'

'It's all planned,' said Edward. 'They are to be married in her home town of Letterkenny in Ireland.'

Victor nodded. 'So, shall I pen an advertisement for the *Times Educational Supplement*?'

'Yes, please. We really need to advertise as soon as we know the outcome of his interview. There's a good chance we could have someone in place for the new academic year.'

Their business concluded, over a cup of herbal tea they discussed the state of the nation, the performance of Margaret Thatcher and the fact that inflation was now running at 9.4 per cent.

*

At seven o'clock Tom and Inger were about to cross the busy road by the Museum Gardens. Behind them, outside the gates, a busker was singing Ralph McTell's 'Streets Of London'.

'He's good, really good,' said Inger.

Tom paused to place a coin in the cap at the feet of the busker, who nodded in acknowledgement. They dodged the traffic and walked down the steps by the Ouse Bridge. Before them the Kings Arms pub was basking in sunshine. Outside on the riverbank stood a dozen tables and Victor was already there enjoying a celebratory drink with Zeb and Owen.

This was one of York's most famous pubs. Just inside the front door was a large plaque showing the height of the water in past years when it had been flooded. That apart, it was unremarkable with its bare stone floors and a long bar.

'Let me get you two a drink,' said Victor.

'Thank you,' said Inger. 'Orange juice for me.'

'And a pint please,' said Tom. He looked at Owen, who was supping deeply on a pint of the local brew. Zeb was smoking a cigarette, a gin and tonic in front of her.

'Congratulations,' said Tom. 'A brilliant win.'

Owen looked thoughtful. 'To be honest I felt a bit awkward shaking hands with Chris. If I'd known, I would have slowed up at the end.'

'Known what?' asked Tom.

'It's only his bloody birthday. He's nineteen today.'

'Ah, I see,' said Tom. 'You stole his thunder.'

Owen shook his head. 'He mentioned it after the race. I told him to call in if he was passing. Inevitably, his mates in the team are taking him on a pub crawl. I told him to enjoy it but be careful and he just grinned.'

'The confidence of youth,' said Tom. 'I remember it well.'

Inger spotted Rosie and Sam walking down the steps from the Ouse Bridge.

They waved and Victor bought another round of drinks. It was a perfect evening and, at times like this, Tom realized how lucky he was to work at Eboracum and have such trusted and respected friends. The evening drifted on amid laughter and more drinks as the story of the pram race grew ever more dramatic in the telling. At eight o'clock, sunset was still an hour away and they were thinking of moving on for an evening meal when Sam pointed up at the far side of the bridge. 'Hey, look at that.'

The bridge had three archways. Small boats were passing through the near two. Beneath the far one the muddy bank sloped down to meet the water. On the parapet above a young man was balancing like a tightrope walker. He swayed from side to side. It was clearly a show of drunken bravado.

'It's Chris!' said Owen. 'What the hell is he doing?'

'I think he's going to jump,' said Tom.

It was Sam who realized the danger. 'My God! Not there . . . not there,' he cried. 'He's right above the stone buttress.'

It was too late. With four pints of beer inside him the young rugby star felt invincible. The river below looked inviting. Almost in slow motion he toppled forward. As he disappeared beneath the surface Tom was already on his feet. Seconds passed. Chris Scully was floating slowly, face down on the water.

'He's hit the buttress!' shouted Sam.

It was Owen who reacted first. He sprinted across the forecourt and dived into the river.

Sam looked at Tom. 'Come on!' Both men kicked off their shoes, Tom threw his jacket on his chair and the two of them raced away to follow Owen.

'Tom, Tom!' screamed Inger.

'Ambulance,' Victor said and dashed into the pub.

Rosie stood up, transfixed in horror.

The water was bitterly cold but Tom summoned the powerful swimming strokes of his youth and managed to catch up Owen as they approached the far side of the river. Owen grabbed Chris and turned him over. Tom and Sam supported Chris's limp figure as they kicked out for the shoreline. Then there was gravel beneath their feet and they dragged him out of the water.

'We mustn't move him,' said Owen. He was kneeling down and had his hands on either side of the young man's head to keep it still. Chris was breathing again after coughing up water and had opened his eyes. His body lay there like a rag doll. Members of the rugby team ran down the stone steps and stood there in a state of shock.

Victor shouted across the river, 'An ambulance is on its way.'

Minutes later an ambulance arrived at the bridge and paramedics were on the scene. Another five minutes passed before two policemen arrived, followed by a second ambulance. On the bridge traffic was being diverted but a crowd had gathered, peering over the parapet at the drama below.

The paramedics took great care in moving Chris on to a stretcher before ascending the stone steps to the ambulance. A policeman began to ask questions and record statements.

'He overbalanced,' said Rod Parfitt. 'We'd all had a drink.'

Owen was distraught, standing there in his soaked clothes

as he watched the ambulance drive away to York Hospital. Slowly Tom and Sam led Owen up the steps, across the bridge and down again to the pub.

Victor was taking charge. 'Inger, Rosie, get Tom and Sam back to the car park and then go home to get changed. Owen, you come with me. I'll need to contact his parents. When I've done that I'll take you home and then go to the hospital.'

Darkness had fallen and it was almost ten o'clock when Tom, Inger, Rosie and Sam walked into the hospital. Victor, Zeb and Owen were sitting in the waiting room drinking coffee.

'Any news?' asked Tom.

Victor shook his head. 'His parents are with him now. I've spoken to them. Told them about the accident. Chris is their only child. They're broken with grief. The doctor indicated it may be serious but we'll know more later.'

Mr and Mrs Scully appeared in the waiting room. Both were ashen-faced. Zeb took Mrs Scully's arm. 'Let me get you a hot drink,' she said and guided her to a seat at the far side of the room.

Mr Scully approached Victor. 'I want to thank your colleagues for pulling my son out of the water.'

'It was fortunate they were there.'

Mr Scully sighed deeply. 'He's always been a bit of a daredevil.'

'Your son is a fine young man,' said Victor. 'An excellent student. You must be very proud of him.'

'Thank you for saying that. I'm aware Mr Llewellyn has

helped him a lot. He's come on in leaps and bounds since he came to Eboracum. We're really grateful.' He looked across at Tom, Owen and Sam. 'I ought to say something to them.'

'Perhaps later. I know they understand but just for now go and sit with your wife. She needs you more.'

It was almost eleven o'clock when a nurse beckoned to Mr and Mrs Scully and they followed her up the corridor. Minutes ticked by. Owen had his head in his hands. Zeb was talking quietly to Victor. Rosie and Inger were standing by the coffee machine.

'Terrible business,' said Sam.

Owen looked angry. 'I told him to enjoy himself but be careful.'

'Just a stupid accident,' said Tom.

'He picked the wrong place,' said Sam. 'Further along he would have been fine.'

'He looked in a bad way,' said Owen. 'I hope to God he will be OK.'

Then they saw Mr and Mrs Scully at the far end of the corridor. They were talking to a doctor. At the end of the conversation a nurse appeared and guided the couple back to the waiting room. Victor approached them cautiously. Mr Scully folded his arms across his chest as if an angina attack was imminent. There was no colour in his face. He rocked from side to side. Mrs Scully was weeping and being consoled by the nurse. It was a desperate scene.

Victor spoke to them quietly and then listened intently.

Finally Victor left Mr and Mrs Scully and beckoned to them all. 'They're taking him away now for an operation. The doctor has told his parents it's a spinal cord injury.'

'That sounds serious,' said Zeb.

Victor sat down and clenched his hands. 'Depends on how many of the nerve fibres cross the site of the injury. His recovery will depend on the extent of the damage.'

'So what can we hope for?' asked Owen.

'The best as always,' said Victor. Owen was clearly very distressed and Victor led him away.

'He's taken it very badly,' said Tom.

'Let's pray he will pull through,' said Zeb. 'He's a fit young man.'

Later, on the other side of the room, Owen looked up at the clock. It was 11.45 p.m. Tom was sitting beside him. 'Nearly nineteen,' whispered Owen.

'Pardon?' said Tom. 'What was that?'

'Nothing really. Just something Chris mentioned earlier.' Owen put his head in his hands once more. 'The signs aren't good. The reality is if it's really bad he may never walk again.'

It was in the early hours before they all drove home. The sense of loss was absolute, a farewell to an age of innocence. There was no going back.

Chapter Seventeen

The Weight of Time

A sliver of golden light touched the rim of the distant hills and caressed the land. It was a new dawn, a new day, and Tom had left early to call into York Hospital to meet up with Owen. It had been a regular vigil for the Welshman. On most days since the accident he had found time to call in and speak with Chris Scully and his parents. The drip-feed of news had gone from bad to worse. The damage to his spine had left him destined to spend the rest of his life in a wheelchair and the long journey of recuperation and healing had begun.

'Any news?' asked Tom.

Owen looked sombre. 'He barely speaks. His parents are here almost constantly, which is a blessing. I bring in cards and letters from the rugby guys to try to cheer him up and tell him he's not alone. I don't think he's read any yet.'

'In time maybe,' said Tom. He looked at his friend. Owen was clearly tired. 'And what about you? How're things?'

'Sue's been brilliant. Problem is I can't sleep. Just keep

thinking about that day. It seems cruel that the life he was destined to enjoy could be snatched away from him in one foolish moment. We've all had experiences like that as young men, a few pints, the sense of bravado, an action you later regret. This guy had a great future and it's gone now. His parents told me he's going to be transferred to a hospital that specializes in spinal injuries.'

They sat quietly as the bustle of the hospital cascaded around them. New arrivals queued at the reception desk, nurses strode past purposefully and porters pushed wheelchair-bound patients along the never-ending corridors. A young woman with long brown hair and an oval face, walked past. Her pale blue eyes reflected a keen intelligence. She was wearing blue jeans, a *Fame* T-shirt and a denim jacket, and she limped slightly as her footsteps clipped across the tiled floor.

'Hi, Maddy,' said Owen and she gave a shy smile and a small wave as she approached the reception desk.

'I've seen her around,' said Tom, 'but I don't know her.'

'That's Maddy Defoe: very bright according to Sam. She's one of his first-year students, hardworking by all accounts. You'll have noticed she still has some difficulty walking. Maddy and her brother, Josh, were victims of a hit-and-run accident when she was a kid. She recovered well, but he took the brunt of the impact and has been in a wheelchair ever since.'

Tom nodded.

'Maddy made a great recovery,' said Owen. 'She's been a regular spectator at our rugby matches, along with a host of other young women who all fancied Chris.'

'I can understand that.'

'She is different, though . . . very quiet. I've seen her most days. Mrs Scully thinks she's wonderful. Maddy comes in and chats to Chris about what's going on in the world and anything that might interest him.'

'Maybe there's some empathy there,' said Tom. 'She must know what it's like to have your life changed in an instant.'

Owen sighed. 'Sadly, you're right.' He stood up and stretched. 'OK, let's meet up later today.'

When Tom arrived at Eboracum he was greeted by the scent of roses filling the air on the winding path towards the entrance. Butterflies hovered above the buddleia bushes and cuckoo spit sparkled on the tall grasses in the hedgerow. It seemed a world away from the antiseptic, sterile environment of the hospital. When he walked into reception, Perkins was sending his assistant, Albert, on an errand. 'And remember, be polite,' he said. 'You're representing Eboracum.' The trainee porter ran off, clutching an envelope.

'Morning, Perkins,' said Tom.

'Good morning, Dr Frith. How's Mr Llewellyn? He's been looking peaky all week. No bounce in his stride any more.'

'He was down at the hospital again this morning.'

'A terrible business,' said Perkins sadly. 'That poor young Mr Scully. My Pauline will be leading the intercessions in church this Sunday and she says she'll include a prayer for him.'

'That's kind,' said Tom. Like ripples in a pond, the news of Chris Scully's accident had touched the lives of many.

By nine o'clock Tom was sitting at a desk in the main hall invigilating the final-year English Literature examination.

Rosie had agreed to take over at ten thirty. The atmosphere was sombre, almost funereal. Small folding tables had been arranged in straight lines and behind each one sat an expectant student. They all looked up at Tom and, as the second hand touched twelve, he announced, 'You may turn over your papers and begin. You have three hours. Good luck.'

There was a scraping of chairs, a few sighs, heads were bowed and the scratching of pens on paper began in earnest. Tom knew all these students well. Some would breeze through this examination, which required them to write three essays in three hours. Others would struggle with the time constraint. Either way he hoped the work he had done with them over the past year had prepared them for this moment. He scanned the room, saw all was well, selected the latest copy of the *Eboracum Echo* from his satchel and began to read.

In the Lodge, the Vice Chancellor and Victor were checking the shortlist for the vacant post of Head of the Art Faculty to commence in September, replacing Royce Channing. Interviews had been timetabled for Friday, 22 June and the candidates had been notified.

'A propitious selection,' said Edward with an enigmatic smile. 'Most encouraging.'

'There're a couple that stand out for me,' said Victor. 'Mr Makepeace from County Durham, who has wide experience, and the young man from London, Mr Laverick. He has an excellent CV and would appear to have leadership qualities. His ideas about embracing new techniques in photography could add much to the range of media opportunities.'

'I agree,' said Edward. 'Mr Makepeace would be the safe pair of hands while Mr Laverick sounds like one of the new breed of artists. If you would organize arrangements for the day I should be grateful.'

'A pleasure, Edward.'

The Vice Chancellor glanced up at the clock. 'How about an early coffee break?'

Victor smiled. 'Good idea.'

Edward stood up and walked across the room. The door to Hermione Frensham's office was open. She was sitting at her desk and looked up. 'With biscuits?' she asked with a smile.

Doesn't miss a thing, thought Victor.

In his office at the far side of the Lodge, Gideon Chalk was not a happy man. He had read the front page of the *Eboracum Echo* and he gritted his teeth. No names had been mentioned but it was clear that he had been identified as the *criminosus*, the guilty man. A survey involving every first-year student had resulted in an overwhelming majority of aggrieved malcontents who rented rooms in his off-site accommodation. Cramped conditions, poor services and a lack of value for money typified the responses. There were many unhappy students and the finger pointed at the mercantile miser.

Ellie MacBride was firmly in his sights and he determined his response would be both swift and resourceful. She had been warned and now must suffer the consequences. He lit a cigarette, stared out of the window and smiled.

At ten thirty Rosie took over from Tom with a whispered greeting and settled down with the revised script for *The*

Importance of Being Earnest. She picked up her takeaway cup of herbal tea and began to read. Meanwhile, Tom set off for the common room where Victor was talking to Richard Head. He collected a mug of coffee and joined the pair of professors.

'How is the exam going?' asked Victor.

'Fine. You could hear a pin drop in there. Rosie has taken over.'

Victor sighed deeply. 'That's good. Call me old-fashioned but to be perfectly frank I prefer the exam system rather than continuous assessment.'

'I agree,' said Richard. 'I loved exams.'

Victor gave him a knowing look. 'I imagine you did, Richard.'

'What about all the coursework during the year?' queried Tom. 'That ought to count for something. Personally I used to get nervous when exams came around.'

'I understand, Tom,' said Victor, 'but essays during term time have recently become a problem. I've come across plagiarism too often, it's egregious behaviour, an abuse of copyright.'

'And we can spot that easily,' said Richard confidently.

'Even so,' said Tom, 'maybe there's room for both, particularly for those students who find examinations really stressful.'

'Fair point,' said Victor. 'We could raise it at the next Student Council meeting.'

'And maybe organize a survey in the *Echo*,' added Richard.

'Which reminds me,' said Tom. 'I've just read an article by Ellie MacBride about student accommodation. There's a lot of discontent out there and I imagine the bursar won't be pleased. According to Ellie he's already threatened her with recriminations.'

'That's a concern,' Victor said but didn't go further.

'Meanwhile,' said Richard, 'on a happier note, I'm looking forward to seeing everyone this evening for our engagement party. Felicity has been working hard on the preparations.'

'Looking forward to it,' said Victor. He glanced at his wristwatch. 'Good to talk but I have to get on.' He stood up and smiled at Richard. 'I'll bring a bottle and Pat will no doubt rustle up one of his famous treats.'

Tom watched him walk away and then looked curiously at Richard. 'So . . . have you set a date for the wedding?'

Richard blushed slightly. 'I'm leaving that to Felicity. We've decided on a long engagement. There's no hurry. She says it's important I have time to adjust.'

'Adjust?'

'Yes, you know . . . to routines that are important.'

Tom nodded. 'You like routine, don't you?'

Richard looked deadly serious. 'Definitely. It's at the core of life.'

Tom studied the perfectionist professor. *He really means it,* he thought.

It was almost one thirty and Tom had enjoyed a late lunch in the refectory. As he walked back to the quad he caught up with Maddy Defoe.

'Hi, Maddy.'

'Oh, hello, Dr Frith.'

'Please, call me Tom.'

She smiled. 'Thanks, Tom. We've not really spoken. I'm always with Rosie for teaching practice.'

'I was with Owen this morning in the hospital. He mentioned your support for Chris.'

'It's just that I know how he feels.' There was a hint of concern in her voice. 'I've been through it all.'

'Owen mentioned your brother.'

Maddy smiled and nodded. From her shoulder bag she took out a leather wallet. In it was a collection of photographs. She selected one. 'This is Josh.'

A young man with a similar oval face and brown hair smiled out at them. He was wearing an athletics vest and had a spectacular upper-body physique – broad shoulders and huge biceps. He was sitting in a wheelchair.

'Josh plays lots of sports. He's outstanding at most of them.'

Tom looked in amazement. 'This is special, Maddy. A great story. Where is your brother now?'

'Stoke Mandeville in Buckinghamshire. It's where they held the Paralympic Games back in 1984. They've got great facilities. Josh loves it there. You should see him play wheelchair rugby. He's brilliant.'

Suddenly there was a call from the archway. Three young women from Science One were waving and appeared agitated. 'Maddy,' was the cry. 'Come on, it's half past one. *Neighbours* will have started.'

Maddy smiled and her eyes were bright. 'Sorry, Tom, must go. It's time for Jason Donovan.'

She linked arms with her friends and they set off for their regular date with the Australian soap. Back in November 1988, twenty million viewers had watched Scott and Charlene's wedding and Maddy Defoe had been one of them. Tom watched her hurry away, but only for a moment. He had had an idea, and he set off for the university library.

At afternoon break, Owen returned from his last lecture of the day and headed for the common room. He was deep in thought. Tom was at the counter collecting a hot drink when he caught sight of the Welshman. He beckoned to his friend. 'I've got something to share with you.'

They found a couple of seats near the pigeonholes. 'Go on,' said Owen. 'What's on your mind?'

Tom took a sheet of notes out of his pocket. 'I've been doing some research on wheelchair sport.'

Owen leaned forward. 'I'm listening.'

'Well . . . Maddy told me her brother enjoys wheelchair athletics. Apparently he's really good at wheelchair rugby – he plays at Stoke Mandeville. So I thought I'd investigate the sport. I've been in the library. I found out it was created back in 1976 for persons with quadriplegia. Then in 1984 there was a competition in Stoke Mandeville for wheelchair athletes with spinal cord injuries.'

'Interesting stuff,' said Owen. 'You've been busy.'

'I read that Great Britain entered a team in Canada last year. Since then wheelchair rugby has been growing worldwide. I think we ought to see if we can get Chris interested. It would give him a new purpose in life. You know his parents. Check it out with them first. Chris's journey to recovery is going to be very long – this could be the first step.'

Owen looked pensive but there was a new spark of interest in his eyes.

*

Tom arrived at Inger's at seven o'clock. He had picked up a bottle of Merlot from the supermarket in Haxby and driven into York. When he pulled up outside Inger's apartment she opened the door with a smile. 'Hi, Tom, almost ready.' She hurried back upstairs while Tom sat down and looked around at the room that had become so familiar. The Challen piano and the print of Edouard Manet's *A Bar at the Folies-Bergère* were special features along with the bookcases full of music manuscripts. Minutes later she reappeared in a summer frock and a headband holding back her long blonde hair.

'You look lovely,' he said with a smile.

Inger kissed him on the cheek, picked up her handbag from the hall table, draped a shawl over her shoulders and they walked out into the evening sunshine.

Tom felt at peace as they drove past the railway station and then queued in the busy traffic outside the theatre and the art gallery. Slowly they passed Bootham Bar and turned left into Bootham Terrace before parking outside a red-brick middle-of-terrace property.

'Have you been here before?' asked Tom.

'No, it's my first time. Should be interesting.'

Tom smiled. 'Knowing Richard as we do, I agree.' He rang the doorbell and Sam answered with a wide-eyed smile.

'Guess what?' He pointed to a clipboard and a list of names. 'You have to sign in.'

Tom and Inger exchanged a knowing glance, but complied before entering the house with its stained-wood flooring and white walls. This was definitely Richard's man-cave: everything appeared to be in precise order and there were coasters on every surface. The walls were filled with books and there was a large open-plan lounge/diner and kitchen. Refreshments had been arranged on the worktop in perfect symmetry. Every bottle had its label facing outward and six identical plates displayed nibbles arranged in concentric circles like edible ammonites. Felicity was welcoming guests while Richard was dividing up a quiche into six precise slices.

Tom went to collect two drinks and fell into conversation with Owen and Sue while Felicity gave Inger a warm welcome. 'Thank you so much for coming,' she said. 'It means a lot to Richard.'

'Hi, Felicity,' said Inger. 'This is lovely. Well done.'

'Thank you. It's been interesting trying to accommodate his obsessions. This is the first-ever party he's hosted here in his home.' She lowered her voice. 'So you have to make allowances. I thought signing in at the door was a bit over the top but I knew you would all take it in good spirit.'

'Not a problem,' said Inger.

Felicity gave a gentle smile. 'That's kind of you to say. I do know that within his organized soul there is a really lovely man, caring, honest and true.'

'I agree,' said Inger. 'His dedication to his work and the faculty is second to none. He is a remarkable man and an outstanding scientist. We're fortunate to have him as a colleague.' She looked across the room where Richard, his lanyard swinging from his neck, had moved on to demonstrating his microscope to an intrigued Rosie. 'So, any plans for the future?'

'Just to carry on as we are. I'm busy teaching in Sheffield and have an apartment there. So we tend to be with each other alternate weekends.' She looked across at Tom who was pouring wine. 'And what about you and Tom?'

Inger gave a cautious smile. 'We're fine.'

'By the way, I'm looking forward to *The Importance of Being Earnest*. Richard has spent hours correlating his sound and lighting script.'

Inger nodded. 'He will be perfect as always. In fact, we're almost ready now and, thankfully, Royce Channing has completed the set. As you would expect, my musicians have worked really hard and Zeb has been busy with her rehearsals.'

The doorbell rang again and all heads turned as Zeb walked in. Beside her was a tall, handsome gentleman in an immaculate linen suit and white shirt. She passed a bottle of wine to Felicity and gave Richard a kiss on the cheek. 'This is Vijay, my new neighbour in Crayke village,' she said. 'He's a consultant at York Hospital . . . fixes hips and knees,' she added vaguely.

'Pleased to meet you,' said Felicity. 'Can I offer you a drink?'

'Just a fruit juice, thank you.'

Victor waved from the other side of the room and studied Zeb's new companion with interest. He also noticed she wasn't smoking.

Sue and Owen walked into the conservatory where Pat was drinking a glass of Sauvignon blanc and admiring the well-kept garden with bright blue lobelia trailing from the hanging baskets.

'Hello,' said Pat. 'Good to see you again. How's your son?'

'He's fine, thanks,' said Owen. 'A year old last month.'

'Time flies.'

'And how are you now?' asked Sue, admiring the handsome, stylish man before her. 'You look really well.'

'I'm just pleased to be here this evening doing normal things among friends and living life as it should be.'

Owen raised his glass of beer. 'I'll drink to that. It must have been a worrying time.'

'Particularly for Victor,' said Sue. 'Owen says he's more relaxed now that you're fit and well again.'

Pat's eyes were soft with sorrow. 'I hated to cause him so much stress, particularly when he was suddenly thrust into his new role.'

'Well, it's fine now,' said Sue, 'and lovely to catch up with your career again, not just the art but your links with the theatre. Owen and I are looking forward to the next musical evening.'

'Thanks. That's kind. Yes, we're planning an extravaganza for next Christmas.'

'Meanwhile,' said Owen, 'Zeb's new man is creating some interest.' They looked back into the lounge where Zeb was sharing news with Rosie while Victor was shaking hands with the newcomer.

'Hello, I'm Victor Grammaticus, a colleague of Zeb at the university.'

'Yes, I've heard a lot about you. May I call you Victor?'

'Of course. Zeb said your name was Vijay.'

'Yes, Vijay Kapoor. Please call me Vijay. Zeb is my new neighbour in Crayke. She speaks very highly of you.'

'She is a remarkable lady and a fine lecturer. We're fortunate to work alongside such an outstanding colleague.'

'She fascinates me: such remarkable energy and zest for life.'

'That's definitely Zeb.' Victor studied this elegant man. 'I understand you work at York Hospital. What's your specialism?'

'Mainly arthroscopic surgery, and I did a trauma fellowship last year in the USA which helps my work. It's very satisfying . . . literally getting patients back on their feet.'

'I'm sure it is. Have you lived in Crayke for long?'

'Five years. I worked in New Zealand before that.'

'You've clearly travelled the world.'

'Yes, but I'm settled here now. It's a very cultural village. Lots of interesting people and Zeb is a great addition to our community. I love her music.' He smiled. 'She plays it non-stop.'

Victor raised his eyebrows. 'Lucky she has a sympathetic neighbour.' He saw the way the doctor looked at Zeb. He was obviously captivated by the dynamic flame-haired dance teacher.

It was later in the evening when Victor caught up with Zeb. 'Vijay is an interesting man. Clearly very talented.'

'He's a bit like Pat in a way. Equally brilliant but not quite as flamboyant.'

Victor smiled. 'Yes, you could say that. Pat is very special.'

Zeb raised her glass of gin and tonic. 'You're a lucky man.'

'True . . . Pat's very knowledgeable . . . and he understands me in a way no one else does.' Victor sipped his wine thoughtfully. 'He said he had spent his life catching fireflies and then he found me.'

Zeb clinked her glass against Victor's. 'I wish I could find someone like that.'

Victor glanced across at Vijay. 'Perhaps you already have.'

*

The evening swept by. Everyone thanked Felicity and Richard for their hospitality and Victor proposed a toast to the happy couple. Gradually the exodus for home began. As they left the sky was changing from red to purple while stars shone down from the vast firmament on this perfect summer night.

Back in Inger's apartment Tom relaxed in an armchair with a glass of wine. Inger kicked off her shoes and walked over to the bureau next to the piano. 'I think I'll have a nightcap.' She took out a bottle of *akvavit* that had been gifted to her by her brother, Andreas. Inger was fond of the traditional Norwegian flavoured spirit. After pouring a glass, she stretched out on the sofa. Then she stroked her long blonde hair from her eyes and looked at Tom. 'I enjoyed this evening. Richard is a lucky man to have found someone like Felicity. Perfect for him.' Tom was swirling his wine around and around in his glass. 'You look pensive.'

'Just thinking.'

'Go on.'

'It's been an eventful day. Seems a long time since I was with Owen at the hospital. I was thinking about that young man and wondering what will become of him. Makes you think about the fact we have one life and have to make the best of it.'

'I agree.'

Tom looked at Inger. 'I'm just happy to be here tonight with you.'

Inger sighed. 'I'm pleased you didn't go to New Zealand.'

'It was just a wild idea. I thought you might want to come with me. It wouldn't have worked.' Tom knew that succumbing to the lure of the job in Christchurch had been a mistake, a patchwork of wrong choices.

Inger gave Tom a wistful look and sipped her drink. 'Our lives are here, Tom.'

'I guess they are but change is coming. We need to embrace it.'

'What do you mean?' There was a long silence while Inger looked intently at Tom. 'You're smiling,' she said softly.

Tom leaned forward and put down his glass. 'When I wake up I see you lying there beside me and I imagine it will always be like this. It's my private dream. It gives me hope. So that's why I'm smiling.'

Inger stood up and stretched out her hand. 'Let's go to bed.'

Chapter Eighteen

Ask the Right Question

It was 8.30 a.m. on Friday, 22 June when Gideon Chalk parked his Audi 100 in his personal parking space at the rear of the Lodge. As he strolled to the entrance, he caught sight of Ellie MacBride walking down the path towards reception. Her script for *The Importance of Being Earnest* was in her shoulder bag and she was hurrying to her early-morning meeting with Zeb. Once again she had agreed to be the prompt for each performance and a busy couple of days stretched out in front of her.

Gideon hurried to catch up with her and called out, 'I read your article, Miss MacBride. Very interesting.'

Ellie stopped and turned. Her eyes narrowed when she saw who it was. 'Good to hear. There will be more to follow.'

The bursar gave an imperceptible shake of the head. 'Very unwise.'

Ellie was determined not to be intimidated. 'Really?' she said coldly. 'I shall make my own decisions regarding the wisdom of reporting concerns raised by the students of Eboracum.'

She turned back towards reception but stopped when he called after her: 'By the way, are you going to the play?' He paused to ensure he had her attention; Ellie looked puzzled. 'Didn't something unpleasant happen last year?' And he smiled as he turned swiftly and walked back to the Lodge.

Ellie remained still for a moment. A year ago, after the dress rehearsal, the previous Head of Faculty, Dr Edna Wallop, had been found at the foot of a flight of metal stairs. The fall had killed her. Ellie stood there, thinking hard. It was a strange question . . . almost sinister. *Was this a veiled threat?* she thought. With a shake of her head she walked on.

When Tom arrived in reception, Perkins was writing in his day book. The friendly porter looked up and smiled. 'Good morning, Dr Frith. Looks like a fine day ahead. Now that exams are over I see there're lots of parties being organized.'

'Yes, happy times for the students.'

'Mr Channing was in early again, making sure the set is in place for the dress rehearsal tonight. I've just seen it and it's one of his best.'

'We're sorry to see him leave.'

'It will be exciting for him. A new life ahead with a young bride.'

Tom nodded and gave a wistful smile. 'Very true – and his successor will be appointed today.'

Peter Perkins looked up at the clock. 'The four to be interviewed are due any time now. According to my day book they're having a guided tour this morning.'

'Eventful times,' said Tom as he set off for the quad.

*

In the music room, Zeb was sitting at a table with Inger and Rosie. They were making some final amendments to the script when Ellie arrived.

'Hi, Ellie. Thanks for calling in,' said Zeb. 'We just have a few additions.'

Ellie looked pale as she sat down. Inger showed her the high-lighted passages. 'There're a couple of pauses,' said Inger, 'one in each act before the orchestra comes in. We've also added a trumpet to the woodwind, percussion, double bass and piano.'

Ellie nodded. 'Sure. That's fine,' and began to update her script.

'Are you OK?' asked Zeb.

Ellie sighed and shook her head. 'Just had a difficult conversation with the bursar. He made it very clear that he didn't approve of my article in the *Echo*.'

'What happened?' asked Inger.

'It was worse this time and felt threatening,' and she explained what he had said.

'This is dreadful,' said Rosie. 'Can't we complain?'

Zeb had a face like thunder. 'Leave it with me. I'll speak to Victor.' She looked at Ellie. 'He's just a pompous little man and you've shaken his cage. It will be fine. Don't give it another thought.' She put her arm around Ellie. 'Now, back to the script.'

Ellie gave a wan smile. 'I think I know it almost off by heart now. Lady Bracknell is my favourite.'

'Mine too,' said Rosie. 'Formidable.'

'Well, it's thanks to Rosie that we've got it down to just over two hours,' said Zeb. 'Having an Oscar Wilde aficionado on the team has been really useful.'

'I heard we've sold out,' said Ellie.

'Yes,' said Zeb. 'There are no tickets left for the two performances tomorrow but we could probably squeeze a few more in for tonight's dress rehearsal.'

'And don't forget the after-show party tomorrow evening,' said Inger.

'Bring a friend, if you wish,' added Zeb.

'Thanks,' said Ellie. Then she sighed. She knew whom she would like to bring.

Owen was looking out of the study window when Tom walked in. 'Look at this,' he said. 'It's the interviewees for the art job.'

Tom peered down at the quad where Royce Channing was talking to three men and one woman. They were an eclectic mix: a grey-haired man in his fifties and another much younger with shoulder-length hair and carrying a camera; behind them was a woman in a flowing kaftan and a tall skinny man in an ill-fitting suit.

'Royce is showing off the set for tonight's dress rehearsal.'

'A brilliant job,' said Owen. 'He's put hours of work into it. Really impressive.'

'He kept his word to Zeb,' said Tom. 'Promised to support her.'

The interviewees were showing great interest in the set that Royce had constructed along with some of his students. There was a stage of wooden blocks, plywood backdrops of various scenes and spotlights had been attached to tubular poles to the side and above the stage. It was unsophisticated but wonderfully effective.

'So, what are you doing today?' asked Owen.

Tom emptied his satchel on to the desk. 'Exam marking. Lots to do. Then Rosie and I will counter-mark the scripts.'

'Sounds busy,' said Owen.

'After that it's a final check of the sound and lighting with Richard for the dress rehearsal. What about you?'

'I've arranged a meeting with Maddy Defoe and her brother Josh at morning break. Chris Scully's parents are coming in as well. I want to let them see how Josh has progressed as a wheelchair athlete. Then I'm hoping we can talk to Chris about the future.'

Tom could sense the determination in Owen's voice. 'Josh sounds to be a good role model.'

'Yes. It's all thanks to Maddy. She kicked off this idea. And you helped too, of course. Early days, though, and there's lots to discuss. I just want Chris to know he can still have a life in sport. As you said, there's a long journey ahead.'

At morning break Zeb called into Victor's study. He was busy at his desk checking anticipated staffing levels for next year but stopped when he saw the expression on her face.

'Hi, Zeb. Time for a coffee?'

Zeb took the hint and boiled the kettle. Minutes later they were enjoying a hot drink and shortbread biscuits. 'Now,' said Victor. 'Why are you looking so agitated?'

Zeb smiled. 'I didn't think it was that obvious.' She looked in her shoulder bag and took out her pack of cigarettes. Then changed her mind and replaced them.

'Smoke if you wish,' said Victor.

Zeb shook her head. 'Vijay has suggested I cut down.'

Victor smiled. 'He's a wise man, very impressive. Is he coming to the play?'

'Yes, he said he would do his best to call in this evening after work. He's a busy man.'

'I imagine he is.' Victor was intrigued. Zeb's latest boy-friend was different to those that had gone before. 'So, what's on your mind?'

'It's Gideon Chalk. I didn't want to talk to him without seeing you first. We have a terrific second-year student, Ellie MacBride, who is on the editorial team for the *Echo*. The bursar clearly upset her this morning. Apparently he was most displeased with the piece she's written about student accom-modation. As you are aware, he's not my favourite person, but I didn't want to go in all guns blazing without putting you in the picture. Someone needs to rein him in. I'm not sure the Vice Chancellor will do it because he seems happy with the way the university finances are being handled. It's what is going on with the students that concerns me. Word has it he's lining his own pockets by subletting the properties he has secured since arriving here and putting too many students into the various houses. He's been a busy man. Either way, he shouldn't be trying to intimidate a student.'

Victor nodded sagely. 'I appreciate you speaking to me first. I'll have a word with him.'

'Thanks,' said Zeb. She got up to leave. 'Must get on. I said I would meet up with Royce after his guided tour with the interviewees. He wanted me to do a final check of the set, which looks brilliant.'

'Sad to see him go,' said Victor. 'Let's hope we get a good replacement. I'm on the interview panel this afternoon with Edward, and Miss Glendenning is representing the govern-ing body.'

Zeb got up to leave. 'Good luck with that, Victor, and thanks.'

'And don't worry, I'll follow this up and we can talk again later.'

*

In the common room, Tom and Inger were enjoying a coffee break.

'That looks an interesting gathering,' said Inger. A group of people were in intense conversation. One of them, a young man, strong in the shoulders, was in a wheelchair.

Tom looked across the room at his friend. 'Owen's organized a meeting with Chris Scully's parents. They've come in to meet Maddy Defoe and her brother, Josh. He's a wheelchair athlete.'

'Owen has really taken it to heart, hasn't he?'

'Chris was his rugby protégé. He's on a mission now to do his best for him.'

'Is he still in hospital?' asked Inger.

'Yes, but he may be transferred shortly. Decisions are still ongoing.'

'I hope he will be OK,' said Inger.

Tom looked down at the the manuscript she was holding. 'Are you set for this evening?'

'Yes. I have a great ensemble, all talented musicians. The music should add a lot to the performance. What about you?'

'Just following Richard's lead with the sound and lighting. He's a perfectionist.'

Inger smiled. 'These are exciting times, Tom. I'm glad you're here to enjoy them.'

Tom looked into her blue eyes. An idea was forming.

Across the quad Victor was striding out towards the Lodge. Miss Frensham was at her desk when he walked in. 'Good morning, Professor Grammaticus. I'm afraid the Vice Chancellor isn't in at the moment.'

'Thank you,' said Victor. 'It's the bursar I wish to see.'

There was a flicker of interest from the efficient PA. 'He's in his office.'

Victor walked down the passageway to the rear of the building, tapped on Gideon Chalk's door and stepped inside. 'Good morning, Gideon. Sorry to disturb you but I need to share something with you.'

Gideon looked up and placed his cigarette in the ashtray. 'I'm rather busy,' he said curtly. 'Can it wait?'

'I'm afraid not.'

'Very well. What is it?'

'It's come to my attention that you exchanged words this morning with a student in my faculty. Is that correct?'

'If you're referring to that ill-informed young woman, MacBride, then yes, I did speak with her. She's becoming a nuisance.'

'In what way?'

'The articles she writes in that student rag are encouraging rebellion. She needs to moderate her language.'

'The *Eboracum Echo* provides a vital voice for our students and Miss MacBride is a perceptive journalist.'

'Nonsense!'

'That may be your view but I'm here to tell you in no uncertain terms that shouting at one of the students outside reception and within earshot of others is unacceptable and must cease. Do I make myself clear?'

'I don't answer to you, Grammaticus. I was appointed by the Vice Chancellor.'

'And I shall be passing on my concerns to Edward in due course. So take this as a warning.'

'You're wasting your time. I'm valued here. Our accounts are in order.'

'Are you going to the play?'

Gideon paused. This was unexpected. 'I haven't decided.'

'You could learn a lot from Oscar Wilde.'

'How so?'

'He once said that there are people who know the price of everything and the value of nothing.' Victor walked out and closed the door quietly behind him.

At six thirty, Rosie and Zeb were sitting on the edge of the stage, having a final conversation about the script. A tall, slim man in his late thirties approached them. He had shoulder-length hair and was wearing a baggy shirt and blue jeans. An expensive-looking camera with a zoom lens swung from a strap over his shoulder.

Zeb looked up. 'Hi, are you press?' She pointed to a reserved section of the seating. 'There're seats over there.'

He smiled. 'No, I'm not press but I was hoping to take some photographs. I'm Ben Laverick. I was appointed this afternoon to replace Royce Channing in the art department.'

Zeb stood up. 'Welcome to Eboracum, Ben, and congratulations on the appointment. I'm Zeb. Dance and Drama. This is my colleague Rosie from the English department. You're welcome to stay for the play if you have time.'

'Pleased to meet you,' said Ben, 'and thanks for the invitation. My train back to London isn't until Sunday morning so this seems to be the perfect way to spend an evening.'

'And yes,' said Zeb, 'take photographs if you wish.'

'It's not just a hobby, it's my specialism. We discussed it in the interview and everyone seemed keen.'

Inger was on the other side of the stage with her musicians and she was waving.

'Good to talk to you, Ben, but you'll have to excuse me. I'm needed elsewhere. There's an after-show gathering tomorrow night in the common room, so come to that too if you can.' Zeb smiled at Rosie. 'In the meantime, maybe Rosie can look after you.'

'Of course,' said Rosie. She looked behind her. The rows of chairs had begun to fill up. There were two empty seats at the end of the third row and they sat down.

'Impressive set,' said Ben.

'Yes. Royce worked hard to finish it.'

'So I guess it will be my turn next.'

'Yes, just talk to Zeb. She's brilliant.'

'Zeb?'

'Elizabeth . . . prefers Zeb.'

'OK. Makes sense. So what's the accent, Rosie, Cornwall or Devon?'

'Definitely Cornwall. What about you?'

'Camden Town in London. I share an apartment with a few other artists.'

'And you're clearly into photography.'

'It's my passion. I'm hoping to progress it in our course structure.'

Rosie found she was enjoying conversing with this intense and attractive newcomer. 'Sounds exciting,' she said.

Ben looked across at Zeb and Inger. 'So I'm guessing Zeb is the producer?'

'That's right – and director. She's with Inger Larson, our music tutor.'

On the other side of the stage Inger was curious. 'Who's the guy with Rosie?'

'Ben Laverick. He's the new Head of Art.'

'Interesting,' said Inger.

'I know what you're thinking,' said Zeb. 'Seriously dishy.'

'Rosie seems to be getting on well with him.'

'I'm not surprised,' said Zeb. 'No doubt you'll meet him later tonight.'

Inger raised her eyebrows and smiled. 'I'll look forward to it.'

At seven o'clock, Zeb stood on the stage in the late-evening sunshine, microphone in hand.

'Good evening, everyone, and thank you for supporting this year's drama festival. Once again, we're fortunate in having many talented students and I know you will be entertained by our final dress rehearsal of *The Importance of Being Earnest*. I should like to welcome our distinguished guests including members of the local press and representatives of various theatrical agencies. A special thank you must go to Inger Larson and her musicians for their superb accompaniment, Rosie Tremaine for adapting the script, Richard Head for sound and lighting and Royce Channing for creating yet another perfect set. Our performance lasts a little over two hours; there will be a twenty-minute interval during which refreshments will be served in the common room. Our play opens outside Green Park in the heart of London in the year 1895. So . . . sit back and enjoy.'

The lights dimmed, Inger's musicians played softly, the young actors walked on to the stage and Oscar Wilde's absurd but wonderfully entertaining plot began to unravel. At the side of the stage, Ellie MacBride opened her script to page one and bowed her head. She was unaware she was being watched. Under the archway at the far side of the quad, Gideon Chalk was standing in the shadows.

Vijay Kapoor suddenly appeared. He had been on call and it had been a demanding day for him at the hospital. Zeb had reserved a seat for him in the front row and it was as if she sensed his presence. She turned, saw him and smiled. Vijay gave a gentle wave, then relaxed as the student actors moved smoothly towards a superb performance.

There was laughter when it was declared that the character Jack Worthing had been found in a handbag at Victoria Station. Predictably he preferred the name of Ernest. Algernon Moncrieff, the so-called idle young gentleman, and the heiress, Gwendolen Fairfax, gave wonderful performances, as did Miss Prism, the family nursemaid. However, it was the otherwise timid young Angela Raynard from Year Three History who surprised everyone by transforming into the redoubtable Lady Bracknell. It was a remarkable interpretation of the part and thoroughly deserving of the standing ovation at the end.

A relieved Zeb was immediately congratulated by members of the press and various agents. Vijay waited his turn patiently and eventually they came face to face in the crowd. 'Congratulations,' he said. 'I'm so pleased for you. An absolute triumph. The audiences will love it tomorrow.'

'Thank you for coming, Vijay,' and she stretched up and kissed him on the cheek.

Owen and Sue had arranged a babysitter and enjoyed the play. They watched Zeb greeting her handsome friend. Sue was intrigued. 'He's so attentive. Different and clearly smitten.'

'Looks a really nice guy,' said Owen. 'I've spoken to him a couple of times. He's a modest man doing a skilled job.'

'I wonder if this is the one?' said Sue.

Saturday morning dawned and Tom was restless. It had been a humid night. He peered out of his bedroom window and saw that an early-morning mist had fallen. The world was still and silent until a shimmer of pearl grey crested the horizon. Hazy sunlight was racing across the land, caressing the treetops and casting fingers of sharp shadows. A day of decisions stretched out before him. He had an important question for Inger. It was simply a matter of picking the right moment.

When he left his wisteria-clad cottage, the scent of roses hung in the air and bright butterflies spread their lacy wings. He felt a sense of anticipation and, as he drove into York, Elton John was singing 'Healing Hands'.

At lunchtime, Tom and Owen met up in the refectory. 'How did the meeting go yesterday?' asked Tom. 'Sorry we couldn't catch up after the play.'

'No, Sue and I had to get back for the babysitter. It went well. Chris's parents have bought into the idea of wheelchair athletics and Josh was inspirational. He's really special. I learned a lot from him. Also, Maddy has made a good connection with Chris. He feels comfortable talking to her. The last thing he said to me was that he wanted to come back to Eboracum to finish his degree. It almost broke my heart when he said that and we have to make it happen.'

'Where would he stay?'

Owen looked thoughtful. 'I need to visit the accommodation he shares with his mates. It's sublet by the bursar and these guys are not happy. They've made lots of complaints but haven't got anywhere. It's about time I had a look for myself.'

'Good idea,' said Tom. 'Or maybe the ground floor in one of the student blocks here on campus might be an alternative.'

'Either way,' said Owen, 'we have to acknowledge that we don't appear to cater well enough for students with disabilities.'

Tom looked around him at all the able-bodied students enjoying their lunch. 'Let me know how I can help,' he said.

At two o'clock the quad was full again with an expectant audience. Final preparations had been completed and Zeb spoke to Ellie at the side of the stage. 'We just need it to go as well as yesterday. All the students look relaxed and they're so pleased about the response they received last night. So we should be fine.'

Meanwhile, Tom was deep in thought. Richard Head was working smoothly through the script and Tom was following his lead but it wasn't the dilemma of the two young actors who were assuming the name of Ernest that was on his mind. His preoccupations continued to dominate his mind throughout the day. It wasn't until much later when the evening performance was about to end that he made a decision.

As the final line about realizing the Importance of Being Earnest was delivered, Zeb breathed a sigh of relief. It was over. There was a standing ovation and gradually the cast, tutors and guests made their way into the common room.

It was Victor who sought out the Vice Chancellor. 'A word, please, Edward.'

'Of course, Victor.'

Victor ushered him to a quiet corner. 'It concerns Gideon. He upset one of my students yesterday morning. There was an exchange of words outside reception.'

'Who are we talking about?'

'Ellie MacBride, Year Two English. A fine student.'

'Are you saying there was a dispute?'

'It sounds like that. Gideon was upset regarding the latest editorial in the *Echo*.'

Edward nodded sagely. 'It would appear there have been complaints about student accommodation.'

'That's correct.'

'But we've always had that, Victor, once young people leave the comfort of home. Perhaps they expect too much these days.'

'That may be so but the evidence is building up that all is not well.'

'You mentioned an exchange of words. Who instigated this?'

'It was Gideon who shouted at Miss MacBride as she arrived.'

'Oh dear. In that case I'll have a quiet word. Perhaps he was overwrought and maybe a little sensitive regarding any perceived criticism of his work.'

'That's possible, Edward, but a word from you will help.'

The Vice Chancellor nodded. 'I'll pick my moment, Victor, but keep in mind he was appointed for his accountancy skills, not his personality.' With that Edward patted Victor on the shoulder. 'Victor, you must enjoy this evening's triumph. Your faculty goes from strength to strength and the appointment yesterday of Mr Laverick as the new Head of Art can only enhance its reputation.'

Ben Laverick was standing alone in the common room taking in the sound and movement of the crowds around him. *So this is Eboracum,* he thought. It was Rosie who spotted him first.

'Hello again,' she said. 'Did you enjoy the play yesterday?'

'Brilliant. A really high standard. You have some very talented students here.'

'Yes. That's thanks to Zeb. She offers wonderful encouragement. This is an annual event so you'll be part of it next time.'

'I'll look forward to it.' He held up his camera. 'I took a lot of photographs and thought I would print them out and post copies on to her in case she wants to use them.'

'I'm sure she would appreciate that.'

'There are also photographs of the musicians. The lighting was perfect for them, particularly some of the zoom shots.'

'We must tell Inger before you leave. In the meantime, would you like a drink?'

'Yes, please, and maybe you can tell me more about yourself and why a Cornishwoman finds herself teaching English in York.'

Rosie smiled. 'Of course,' she said, 'but my story is probably similar to yours; I simply responded to an advertisement in the *Times Educational Supplement* for what appeared to be a great job.'

They moved through the crowd towards the serving

counter, collected two drinks and continued their conversation. Rosie found she was enjoying listening to the stories of this handsome newcomer.

At the far end of the room and in amongst all the excited chatter, Inger was congratulating her musicians while Tom waited to pick his moment to intervene. 'Inger, can you come outside with me for a moment? There's something I want to ask you.'

'Outside?'

'Yes, away from all this noise.'

She picked up her shawl from the back of her chair and followed Tom into the quad. It was a still, balmy midsummer night and they walked across the grass to the edge of the stage. 'What is it?' asked Inger.

Tom took her hand. 'Let's sit down.'

There was a pause while Tom searched for the right words. 'It's been on my mind for a long time.' For Tom it had indeed been a long journey towards this moment. He had thought about it for many months. His fear as always was rejection, but he had decided the time was now.

There was a brief silence. Inger sat calmly on the edge of the stage. She was curious.

Eventually Tom took a deep breath and asked the question that had been on his mind for so long.

He held Inger's hand and looked into her blue eyes. 'I love you, Inger Larson, always have, always will. You're also my best friend. That should count for something. We're good together.'

She smiled. 'We are, although I am not too sure where this conversation is going.'

'Inger . . . will you marry me?'

There was a long pause. 'That's a surprise, Tom. I've not considered marriage.'

'Well, can you consider it now? I'm serious.'

'What you're asking is a big commitment. I'm not sure I'm ready for that.'

'I see. In that case I'll take that as a no.' Tom stood up and stared at the sky. 'Sorry, that didn't come out right.'

'Don't worry. I understand,' said Inger. 'Come on. Let's go back inside.'

Tom felt a little deflated as they re-entered the common room.

Later, Victor spotted Tom sitting alone in the far corner of the room and he walked over and sat beside him. 'What's wrong, Tom? You're looking a little preoccupied.'

'Yes. Life's never simple, is it?'

'Go on. What's on your mind?'

'I've just asked Inger to marry me.'

'From the look of you I presume she said no.'

Tom nodded. 'Yes. I was hoping she would have liked the idea.'

Victor placed a hand gently on his shoulder. 'Oscar Wilde once said that the answers are all out there but we just need to ask the right questions.'

'I thought that's what I did.'

'Almost, Tom. I think you asked the right question but not necessarily at the right time.'

Chapter Nineteen

None Shall Sleep

As Tom drove into York the cars in front of him had flags of St George fluttering from their windows. Shopfronts were covered in messages for the England football team and on the radio Luciano Pavarotti was reaching a crescendo with his stirring performance of 'Nessun Dorma'. A life-size cardboard cut-out of Paul Gascoigne stood in the doorway of the students' common room and even Perkins in reception had decorated his counter with bunting. England had reached the semi-final stage of the Football World Cup in Italy and the manager, Bobby Robson, was confident he would lead out a team that could defeat West Germany and book a place in the final. It was Wednesday, 4 July and Italia 90 had captured the hearts of the nation.

Owen was rummaging through the filing cabinet when Tom walked in.

'Hi,' said Owen, 'big day. England versus Germany.'

'That's right,' said Tom. 'So where are you watching the game?'

'I'm staying here. Sam mentioned the Students' Union has arranged with Perkins and Charlie the caretaker for a large-screen telly to be set up in their common room. Anyone can go, including staff.'

'That's great.'

'It gets better. Zeb mentioned beer and refreshments have been organized and it should be lively with both the rugby and football teams in there. Kick-off is at seven.'

'Fine. I'll join you.'

'Let's meet back in here just before the game and go in together,' said Owen. He found what he was looking for in the filing cabinet and sat at his desk. 'So what have you got on?'

'A meeting with Victor and Zeb about next year's timetable.'

Owen nodded. 'Let me know if I can help.'

'What about you?'

'I've arranged with one of the guys in the rugby team to check out Chris Scully's accommodation. It's up the Hull Road somewhere. I'll cycle there at morning break.'

'OK, we can catch up later.'

Tom tapped on Victor's study door and walked in.

'Morning, Tom,' said Victor, 'thanks for calling in. Take a seat. It's just a preliminary meeting regarding next year's timetable and an update concerning school teaching-practice placements.'

'Coffee?' asked Zeb.

'Yes, please,' said Tom. 'I've just heard from Owen that tonight's World Cup game will be shown in the students' common room. I'm looking forward to it.'

'That's right,' said Victor. 'It's thanks to Zeb. She could charm the birds out of the trees,' he added with a smile. 'Perkins and Charlie the caretaker were putty in her hands. It's all organized.'

'And I don't even like bloody football,' said Zeb as she served up the coffee.

'Anyway, it sounds like a good social evening,' said Tom. 'So thanks, Zeb.'

'I'll be there, hanging around the bar and making sure everyone behaves,' said Zeb.

'And I'll call in at some point,' said Victor. 'I mentioned to Pat I might be late home.'

Tom sipped his coffee and sat back in his chair. He liked this tidy room with all the bookshelves, well-chosen artefacts and a vase of sweet peas on Victor's desk.

Victor gave Tom a bundle of A4 sheets of graph paper with neat colour-coded columns. 'This is as far as we've got with next year's timetable, Tom. It's definitely a first draft but we need to coordinate with the dates of teaching practices for all the year groups. So that's the next job. I need you to see what's possible for teaching placements while ensuring every student gets the best opportunity for first-hand experience in the classroom.'

'So, where are you up to, Tom, and can I do anything?' asked Zeb.

'I'm fine,' said Tom. 'Last year's experience helped. Knowing a lot of the headteachers means I can move faster with securing placements.'

'Good to hear,' said Victor. 'Let's arrange to meet again a week from today, same time, and see how far we've got.'

The three of them visibly relaxed. Meetings led by

Victor and Zeb were often brief and to the point. Without being aware of it, Tom was learning much about the art of leadership.

'On a lighter note,' said Victor. 'Have we all got our tickets for the dance? It's not black tie so the dress code is simply smart casual, a bit more relaxed this time.'

The end-of-term Faculty Dinner Dance at the Assembly Rooms in York was just over a week away.

'I've got mine,' said Zeb. Both Victor and Tom gave her an enquiring look and smiled. 'And yes, I'm bringing Vijay.'

'Good choice,' said Victor, 'and what about you, Tom?'

'I'll be there with Inger.' He didn't mention it had been Inger who had reminded him about the tickets. They finished their coffee and Tom stood up to leave. 'I've got a few tutorials now with English Three so if you'll excuse me I'll get on.'

'Thanks, Tom,' said Victor.

'And I'll see you tonight,' added Zeb.

Owen was cycling up the Hull Road looking for a cul-de-sac with the street name Lavender Close. He found it, propped his bicycle against the gate and stared up at a semi-detached three-bedroom house with a bay window. From the outside it looked to be a tidy property.

He rattled the door knocker and Rod Parfitt, the short, stocky rugby scrum half, answered. 'Hi, Owen. Come on in. All the guys are out so it's just me.'

'Thanks, Rod, I appreciate your time.'

'What is it you want to see?'

'Chris is talking about coming back to uni to finish his degree.'

The young man's eyes lit up. 'That's brilliant. What can we do to help?'

'Well, he would need wheelchair access for a start.'

They both stared down at the steep front step. 'Tough but possible, I suppose,' said Rod, 'if a ramp was installed.'

'Let's have a look inside,' said Owen.

Off the hallway was a tiny kitchen. 'The tap's loose,' said Rod. 'Keeps falling off. We told the bursar but nothing's been done.'

Owen frowned as they stepped back into the hallway. 'Is there a loo down here?'

'No, that's upstairs.'

'Let's check it out,' said Owen.

They climbed the stairs to the landing and stepped into the bathroom. The paint was peeling off the walls and there was a damp patch on the floor. Next to the toilet was a bath. It was full of dirty clothes. 'The plumbing's knackered,' explained Rod. 'We dump our dirty washing in here and take turns to go to the launderette.' He pulled a mat from under the bath. It was covered in black mould. 'There's a leak somewhere.'

Owen frowned. 'What are the bedrooms like?'

'Bit cramped,' Rod said and opened all the doors. Each of the three rooms had two single beds and a cheap wardrobe with the door hanging off.

'So, there's six of you in the house?' asked Owen.

Rod looked surprised. 'No, eight.'

'Eight? Where do the other two sleep?'

'In the lounge although it doubles up as a meeting place.'

They walked back downstairs and stepped into the lounge. There were two single beds, a scattering of cushions on the floor and a small portable tv on a plywood table. Owen kept his thoughts to himself. It saddened him that somehow the amiable rugby player had learned to cope with the deplorable conditions.

'None of us want to stay here next year,' said Rod with a rueful grin. 'All the guys are looking elsewhere but decent accommodation is hard to find.'

Owen had seen enough. 'Thanks for your time, Rod. This has helped.'

Rod looked a little shamefaced. 'Sorry it's a bit of mess. We do our best.'

'I know you do,' said Owen. He climbed on to his bicycle and headed back to Eboracum.

Inger and Rosie were in the common room at morning break. The place was strangely quiet. Everyone seemed to be in meetings while outside in the quad Albert, the assistant porter, could be seen hurrying back and forth to the students' common room, carrying heavy boxes. Charlie had pushed a giant television with tall tubular legs on wheels to the front of the huge space. The room was being transformed for the big event.

'It's for the football,' said Rosie.

'Football?' queried Inger.

'It's the World Cup. England are playing Germany tonight at seven.'

'Oh yes, I saw it on the news. Everyone seems very excited.'

'Sam told me. They're setting up a television set in the students' common room. I said I would go. Why don't you come? Tom is sure to be there.'

'I've not seen him today. He's had meetings and tutorials. Sounded busy.'

'It would be good if you came. I would have someone to talk to while they're shouting at the telly. Zeb will be there as well. She's organized a bar.'

'Maybe I will.'

They drank their coffee while the world of academia drifted around them. Tutors checked their pigeonholes for mail; colleagues from various departments looked at the timetable noticeboard.

'So, I'm almost there,' said Rosie. 'End of my first year.' She gave a wry smile. 'It's been eventful, hasn't it?'

Inger nodded. 'You could say that.'

'Sam asked me to go to the dance with him. I said yes.'

'That's good.'

Rosie put down her coffee cup and thought for a moment. 'He's a good guy. Interesting in a quirky sort of a way.' She paused. 'Very different to Julian.'

'You're better off without him. You were too good for him.'

Rosie smiled, sat back and reflected. 'Sometimes with Julian I felt that my heart would burst through my chest, it was so intense.'

'Maybe that's not always a good thing,' said Inger quietly.

At lunchtime, in the refectory, Sam and Richard were deep in conversation about how galaxies co-evolve with their supermassive black holes. The subject changed when Owen sat down opposite them. 'So tonight's the night.'

As always, Richard went down the literal route. 'Quite right. The Earth is at aphelion.'

'At where?' said Owen.

'It's the point in the orbit of a planet at which it is furthest from the sun,' explained Richard.

Sam grinned. 'I think Owen was talking about tonight's football match.'

'Ah yes, I calculated the odds from the reports in this morning's papers. England have a 43.5 per cent chance of winning.'

Owen looked at Sam and raised his eyebrows. 'That's encouraging,' he said.

It was then that Rosie and Inger arrived at their table, both carrying a tray with a summer salad.

'Hi,' said Rosie. 'I guess you guys are talking football.'

'Not exactly,' said Owen with pronounced irony. 'We were discussing the Earth's orbit when it's furthest from the Sun.'

'Obviously,' said Inger.

'So, are you both coming tonight?' asked Sam eagerly.

'Yes,' said Rosie. 'Inger's going to keep me company as I'm guessing your attention will be elsewhere.'

Sam couldn't think of an appropriate answer.

It was one thirty when Owen knocked on Victor's door and walked in.

'Hi, Owen, take a seat. What can I do for you?'

'Thanks, Victor. It's about Chris Scully.'

'I'm aware of your high commitment towards helping the young man. So what's the latest?'

'He wants to come back as soon as he can to complete his degree.'

'That's positive news.'

'So I've been looking at wheelchair access this morning.'

'That's good. What did you find?'

'I started by checking out his current accommodation up the Hull Road. It's a semi that looks fine from the outside. Inside it's not so good. Faulty plumbing and only one toilet and that's upstairs. There're two men in each of the three bedrooms plus the lounge has been converted into another bedroom with two more beds. There's eight men in there with one toilet, a bath that leaks and a tiny kitchen. It's over-crowded and entirely unsuitable for them. With regard to Chris Scully, it's impossible. Even if we built a ramp to the front door, it's not wide enough for a wheelchair.'

'I had no idea it was that bad. Thanks, Owen. Let me have the address, will you?'

Owen scribbled it down and passed it to Victor. 'So I'm guessing Chris would have to be in halls.'

Victor nodded. 'F Block is the latest and that's got three ensuite rooms on the ground floor. I would need to check with the housekeeper to ensure wheelchair access is possible and discuss it with the Vice Chancellor. That way we may have a solution.'

'OK, Victor. I hope that works out.'

Victor stood up and shook Owen's hand. 'You've gone the extra mile here, Owen. I appreciate all your efforts.'

Owen paused by the door. 'Are you calling into the students' common room tonight for the football? Should be a lively affair. Most of us are going. I think Zeb suggested she may prop up the bar.'

'I have a ton of paperwork but I'll be there at some point.'

Owen smiled and closed the door. As he walked back to Cloisters corridor he reflected on the conditions in the house on Lavender Close. The bursar had a lot to answer for and the net was closing in.

Meanwhile, Victor sat back and sighed. His thoughts drifted on a stream of consciousness and he thought of Pat. It had been a difficult year but his partner had responded well to his course of treatment. The thought of life without him had been almost too much to comprehend. Now he could foresee happy times ahead. The clock on his mantelpiece ticked on. *Time is a great healer,* he thought.

At four o'clock Tom drove back to Haxby and collected a fish-and-chip supper en route. He settled down with a mug of tea before getting changed into jeans and a T-shirt and returning to Eboracum. At six thirty he climbed the stairs to Cloisters and met up with Owen again, who had followed exactly the same routine: fish and chips and a clean T-shirt.

Owen was sitting at his desk when Tom walked in. 'All set?' he asked.

'Fine,' Tom said and sat down in one of the armchairs. He looked preoccupied. It was clear his mind was elsewhere.

'Hang on. What's wrong?'

'Why?'

'You've been wandering around like a wet weekend the last few days.'

'I hadn't noticed.'

'Well, I bloody have. Come on. We've been mates long enough. It'll stay between these four walls if you like.'

'I've had a bit of a set-back.'

'That's life, Englishman. Shit happens. So what is it?'

'It was during the after-show party after the play. I took Inger out into the quad where it was quiet and I asked her.'

'Asked her what?'

'To marry me.'

'What, just like that? No preamble? Just straight in like a bull in a china shop?'

'She said no.'

'What, a complete no or a possible maybe?'

'She said it had come as a surprise. It was a big commitment and she wasn't sure she was ready for something like that.'

'Makes sense. How are things now?'

'Fine. We still spend time together at weekends.'

'Maybe that's all she wants at present. Marriage is a hell of a big commitment. I know that and I was lucky. Sue was as keen as me.'

'I'm pleased for you, Owen. At times I wish I had what you have.'

Owen laughed. 'What . . . changing nappies and waking up in the night?'

'You know what I mean: something stable, a life to look forward to with someone you really love.'

'Have you told her that?'

'Pretty well. I think I did.'

'Well, take my advice and bide your time. Inger's a fantastic woman but she's chosen what seems right for her at this point in time. Don't push her. Give her some space.'

'Is that what you did with Sue?'

'Not exactly. I think she realized I was God's gift to women and she needed to get in first.' Tom smiled and Owen patted him on the back. 'That's better. Now come on, you limp stick of rhubarb, let's have a pint before the game.'

When Tom and Owen walked into the students' common room they found all of the front seats had been taken. Dawn

Jenkins, President of the Students' Union, was behind the bar and Zeb was serving a can of beer and an orange juice to Sam and Rosie. Inger was standing alongside drinking a plastic beaker of red wine.

'Hi,' said Sam. 'It'll be standing room only soon.' A surge of students had just flooded in and many had settled on the floor in front of the screen.

'Two cans of beer, please,' said Owen and Zeb gave him a grin.

Tom walked up to Inger. 'Barely seen you today. We've both been busy.'

'Rosie was keen for me to come along. Bit of companionship while you boys are watching the football.'

'It's good to see you. We could go for a walk later.'

'When?'

'At half-time. There's a break of about fifteen or twenty minutes.'

Inger smiled. 'I know my place.'

'Sorry, didn't quite mean it like that.'

'Go and enjoy your football. I'll be at the back here with Rosie.'

'Thanks.'

Owen and Sam were waving from the far side of the room. 'Come on, Englishman,' shouted Owen. 'Kick-off's in five minutes. There're a few seats here.' Tom hurried over and sat down.

Rosie looked at Inger. 'It's a lovely evening. Let's sit in the quad.'

They both glanced across the room where Owen, Tom and Sam were staring at the screen. The broadcast was from Turin and anticipation mounted as kick-off approached. Suddenly there were loud cheers as the teams walked out.

'I prefer chess,' said Rosie. 'Much less noisy.'

'I agree,' said Inger and they walked out into the evening sunshine.

The England team stood side by side for the national anthem, all household names: Shilton, Parker, Walker, Wright, Butcher, Pearce, Platt, Gascoigne, Waddle, Lineker and Beardsley. In the ground there were forty thousand German fans compared with only four thousand supporting England but they could be heard singing and encouraging their team.

When the game began, hopes rose every time Paul Gascoigne received the ball but the teams cancelled each other out and at half-time there was no score. The room was full now with young men and women and a smattering of tutors from various departments. Almost everyone was clutching a can of beer or a beaker of shandy. Latecomers were standing at the back.

Tom looked for Inger but she wasn't there. He bought three more cans of beer from Zeb and returned to Owen and Sam.

In his study Victor closed a Manila folder and stretched. It had been a long day. His window was open and he could hear cheers and shouts coming from the students' common room. It was time to make an appearance down there but first he rang Pat. 'How are you?' he asked.

'Fine. I've just come in from the studio. Had a good day. What about you?'

'Busy as always. The harsh reality of catering for students with a disability came home today.'

'Are you talking about the young man who's now using a wheelchair?'

'Yes. We need to find suitable accommodation for him. He wants to finish his degree here.'

'A brave decision.'

'Yes, I thought so. That apart, it's the timetable again and I've promised to stay late. It's the big football game. Everybody seems to be watching it here. So I'll call in shortly. The students need to see I'm interested.'

'I thought you hated football.'

'Not really, but I prefer athletics. At university I wanted to run a sub-four-minute mile like Roger Bannister but never quite made it.'

'Never mind. By the way, have you eaten?'

'Zeb brought me a sandwich a while ago.'

'I'll save you some of my home-made quiche. It will make a nice supper.'

'Thank you. I couldn't manage without you.'

'I know,' said Pat. 'Aren't you lucky?' They both laughed as he rang off.

Victor locked his door and went downstairs. He found Rosie and Inger sitting on one of the benches in the quad.

'Not watching the football?' he said with a smile.

'No, we decided to unpick the intricacies of men.'

He smiled. 'Ah, well, good luck with that. I'll leave you to it.' When he entered the students' common room a hubbub of noise greeted him and Zeb poured him a beaker of wine. 'Welcome. You'll need this,' she said with a smile. 'It's bedlam in here and nobody has scored yet.'

He walked behind the bar and stood next to her. 'I'll stay here until someone does and then I'll slope off.'

Zeb raised her glass. 'Yet another good decision, Victor.'

During the second half there were groans and cries of 'Oh, no!' Germany had scored and Victor, true to his word, left for his quiche supper. The England goalkeeper, Peter Shilton, had been desperately unlucky as the ball ballooned freakishly high above his head before bouncing into the back of the net. The cheering became more frantic as students and staff urged on the team. Then, with ten minutes to go, the room erupted with cheers. Gary Lineker had scored an equalizing goal. The BBC commentator, John Motson, the voice of football, summed up the moment: 'The ace marksman keeps England in the World Cup.'

'Bloody tense,' said Owen.

Sam shook his head. 'Now we've got extra time.'

'Three more beers,' Tom said and headed for the bar.

Desperate moments followed during the period of extra time and there were groans again as Chris Waddle hit the post. At that moment England were inches away from a win. Then came a moment of drama that was destined to sum up the heartache of the nation. In the ninety-ninth minute Paul Gascoigne was booked for a tackle which meant he would be suspended for the final. He grabbed his shirt to wipe away the tears. Finally the referee blew his whistle and it was time for a penalty shoot-out.

The room went quiet.

'This is it,' said Sam. 'All or nothing.'

Everyone held their breath as Gary Lineker, Peter Beardsley and David Platt all scored their penalties. Then

Stuart Pearce blasted his against the diving legs of the German goalkeeper and there were cries of disappointment. The England goalkeeper anticipated the right way to dive for every one of the German penalties but he was always a fingertip away from making a crucial save. Then Chris Waddle blasted his penalty over the bar and it was over. England had often looked like the better team, but they had lost and the room was filled with bitter disappointment.

'So close,' said Sam.

'Unlucky,' said Tom.

'Bloody Germans,' muttered Owen.

Slowly the common room emptied. England had saved their finest performance for this epic semi-final but finished up with broken hearts. Everyone said their farewells. Groups of students headed off into York singing songs, sad at the result but consoled by the fact they had watched a game that had restored the pride of English football.

Tom and Inger walked out to the car park and Inger leaned against her Mini. Above them was a purple sky and the hint of a gentle warm breeze.

'It's late,' said Tom. 'Thanks for coming. Not really your scene.'

'I guess not but Rosie and I had a good heart-to-heart.'

'How is she now?'

'Sam has invited her to go for a walking holiday in the Lake District.'

'That's a bold move. What did she say?'

'That she would think about it.'

'I hope she goes. He's a really good guy.'

'I agree. It would be a perfect ending to her first year.'

Tom took a step back and looked at Inger. 'So have you managed to enjoy the evening after all?'

'To be honest the best part for me was the chat with Rosie and hearing Luciano Pavarotti singing "Nessun Dorma".'

'What does "Nessun Dorma" actually mean?'

Inger smiled. 'It's an Italian phrase, Tom. It means "None shall sleep" and it's the title of an aria from the opera *Turandot* by Puccini.'

'I didn't know that. It's a wonderful piece of music.'

'It's sung by a prince who is in love with a cold princess.'

'Really?' said Tom. 'So, appropriate for tonight,' he added with a smile.

'Maybe not.'

'True enough . . . I'm certainly not a prince.'

'And I'm definitely not a cold princess.' She held his hand. 'It's too late for you to travel back to Haxby. Just follow me.' She was smiling and so was her heart.

Her words were like sweet summer rain and he followed Inger's car back to her apartment. *None shall sleep,* he thought and smiled.

Chapter Twenty

The Way Ahead

When Tom looked out of his bedroom window a rim of golden light appeared over the distant hills and cast bars of amber and shadow across the room. In the distance, fields of ripe barley swayed in sinuous rhythm and the branches of the tall elms stirred with a gentle whisper. On the radio the Charlatans were singing 'The Only One I Know' and he thought of Inger. Last summer they had enjoyed a holiday in Norway but nothing had been discussed for the coming vacation and the academic year was all but over. It was Friday, 13 July, the end of the summer term and a day of unexpected outcomes lay before him.

Perkins was behind his counter when Tom walked into reception.

'Good morning, Dr Frith. Well . . . we've made it, another year.'

'Yes. Thanks again for your support.'

'My pleasure. Are you all set for tonight? My Pauline has been teaching me the quickstep.'

'Looking forward to it, although I'm not a dancer.

I'll watch you and pick up some tips.'

'Good luck with that,' said Perkins. 'Mr Llewellyn was in bright and early. Have a good day,' and he smiled as Tom made his way into the quad.

Owen was sitting at his desk when Tom walked in.

'All set for tonight?' asked Tom.

'Yes, fine,' said Owen, 'and it's a relief we don't have to wear those penguin suits. Casual gear tonight. Sue has booked a taxi for us and we're collecting Sam and Rosie on the way in. How about you?'

'Inger's ordered a taxi for half seven from her place so we're fine.'

Owen looked quizzically at his friend. 'Have you got plans for the holiday?'

'Not yet.'

'Speak to Inger. Get it sorted.'

Tom stared out of the window. 'She's never been quite the same since I hesitated about that job in New Zealand.'

'That's a long time ago.'

'Maybe.'

At nine o'clock, Zeb held a meeting with Inger and Rosie in her study. 'Just looking ahead to next year,' she said. 'I was considering *Twelfth Night*. What do you think?'

'"If music be the food of love,"' recited Inger with a smile.

'Spoken by Duke Orsino,' said Rosie, 'definitely a conundrum.'

'How so?' asked Inger.

'He was more in love with the *idea* of being in love than with any person.'

'I know a few men like that,' said Zeb.

Rosie considered this for a moment. 'Don't we all?'

'*Twelfth Night* is a good choice,' said Inger with a wistful smile. 'A tale of unrequited love, both hilarious and heartbreaking.'

'Very true,' said Zeb. 'Anyway, I've just seen that it's on in Stratford in April next year.'

'Why don't the three of us go?' said Rosie. 'Could be fun.' Inger smiled. 'I would love to.'

'In that case,' said Zeb, 'we could book it either for us or for field week with the students.'

'Either could be perfect,' said Inger.

Rosie nodded. 'The students would love it.'

Inger frowned. 'As long as the bursar releases the funds.'

'That's a battle for another day,' said Zeb, 'and I'm ready for it.'

Rosie glanced at the clock. 'Sorry, must fly. A couple of students in English Four want to see me. Catch you at break. Thanks, Zeb,' and she hurried away.

'Good to see her come through a difficult time,' said Zeb. 'She looks settled now. You've put a lot of time in, Inger. It's just what she needed: a friend she could trust.'

'She's a different woman,' said Inger, 'and I think she may be interested in Sam. He's clearly besotted with her.'

'I noticed,' said Zeb. 'They're going to the dance together tonight so that's a step in the right direction.'

'Could be good for both of them. Are you going with Vijay?'

'Yes. Strange, really. He must be the first man who didn't want to get me into bed on a first date.'

Inger raised her eyebrows in mock surprise. 'I always thought it was the other way round.'

Zeb grinned. 'Fair point. Anyway, what about you and Tom? How's it going these days?'

'OK.'

Zeb gave Inger a searching look. 'Inger, whatever happened in the past . . . don't let that influence what you do in the future. Tom's a hell of a guy and it's obvious he worships the ground you walk on. For such a great handsome hunk it's almost sad to see him go misty-eyed when he sees you. He's seriously bright but like all men he just needs pointing in the right direction.'

Inger looked at her perceptive friend and gave a wry smile. 'I can see why Victor wanted you as his deputy.'

They both laughed, gave each other a hug and headed off for their next meeting.

At ten o'clock in Room 2 on Cloisters corridor, Rosie was sitting at her desk when the phone rang.

'It's Ben Laverick here, ringing from London.'

'Oh, hi, Ben. Good to hear from you.'

'I was hoping you might be able to help me.'

'If I can.'

'I've arranged viewings on a few flats this weekend. I wondered if you might be about to act as a guide.'

'Yes, I'm around for a few days. What have you in mind?'

'I'll be at York railway station at midday tomorrow and hoped we could meet up and maybe have a bite of lunch, then check out these properties. If you can spare the time I should be most grateful.'

'That's fine, Ben. Glad to help.'

'OK, I'll see you then. Bye.'

Rosie sat back and smiled.

*

At morning break, Tom was in Victor's study going through the list of school placements for the next academic year.

'Well done, Tom. We look to be almost there.'

'There's been a cluster of headship appointments this term so there'll be a few new faces next September. I'll get in there early and make contact, probably during Freshers' Week.'

'Good plan.' He closed his Manila folder. 'How about a coffee?'

'Yes, please.'

Soon they relaxed with conversation that ranged far and wide. Eventually Victor gave Tom a fixed stare. 'Tell me, Tom. You and Inger have spent a lot of time together.'

'She's very special.'

'I know that. I guess what I'm really asking is what is it you want, not just in your work but in life generally?'

Tom put down his mug of coffee and sat back in his armchair. 'It's fairly simple really. I love my work but I would like a future with a family.'

'I understand,' said Victor. 'You mean everything that makes up the simple tapestry of life.'

'I imagine so.'

'Have you ever mentioned this to Inger?'

'Not in so many words.'

'Perhaps you should.'

They finished their coffee in silence.

Meanwhile, Sam Greenwood and Richard Head were in the science block storeroom doing a stock check of various ammeters and electrical equipment. Richard's annual stocktaking involved a very detailed system of checking and recording. There was a place for everything and Sam had grown used to ensuring that every battery had its label facing outward on the shelf. They had an hour to spare before meeting up with their final-year students for a liquid lunch in the Cross Keys on Goodramgate.

'The country's going mad,' said Sam. 'Electricity used to be a public monopoly, now it's a private monopoly. Did you know that Sir Trevor Holdsworth, Chairman of National Power, gets £185,000 for a two-day week?'

Richard didn't look up from arranging a collection of pipettes in order of size. 'Assuming a two-week holiday, that's £1,850 per day.' He had always been good at mental arithmetic.

'And he can top that up as Deputy Chairman of the Prudential,' continued an irate Sam.

'But does he have our job satisfaction?'

Sam sighed as the thought of cleaning the Bunsen burners crossed his mind. 'I suppose not,' he replied. However, while stocktaking with the fastidious Richard wasn't everyone's cup of tea, he had the elegant Rosie for a partner this evening at the dinner dance and he had an interesting proposal to put to her.

Owen had gone to the common room for morning break and was flicking through the pages of his *Daily Mirror* when Zeb sat down to join him. She lit up a cigarette and began to drink her coffee. 'So, what's the news in your socialist rag?'

Owen grinned. 'According to Jack Straw, Labour is planning to scrap the poll tax and bring back rates.' The Shadow Education Secretary had made it clear it would be one of their first acts when they returned to power.

'About time too,' said Zeb. She was obviously enjoying her cigarette and puffed it contentedly. 'I'm trying to cut down. Promised Vijay. Anyway, is there anything else to cheer us up?'

'Well, Madonna wants to start a family with Warren Beatty.'

'Wouldn't we all,' said Zeb with a smile.

'And Edwina Currie has been involved in some spicy chat on the radio about bananas and condoms.'

'Predictable,' said Zeb.

'They're calling her Blunderwoman now,' said Owen.

'She asks for it.'

Owen put his paper to one side. 'There's something else I need to share with you.'

'Go on.'

'It's about student accommodation. I've been checking where Chris Scully could live while he completes his degree. The house he was in up the Hull Road was a disgrace, over-crowded and in need of urgent repair, but nothing is being done about it. It's one of the bursar's properties.'

'Greedy sod,' muttered Zeb.

'So now I'm looking here on campus.'

'F Block is probably the best we've got,' said Zeb. 'Even so, the ground floor would need some work.'

'That's where you come in, Zeb. I want you to use your charms on the Vice Chancellor so he can raise it with the governors. It's a project that would need serious funding. I've already mentioned it to Victor. Work would have to start very soon to be ready for September.'

Zeb looked thoughtful. 'It begs the question of how we cater for students with disabilities. Have they got equal opportunities?'

'That's what we need to find out,' said Owen. 'So any support would be gratefully received.'

'I'll do what I can. In the meantime Gideon Chalk needs to be brought to heel. Did you know he's giving Ellie MacBride a hard time?'

'Why, what's happened?'

'He didn't approve of her articles in the *Echo*. Made it clear he wanted her to stop.'

'I've heard Tom talk about her. There's no way she'll be muzzled by an evil little bastard like Chalk.'

'Exactly.'

Gideon Chalk knew that he had to curb the antics of students who were reporting for the *Echo*. He could not afford for them to scupper his plans and lucrative second income. His office door was slightly ajar. He heard footsteps approach and then the sound of a gentle knock.

'Come,' Gideon called out.

James Spofforth, a Year Two student, walked in. He looked dishevelled, which did not surprise Gideon as he knew the young man was barely surviving on his grant.

'What is it this time, James? You know the condition for letting you defer payment of your rent for the next couple of months.'

'Yes, Mr Chalk,' James replied.

'So, why are you here?'

James looked uncomfortable. 'I have some information which you might be able to use.'

'Really? Well, it would have to be good to persuade me to go along with you not paying me the money you owe.'

'It's only until my grant comes in, Mr Chalk. Not to let me off payment.'

Gideon laughed. 'That would never happen, James. What is it you have for me?'

'You know Mr Channing is leaving college and that he is due to marry one of the students who he had an affair with?'

'That's old news, James, and is of no interest to me at all.'

'But this might be. It's about Ellie MacBride, who you had mentioned specifically.'

'Really? Go on.'

'One of my friends is in her English group. Their tutor is Tom Frith. Rumour has it that she's having an affair with him. So, who knows, the same might happen to them as happened to the other pair.'

'That *is* of interest, James.'

'So will you defer payment of my rent?'

'On this occasion I shall. But do not think I will make a habit of it. My generosity only goes so far.'

'Thank you, Mr Chalk,' said James and he walked out of the office.

Gideon Chalk smiled. This was a perfect opportunity. He knew exactly what he was going to do. He reached for a sheet of writing paper with the Eboracum crest.

'A note from the university to her parents expressing polite concern for her welfare,' he murmured to himself as he typed. 'And the final flourish . . .' He smiled as he typed Victor's name at the end. 'They will think he just forgot to sign it.'

Gideon Chalk read the letter. Pleased with it, he sealed the envelope and walked towards reception. He knew that the hardworking Mr and Mrs MacBride would want to save their daughter from potential ruin and likely forbid her to return. If they made a fuss, so much the better.

'I would be getting rid of that bastard Tom Frith as well.

What a morning!' he said to himself as he handed the letter to Albert.

'Make sure this is posted today,' said Gideon with as much authority as he could muster.

'I will, Mr Chalk,' replied the assistant porter. He couldn't help notice that the letter was addressed to Ellie's parents. He had a soft spot for this lively student. She was so bright and cheerful and always spoke to him when she passed. He hoped there wasn't a problem.

At one o'clock Tom walked into the Guy Fawkes Inn where he had responded to an invitation from his English Two group. Ellie MacBride was the first to greet him. 'Thanks for coming, Tom. Can I get you a drink?'

'Just a small beer, thanks.' He looked around. 'Are you making this an annual event?'

'Probably. It's good to meet up and let our hair down at the end of a busy year.'

'I agree.'

Tom sipped his beer and Ellie gave the barman a fifty-pence piece.

'Can I buy a round?'

'You're our guest, Tom.'

'Even so, I should like to contribute.' He glanced at the barman. 'Can I have a couple of large jugs of bitter, please, and another of lemonade?'

'That's kind, Tom. So, any plans for the vacation?'

'Not yet. Work to complete, then I'll make some decisions.'

'So, not Oslo again?'

Tom was surprised. He hadn't mentioned last year's holiday in Norway with Inger.

Ellie smiled. 'Sorry, Tom. The members of Inger's choir are always first with gossip.'

'No secrets at Eboracum then,' he said.

'Maybe there are still a few,' she said and her green eyes were bright with expectation.

The jugs of beer and lemonade arrived and they carried them to the table.

A lively half-hour followed for Tom while he caught up with their holiday plans. In a way this was his favourite group of students. They had arrived with him back in 1988 and had shared his journey. Stories were told and there was laughter as they recalled the highs and lows of teaching-practice experiences in school. Once again Tom regretted ever having considered the post in New Zealand. His life was here at Eboracum with these students and, hopefully, beside Inger. It belatedly occurred to him that it would have impacted on not only his friends but also his family. His parents would have supported him but they would also have been heartbroken. He owed them a loyalty that he had almost forgotten.

After saying goodbye to the group, Tom walked back to the university. He saw Dawn Jenkins, President of the Students' Union, speaking with Gideon Chalk outside reception. He was wagging a finger in her face and the conversation appeared to be heated.

'No more warnings,' he was saying as Tom approached.

'What's going on?' asked Tom.

'Oh, hello, Tom,' said Dawn calmly. 'No worries. Mr Chalk is simply trying to use his influence to close down the *Echo*.'

'That's nonsense,' said Tom.

Gideon was furious. 'This has nothing to do with you. I'm having a private conversation with a representative of the student body.'

Tom took a step forward. 'Dawn, is everything OK? I don't want to interfere unless you want me to stay.'

'Thanks, Tom, but I can handle this.'

'Very well, but let me know if I can help.' Tom gave Gideon a hard stare and walked on while Gideon responded with a look of pure hatred.

Gideon turned back to Dawn. 'You don't know what you're dealing with here. I have significant influence and I'm prepared to use it if provoked.'

'*Provoked*? What do you mean?'

'Those inflammatory articles in that apology for a student newspaper. It's gutter press and full of innuendo. I've been made a target.'

'Which you have brought on yourself,' said Dawn quietly. She stepped back and smiled. 'As this is my last day at Eboracum I'll report this conversation to my successor, Jonny Halliday. No doubt he will be interested to hear your views next term.' Then she turned and walked away.

Gideon shouted after her. 'No more warnings. You will be closed down soon enough. I shall see to it.'

At seven o'clock Inger was in her bedroom putting the final touches to her make-up while Tom was in the lounge watching television. It was the *Wogan* programme and Terry was interviewing the stars of the recently released hit movie, *Back to the Future Part III*. Tom recalled once again the happy times he experienced in Norway last summer and sat back on the sofa enjoying his private stream of consciousness.

Their taxi wasn't due until seven thirty so he had plenty of time to savour those memories. When Inger emerged he drank in the image before him. 'You look beautiful,' he said. 'Love the outfit.'

She stood there in a simple but elegant black dress. Her hair hung freely over her shoulders. 'Thank you, kind sir. Rosie and I picked it out last week.'

There was the sound of a car horn outside and they walked out together into the sunshine.

By seven forty-five a stream of taxis had pulled up outside the Assembly Rooms in York city centre. Victor and Pat arrived first. The dress code was smart casual this evening and Pat had decided upon a sky-blue linen suit and a white collarless shirt. Victor had gone for his predictable waistcoat, black jeans, white shirt and red bow tie. His ponytail was neatly gathered in a black bobble.

Pat was particularly fond of this neoclassical building. He felt as though he was walking into a Roman forum. The doorman smiled in acknowledgement as they stepped into the Great Assembly Room bordered by Corinthian columns. Above the ballroom floor were sparkling chandeliers and the light and warmth surrounded them. Close to a hundred people had arrived and were sitting at tables around the edge of the dance floor. After collecting a bottle of Merlot and two glasses they found seats at the head of one of the larger tables.

Next to arrive were Richard and Felicity. Richard had undergone a transformation. Clean-shaven and with a neat haircut and a new cream suit, he looked as if he was dressed for the Henley Regatta or Wimbledon. Felicity had clearly worked wonders on him. Hand in hand, they approached the bar, collected drinks and went to sit next to Victor and Pat.

'Good evening, Felicity,' said Victor. 'Hello, Richard. I'm so pleased you're here.'

'We've been looking forward to it,' said Felicity, 'haven't we, Richard?'

Richard was rearranging his place mat so it was exactly parallel with the edge of the table. 'Yes, we have,' he murmured.

'Love the suit, Richard,' said Pat. 'Very summery.'

'Precisely,' said Felicity. 'I've told Richard he must make an effort to look smart when the occasion demands.'

'Well, you've definitely succeeded this evening,' said Victor with a smile.

Owen and Sue's taxi arrived next. They were sitting in the back with Rosie while the long-legged Sam was in the front passenger seat. In front of them was a chauffeur-driven limousine from which emerged Gideon Chalk and his latest acquisition, a slim young woman with long dark hair who was wearing too much make-up and too little clothing. Gideon, in a black shirt and an ash-grey linen suit, strutted in as if he owned the place.

Owen was fuming as they followed them beneath the portico of grey stone towards the entrance. 'Looks like a bloody nightclub owner,' he muttered. At the far side of the bar were a few tables for two. Gideon led his partner towards one of them and then ordered a bottle of champagne after engaging the Vice Chancellor in friendly conversation.

*

Owen was collecting a round of drinks at the bar when Zeb and Vijay arrived. Zeb looked stunning in an off-the-shoulder black dress with a red sash around her waist. Vijay was wearing a linen suit, the colour of moss on limestone, and a crisp white shirt. They stopped in the centre of the dance floor and looked around them.

'Shall we sit with Victor?' asked Zeb. 'He and Pat are great company.'

'Of course,' said Vijay. 'Let me get some drinks. Is it a G and T?'

'Yes, please, although I know you won't be drinking as you're driving.'

He took her hand. 'That's OK. There's something I want to ask you before we settle down with your friends.'

Zeb was curious. 'What is it?'

'I have a conference in New York next month. I wondered if you would like to join me.'

It came as a surprise and Zeb paused before responding. 'Are you quite sure, Vijay? I think we're both aware I have something of a reputation regarding partners.'

He smiled. 'That's part of your charm,' he said quietly and squeezed her hand. 'Please say yes.'

'In that case, of course I'll come. How exciting.' She kissed him on the cheek and set off for Victor's table.

As Inger and Tom stepped into the Assembly Rooms they paused to take in the bustle of activity and the grandeur of the setting. 'I love this place,' said Inger. 'It's so elegant.'

'Like you,' said Tom with a smile and he spotted Owen waving in their direction. 'Shall we join them?' While Tom collected a round of drinks Inger was soon catching up with

Sue and Rosie. By eight o'clock waiters and waitresses had served up the prawn cocktail starter and the meal began with relaxed conversation.

Rosie and Sam were sitting side by side and he spoke quietly to her. 'You'll recall I'm planning a walking holiday in the Lake District. I wondered if you had decided whether or not to join me. I know you'll be going back to Cornwall so we could go when you're free.'

Rosie smiled. 'Thanks, Sam. That sounds lovely. I would be back here from Cornwall in the middle of August if that fits in with your plans.'

Sam's face lit up. 'That's brilliant. Are you around tomorrow? We could make arrangements, maybe have some lunch in the Dean Court.'

'Sorry, I have a commitment tomorrow. I'm meeting the new art guy, Ben Laverick. He rang asking for some help with viewing a couple of apartments. He's coming up on the train from London.'

'Oh, right, I understand,' said Sam, clearly disappointed while considering over his starter that he might have a rival.

After the meal the music began and a few couples took to the floor. The DJ had selected some tunes from his ballroom selection to get the dancing started. Soon Peter Perkins was skipping around the floor with his wife, Pauline, and doing a passable imitation of a quickstep. In the centre of the floor Vijay was showing Zeb he was an accomplished dancer and they moved effortlessly and in perfect harmony.

'Now that's how to dance,' said Inger to Tom.

Pat had sat down beside them on his way to the bar. 'Vijay is impressive,' he said. 'He knows all the moves.'

'Sadly, I don't,' said Tom, 'but I'm willing to try,' and he took Inger's hand.

'Well done,' Pat said and spoke quietly to Inger. 'So pleased to see you and Tom happy together. You make a good team . . . a perfect couple.'

Inger smiled as Pat walked away to the bar.

'A pity that he doesn't feel able to dance with Victor,' said Inger. 'One day maybe,' she mused as she followed Tom on to the dance floor which was crowded with couples.

Later in the evening, Zeb sat down with Tom and Inger while Vijay was making conversation with other guests.

'Just look at him,' said Zeb, staring at Gideon Chalk in disgust, 'chatting with the Vice Chancellor and reeking of self-importance, then returning to his table and drinking champagne all evening. Have you seen his partner? She doesn't look happy.'

'That's not all,' said Tom. 'I overheard him giving Dawn Jenkins an earful this afternoon. He was threatening her with shutting down the *Echo*. I asked her if she wanted me to stick around but I wasn't needed.'

'Dawn can handle herself in situations like that,' said Zeb.

'He really is a nasty piece of work,' said Inger.

'The way things are going,' said Zeb menacingly, 'he will run out of luck and not be with us for much longer. He's stepped out of line once too often.'

'Why? What's happened?' asked Inger.

'Watch this space,' said Zeb. 'Owen's on his case and he's determined.'

'That's good,' said Tom.

'What about Ellie MacBride?' asked Inger. 'Is she OK? The bursar was giving her a hard time too.'

'That's another reason we need to stop him.'

As the evening progressed the dancing slowed and couples were holding each other in the semi-darkness while the DJ played Michael Bolton's 'How Can We Be Lovers' followed by ABBA's 'The Winner Takes It All'. Tom and Inger held each other close as they moved around the floor.

Suddenly, shouting could be heard from the bar area.

'How dare you!' yelled a young woman.

'I wonder what's going on over there,' said Tom.

'Probably someone a little worse for wear.' Inger smiled. 'It will sort itself out.'

'I'm not so sure,' said Tom as a highly pitched scream pierced the air. He looked over to see Gideon Chalk recoiling from an angry young woman. 'Get off! Get off me!' she yelled.

'What are you talking about?' Gideon shouted. 'I was putting my glass on the bar. I never laid a finger on you.'

'You did,' said the young woman. 'I know it was you. You're a dirty old man.'

Gideon raised his hand as if to strike her and, as he did so, Robbie the barman intervened and swiftly grabbed his arm. 'I wouldn't do that, sir, if I was you.'

Gideon began to struggle violently. 'Let go, you idiot. It was this bitch that started it.' With that he pushed the woman away and she fell backwards over one of the bar stools. Her friends rushed to her aid.

The barman leaned over and grabbed Gideon by the lapels. 'Call the police, Sarah,' he said to his wife who was serving drinks beside him.

'Ringing them now,' she called out.

'Who the hell do you think you are?' yelled Gideon. 'Involve the police and you'll be the one who is sorry. I shall make sure of that.'

'I don't think so, sir,' replied Robbie as he tightened his grip.

Tom and Inger watched in astonishment as within minutes two policeman walked in and made their way to the bar. A furious Gideon Chalk was escorted out and bundled into a police car. The young woman who had been assaulted was being comforted by Robbie and Sarah and her friends while Gideon's escort was seen making a hasty exit.

'What was all that about?' asked Inger.

'Beats me,' replied Tom. 'But it looks like Gideon touched some woman while at the bar and she took exception to it.'

'I don't blame her,' said Inger, 'but what a way to end the night.'

'That won't have done his image much good,' said Tom. On the other side of the room the Vice Chancellor was watching in horror.

'I hope they throw away the key,' said Inger with feeling.

It had been an unexpected end to the evening, but finally they said their farewells, collected their coats and made their way home.

It was midnight when the taxi dropped off Inger and Tom and they walked up the path to her front door. They stood there standing face to face and a gentle breeze stirred Inger's hair. She gave Tom that direct stare he had come to know so well. 'Before we go in there's something I want to say.'

'I'm listening,' said Tom.

Inger leaned forward and kissed him, gossamer-soft and then again with feeling. Tom stood there transfixed.

'A while ago you asked me a question,' she said.

'Did I?' Tom was puzzled and simply looked intently at this beautiful woman. They stood there in the darkness as moonbeams caressed her face.

'Tom . . . it was after the play. We sat outside in the quad. You asked me to marry you.'

'That's right, I did.'

There was a long pause and then the flicker of a smile. 'So, Dr Frith . . . would you like to ask me again?'

About the Author

Jack Sheffield grew up in the tough environment of Gipton Estate, in north-east Leeds. After a job as a 'pitch boy', repairing roofs, he became a Corona Pop Man before going to St John's College, York, and training to be a teacher. In the late seventies and eighties, he was a headteacher of two schools in North Yorkshire before becoming Senior Lecturer in Primary Education at the University of Leeds. It was at this time he began to record his many amusing stories of village life as portrayed in the Teacher series, comprising: *Teacher, Teacher!*, *Mister Teacher*, *Dear Teacher*, *Village Teacher*, *Please Sir!*, *Educating Jack*, *School's Out!*, *Silent Night*, *Star Teacher*, *Happiest Days*, *Starting Over*, *Changing Times*, *Back to School*, *School Days* and *Last Day of School*.

University Challenges is the second novel in the University series and follows on from *University Tales*.

In 2017 Jack was awarded the honorary title of Cultural Fellow of York St John University.

He lives with his wife in Hampshire.

Visit his website at www.jacksheffield.com.